Lady Len & the Mysterious Mac

Lady Len & the Mysterious Mac

ROSE PRENDEVILLE

First published by Eridani Press.

LADY LEN AND THE MYSTERIOUS MAC. Copyright © 2023 by Jean M. Ward. All rights reserved.

Cover by Poshie

Names: Prendeville, Rose, author.

Title: Lady Len and the Mysterious Mac / Rose Prendeville.

Description: First edition. | Nashville, Tennessee : Eridani Press, 2023.

Identifiers: ISBN 978-1-955643-09-2 (trade paperback) | ISBN 978-1-955643-10-8 (ebook) | ISBN 978-1-955643-11-5 (audiobook)

Subjects: LCSH: Highlands (Scotland)—Fiction. | Man-woman relationships—Fiction. | Romance fiction. | Historical fiction. | BISAC: FICTION / Romance / Historical / Scottish | GSAFD: Love stories.

Classification: LCC PS3616.R452 | DDC 813/.6—dc23

LC record available upon request.

For everyone who was made to feel like you were not enough. You are.

Chapter One

Silas MacKenzie was used to people staring. They couldn't help themselves, just like they couldn't help offering all their unsolicited advice. Like leaning too far over the edge of a cliff or taunting a feral boar, they slung their wisdom from fifty paces, just to prove their bollocks' worth.

Much like Goliath in the Book of Samuel, Si was feared on account of his size, but he was also dismissed as simple and wild—from his first tutors, and later, professors at King's College, to his fellow scholars whose jaws hung slack upon hearing any cogent rebuttal. And maybe they were right. At any rate, strangers recoiled, even as they itched with a moral duty to guide him, and now that he was back after seventeen years away, even his own kin were as good as strangers.

Yet another stranger was the lass who had run terrified from the kirk, escaping her own betrothal ceremony, drawn like a moth to his mother's grave. Each MacKenzie and Mackintosh present had an opinion on the matter. Si watched her through the doorway, whilst everyone else watched him. Wind rattled the eaves and benches creaked as they shifted restlessly, waiting for him to do something but too afraid to say it for once. And why? Because this time there was nothing to be done?

If he were silver-tongued like his father's steward, or even warmly commanding as the laird had been in his prime, before the ravages of war, before succession and political exile had gotten their talons in him, then perhaps he'd have stood a chance. But Si had never mastered the art of endearing himself, preferring instead to shrink into the background, and how well had that ever worked?

So there they were. The lass had taken one look at him and fled. Now everyone stared at him, buzzing with unvoiced counsel on how to play the part of laird and master and coax her back inside, to command her obedience, when he had no business wedding the wee slip of a girl in the first place. Lord knew she'd end up in the ground right alongside where she was standing, because Silas MacKenzie broke everything he touched. If it hadn't been evident before her flight, she would surely work it out soon, as she studied the cross-shaped headstone of Iona MacKenzie.

Blast and damnation. She was better off staying outside.

He sat beside his father, taking up far too much space in the tiny pew. Like everything else, the benches were much smaller than he remembered. His knees kept banging into the back of the next row, and he was all angles and elbows, like the adolescent boy who had departed Ross so long ago. What was it about coming back to a place you left behind as a child that put you right back there, in time as well as space, making you feel more immature than you ever had back then?

Outside, the skies darkened, ushering in damp air that set his father coughing. It sounded as though his ribs were rattling together like a pair of dice. He'd lived in the temperate climes of France far too long, and a fresh wave of a guilt washed over Si. If he'd returned home sooner to take up the mantle of Kintail, the laird needn't have returned to the brisk Highland weather that seemed to be making his lungs work double time.

Father Sinclair cleared his throat. "Perhaps we might continue the ceremony? Do we really need the bride for this part?"

Si raked a hand through his hair and counted his exhale—*one, two, three*—but it came out as a growl that made the priest flinch. He wasn't wrong. Everything about this charade was based in tradition, and traditionally the bride was no more than an accessory at her own betrothal, and later, her wedding, whether she wished to be involved or not.

The rèiteach was meant to be lighthearted and jovial. Then Mr. Mackintosh had insisted they hold it in the kirk with a priest. He hoped such pretense of officiousness could elevate his own status in the Chattan Confederation.

"She just needs a moment," the girl's mother whispered, stroking her husband's arm with a placating hand, as though they hadn't all been waiting half an hour already.

"Wee Ellen *always* needs a moment," the younger sister moaned, earning a slap from one of her parents that made Si flinch. "Well she does," the girl sniffed.

Si's father, the Laird Kintail, coughed again, his hunched shoulders wracking. They'd need to get the physician in with some kind of poultice or potion to stop the crackling sound coming from the old man's chest.

Despite age and infirmity, though, his old grey eyes were clear and sharp, urging Si to get on with it, just as they'd urged him to stop begging off the arrangement when he'd gone to his father at dawn. If he'd known this was part of the plan, he'd have never returned home from Aberdeen.

When the laird finished coughing, he nudged Si's young cousin, Bram, and whispered in the lad's ear.

"Do I really have to?" the twelve-year-old whined, annoyed with the ceremony and his part in it, but for all the wrong reasons. With a familiar jerk of his head, the laird confirmed the boy must play his part, requesting her hand be given to Si.

Knowing better than to argue, Bram dragged himself on his too-large feet over to the bride's family. He winked roguishly at the younger Mackintosh daughter, at least four years the lad's senior if she was a day, and she erupted into her own fit of coughing until her father stamped his foot.

Bram shrugged, peeking out from the black hair that hung in his eyes. "So can we, aye?"

The father's mouth pursed into a solid line, lacking even a hint of amusement.

"Like we practiced," the laird choked before coughing some more.

Mercy, it was starting to sound like a hospital inside the kirk.

Bram rolled his eyes at his uncle and turned back around. "Good sir, on behalf of my cousin, heir to the chief of Clan MacKenzie," he began, without the slightest irony, which made Si twitch, "can we have the honor of your daughter's hand?"

Mackintosh lifted his chin self-importantly. He certainly enjoyed standing on ceremony and all the attention it entailed. "Which daughter?"

"The one outside. Ellen, is it? But I'll take that one for meself, if ye like," the brat added cheekily. The sister uttered a horrified squeak and buried her face in her lap.

The one outside indeed. Neither of them might have much say in the matter, but she wasn't a lamb to be bought and sold at auction, without even being present for the transaction.

"Enough," Si thundered, standing up and pulling his shoulders straight, his head nearly cracking against the rafter, and his voice booming through the tiny kirk.

Mackintosh's eyes widened and he shrank back a little. "Fine, yes, granted," he stammered quickly, before Si could insist on yet another delay while he retrieved the girl.

Outside, she turned her face up towards the light rain that had begun to fall, like a bluebell welcoming the dew. Tiny as she was, she'd be soaked through in no time if he left her out there on her own, and then he'd have two patients in the sick ward to contend with. But she didn't appear bothered by the drizzle. If he wanted her back inside, he would have to go and fetch her just like everyone was expecting him to do.

She seemed to sense his arrival before he drew even with her, as though the ground shook when he walked, and she instinctively shrunk away, toward the rowan tree that stood sentinel over his mother's grave.

"Milady Ellen?" he asked, his voice rough and scratchy from disuse, unrefined even to his own ears. No wonder lowlanders thought him an insensible oaf, little better than the giants of faerie stories. "Nae better?" he tried again, and she shrugged a little, her lovely blonde hair darkening and beginning to curl in the damp as she stared down at the headstone.

Of course she wasn't better. The lass no more wished to wed than he did.

His father was sympathetic, but he'd also made it clear—the clan had grown restless during his years in exile, and tolerance for the heir's coastal malingering had run out. They were impatient for some sign that the Kintail was preparing a tanist to succeed him and restore the lands of Ross-shire to their former glory.

Even his father's sympathy ran short, however, when Si protested that it should be Bram who was next in line, and not himself. Clearly, that was a battle for another day, after the Kintail's health improved and the clan's unrest was mollified. If a marriage would appease them for a time, then Si supposed it was the lesser of evils, and wouldn't such a comparison delight any bride?

He looked down at the lass, whose head might almost reach his oxters if she stood on her toes. Her nose was dripping blood as bright as rubies. They'd mentioned she was sickly. Perhaps this was his penance, then, for killing his mother—a lifelong reminder of human frailty.

When he held out his handkerchief to her, she merely stared at it, and so he reached for her face himself. The lass jerked back, hitting her head against the tree. Her eyes widened, but she didn't cry out or move her hand to rub the spot, and Si raised his palms in surrender.

She was more skittish than a day-old foal, but this time when he reached out, she didn't flinch, and so, as gently as he was able, he tipped up her chin and held the cloth to her face to stop the bleeding.

"All right, milady?" he asked, hating the way the words seemed to stick in his throat.

It was the same shame as when his tutor once filled his mouth with river pebbles and ordered him to recite his psalms, until the man realized that Si would just swallow the rocks along with his syllables. The tutor had given up after that, and Si's father, not yet the Kintail, sent him away to board with a more renowned scholar in Aberdeen before his twelfth birthday. He could still taste the pebbles now, all algae and earth.

The lass reached up to take the handkerchief for herself, and Si withdrew his hand, but not quickly enough. Her fingers brushed against his as the sky finally rumbled, and lightning scorched down his arm, straight to his stomach. His eyes shot to hers before he stepped away and unfurled the back of his plaid to protect her from the rain.

Si hated too the way she instinctively shrank from him, as though a man of his size could only be meant for violence. He wished she'd look at him, so he could know the color of her eyes and show her that he meant no harm.

If he ever did want to see them, he supposed he needed to get her out of the rain, and into that kirk, where their families were growing more restless by the second.

"I'm not," he began, and then cleared his throat. Not what? So many things.

He swallowed and tried again.

"I know I'm not what you must've had in mind."

She snorted, a soft, quick laugh that erupted unexpectedly before she clapped one hand over her mouth to keep the rest inside.

He tore his gaze from her face, focusing instead on his mother's headstone. "I'm not a bad man," he whispered. "I willnae hurt you, nor let any harm come to you." She couldn't know just how deeply he meant those words. And why should she believe him, when they'd never laid eyes on each other before today?

"Gawyn would say, if there's something you dread, best to have done with it quickly," he said, mostly to himself, but she nodded slowly, as though agreeing with him. "I ken you're not keen, but unless you're planning to make a break for it, the fastest way to bring this infernal day to its conclusion would be for you to come back inside the kirk."

He hadn't meant to sound so cold. She looked past the headstone, to the kirkyard fence and the soggy fields beyond, as though considering the option of escape.

Si scrubbed a hand over his beard. Should he have shaved it off? Would a younger face make him look less severe, or all the more terrifying with the countenance of an overgrown bairn?

"Sure you'd prefer your own kirk near your own home," he offered. "Inverness, aye?" Had she been there when Fraser of Lovat had laid siege to the city back in 1715? Had the siege forever altered her young life as it had the MacKenzies', snatching away a beloved laird before his own babe had drawn its first breath? With an heir not yet born, the tanist became laird—Si's father, Alex—and Silas became the new heir.

She stopped dabbing her face and began folding the handkerchief into smaller and smaller squares.

"I want to thank you for being so accommodating on account

of my father's recent poor health," he went on, in case no one had explained to her why she'd been brought to Ross before the wedding instead of after.

The lass snorted again, and Si would almost swear he could hear her thoughts on the wind, a muttered, "As if it matters what I want."

But no, perhaps he was only hearing his own thoughts outside his head.

Another clap of thunder pealed across the sky, and this time the lass shrunk towards him instead of away, and it cracked something open inside him as the rain began to fall harder, the scent of lavender wafting up from her wet hair.

"If you will," he whispered, making to turn back towards the kirk, and at last she relented.

Hushed voices fell silent as they entered. Bram scratched his ankle with the toe of his other boot.

"Ask again," Si ordered his cousin, who glared at him, but rolled his head sullenly towards Mackintosh.

"Can we?"

Puffing up once more, the father said, "Well now, that all depends—"

"Jesus—"

"Silas," his father warned, jerking his head towards the crucifix.

"Begging your pardon," Si mumbled to the priest, the father, and God Himself, but mostly to the lady, for she stared intently at the floor, no doubt humiliated by all of it. "Mr. Mackintosh, the hour is late, the lasses are clearly exhausted, and my father should be out of the damp. Unless you mean to revoke your consent, might we have it and have done?"

It was an offer as well as a challenge. One final chance to save the girl from a fate of being tied to him, and she knew it, finally lifting her watery eyes to his, the unexpected sapphire shades of the North Sea. She was a Mackintosh, he should've known they'd be the purest blue, and he realized with absolute certainty that he'd do anything to protect her, even from himself.

"It is indeed an auspicious day for our two families," her father blustered, but eventually he gave his consent once more, and everyone except the bride and groom sighed with relief.

She didn't withdraw her gaze from his the entire time, and it made his mouth dry.

They were officially betrothed, before God and in the sight of his blessed mother, buried these twenty-eight years. Her death had cast a shadow over Si his whole life, one that he could never outrun, not even a lifetime away in Aberdeen. Would she rest easier now he was settled? Or would her spirit be overcome with fear for the Mackintosh lass?

Father Sinclair gripped Si's elbow in a friendly way that would've been a shoulder clap on an average-sized man, and he bent to hear the whispered words. "Perhaps smelling salts in your waistcoat on the day. Will it be the boy standing up with you?"

Si cast his gaze to Bram, watching from the doorway as the Mackintoshes piled into a carriage for the short journey back to their inn. Young Bram had been the heir to all of this, until that fateful day.

"He's not too young?" Si asked.

"He is *very* young, but needs must," Father Sinclair said, turning away to tend other priestly matters.

Well, and maybe he was, but Si intended to make a man of him and restore him to his rightful place the moment he came of age.

ELLEN'S FATHER WAS FUMING WHEN THEY BOARDED THE carriage.

He could never abide disrespect in any form, but worse was the appearance that he wasn't in complete control. Bad enough she'd stepped out of line in the kirk—unthinkable—but then Silas MacKenzie had stepped in to stop his opprobrious hemming and hawing—unforgivable.

Only her cousin Jory had ever dared risk the fury of Rupert Mackintosh on Ellen's behalf. Though she supposed standing up to bullies wasn't such a great risk for a man so big and braw as this MacKenzie.

When the carriage lurched away from the kirk, Ellen gazed out at the sea of scattered headstones. Standing there trying to catch her breath, she had prayed for the ground to open and entomb her with its denizens below. But as usual, the answer was *No*. She remained steadfastly earthbound and betrothed.

"I've never been more insulted," her father huffed.

"I'm sure he meant no offense," her mother soothed, stroking his arm tentatively, like you might pet a temperamental cat. "A man like that can't help being gruff. It's just his way."

A man like that. They didn't even know him.

For years, her father had threatened her with the specter of a MacKenzie husband, with no particular man in mind. He only liked the idea of allying himself with the clan. None of them had ever imagined he'd actually produce a MacKenzie groom, let alone the son of a laird.

But then Old Kintail had returned from the continent and word began to spread that his son sought a bride, and the next thing Ellen knew she was standing in the kirk being stared at by her soon-to-be kin.

She didn't know what to make of *a man like that*. It was all a bit too much.

"A man so big and fine, you mean?" Maggie asked, unhelpfully. "His cousin's awfully forward."

"Sure and all, he's the manners of one who knows he'll command the clan someday soon," her father conceded. "And you, young miss, are lucky he'll still take you off my hands after such a display."

Young miss. When Ellen was three and twenty, and hadn't he been telling her for years she was getting too old to make a desirable match? Too old, too quiet, too frail.

When he didn't force her to wed Logan Mackintosh last year, she'd almost dared hope he was considering her request to go abroad and take holy orders at Abbaye Notre-Dame-des-Chelles in Paris. But then, on an otherwise ordinary sunny Wednesday, he gleefully announced the awful news: the MacKenzie heir was returning to the Highlands to wed, and even more remarkable, he was willing to settle for an old maid like Ellen.

Silas MacKenzie. She'd no idea what to do with him. Or what was in it for him, with his deceptively gentle voice that could be laced with steel when he wanted it to, his scraggly beard, and hooded eyes the color of heather honey.

He didn't seem to want to marry any more than she did. And who could blame him, when she was half his size and afraid of her own shadow—too small, too timid, too lachrymose? She was a drab little dormouse, best suited to hiding away inside cloister walls, not playing lady of the castle.

"Wee Ellen, I know you can't help it. I know you've a weak constitution, but you must pull yourself together," her father scolded. "Now isn't the time to give into one of your missish fits."

"The wife of a laird must be strong indeed," her mother agreed. "He can't be forever looking after you *and* the whole clan as well."

"Then why saddle him with me," she muttered. Nobody heard her. No one ever did.

"You've gone and ruined his good handkerchief." Maggie nodded at the cloth still balled in Ellen's fist.

She unclenched her hand to study the blotchy, crimson stain. Was her blood the most vibrant thing about her?

"I dare say he has more than one," her father chortled. "And a good thing, too. He'll have to get used to ruining them, being wed to our poor Wee Ellen, won't he?"

"I suppose he must," her mother chuckled.

Ellen's fist tightened around the wadded-up handkerchief once more, but she froze her lips into what she hoped resembled a pleasant smile and swallowed down her screams.

"Jory will have to teach that big MacKenzie how to make her special lozenges," Maggie said, even though by now Ellen was perfectly adept at making her own yarrow capsules to staunch a bloody nose.

When her sister called him *that big MacKenzie*, it set her stomach in disarray. His size certainly hadn't escaped her own notice. Compared to *her* it all seemed rather impossible. She knew just enough about the mechanics of the marriage bed to know that it couldn't possibly work. If the ground refused to swallow her up, then she would have to try and convince him, as she'd been unable to induce her father, to send her away to France.

"What do you think kept Jory?" her sister prattled on.

"Edinburgh's far away," their mother said, echoing Ellen's own thoughts.

If she were brave like her cousin Jory, she'd not have stopped at the grave of some long dead MacKenzie. No, she'd have leapt the old stone fence and kept right on running until she reached a ship bound for the continent, and then she would have stowed herself aboard without concern for rats or sea sickness.

Indeed, if she were brave like Jory, she might never have arrived at the kirk today. She might have made her escape the moment her fate was announced, taking her future in her own two hands and forging a path forward alone. Of course, if she were anything like Jory, she wouldn't yearn for the safety of a convent at all.

"I suppose their journey takes twice as long, with the Shaw Wretch stopping every few miles to tup her in the woods along the way."

"Margaret Mary Mackintosh!" their mother gasped.

"What? We were all thinking it."

Ellen had most certainly *not* been thinking it, but her father chortled and nodded his agreement as though he'd had any hand in their match, other than ordering Jory's exile which ultimately led to her betrothal to Finlay Shaw.

"All of sixteen, and sure you'll never catch a husband with a mouth like that," Mother warned Maggie.

"She'd better find someone to take her off my hands after the business with Bearradh Dearg fell through," her father lamented.

Ellen shivered. Her sister had been expected to follow Jory to the convent on the Scottish coast until the whole thing turned out to be a nefarious ploy by Clan Gordon.

If only their father hadn't gotten it into his head that he had to have *this* specific MacKenzie for a son-in-law. The man was already several years older than Ellen. Given the choice, she'd have gladly stepped aside and let Maggie use her dowry in a year or two. But this one needed a wife now, and so Ellen was to be handed off like a side of mutton.

"I ought to have forced that cheeky little MacKenzie cousin to make good on his offer."

"Da, no! He's practically a bairn," Maggie exclaimed, just as he knew she would.

"Oh, but he'll grow, my girl. He's all limbs now, but he'll be almost as big as his cousin, I'd wager. He'll grow, you'll see."

"Not fast enough to suit me," Maggie grumbled, straightening her skirts.

If he was anything like his older cousin, the boy would indeed grow, and keep right on growing until he was practically a giant holding up the sky.

Ellen took great gulping breaths, trying to settle her nerves. There was no possible way it could work.

Chapter Two

Back at Castle Leod, Alex MacKenzie, the Laird Kintail, fairly collapsed the moment he stepped inside. With the help of Gawyn, their oldest and most faithful groom, Si carried him to his second-floor chamber.

He sent Bram to the kitchen, and the lad soon returned with Mrs. Kynoch, the cook, who busily took over. She covered his father's chest in a mustard plaster and ordered him to drink some vile-smelling concoction. That the laird managed to choke the brew down was a testament to his iron will—as well as to the fact that no one was foolish enough to argue with Morag Kynoch. No one except Si.

The ruddy-cheeked woman had been their cook since he was small enough to hide inside a cupboard. She had remained at Leod even when the MacKenzies had abandoned it for their own separate exiles. She had probably single-handedly kept the place from falling into rubble, helping Bram's mother bring him up, waiting patiently for the day when Alex and Si would return. Now he was back, Si couldn't get used to her insistence that at twenty-eight he was nigh on old enough to address her by her Christian name.

"Has he fever, d'you think? Should I send for a physician?" Si asked, hovering over her shoulder as she tended his ailing father.

The cook cast him an affronted glare. "A physician, is it? And here's me slaving away night and day to care for Himself as well as cook all the meals."

"Och, you've done it now, laddie," his father teased.

Si did his best to look chastened, but the way she spoke, it sounded as though the laird had been poorly ever since he'd returned.

When Alex was wounded fighting with the Jacobites at Glen Shiel eight years ago, his steward, Norval MacKenzie, had messaged Si that his father might not survive the week. But they smuggled him aboard a ship and he soon rallied, as he always did, finding the temperate clime of Nice surprisingly agreeable. Si hadn't visited Leod since.

Did his father regret the king's pardon which now permitted his return to the Highlands? Or was he relieved to come home? Could a man feel both things at once? Would he have returned to Scotland at all, had Si not dragged his heels leaving Aberdeen to face the role that awaited him here, with only Norval MacKenzie by his side?

"You look tired, Da."

"I'm all right." His father patted his hand in a comforting way, even though Si should be the one doing the comforting. "It did my heart good today, seeing ye with the lass. I ken she'll make you happy, if ye let her."

Si turned away, so his father wouldn't read the emotion in his eyes. "A more mismatched pair never graced the kirk door." He managed to say it like a joke.

"She can help ye prepare to take over all this."

"Psssh," Si tsked. "We've talked about that, Da. Norval and I can help you prepare Bram to take it back when he's of an age."

He glanced towards the door, where a shock of black hair ducked out of sight, pretending not to eavesdrop.

"You've talked about it," his father said dryly. "I've made my peace with what's coming, and it's time you did too. The clan willnae wait. If I don't name you, they'll demand someone else, and it won't be Bram."

Like Mrs. Kynoch, the steward had remained in Strathpeffer the last eight years, where the crofts and the rents were his domain. By rights, he was the real tanist, and if Bram wouldn't do, Norval should become laird, though he was only a few years junior to Alex. Or, if Norval was too old and Bram was too young, perhaps they'd settle for Si's cousin Cedrick, the piper. Anyone would be a better choice.

"They'll have to wait a bit longer to be rid of you," Si said. "I've a friend coming up for the wedding."

"Have ye son? All the way from Aberdeen?" his father's eyes lit with pride whenever the topic of Si's studies arose, unlike the rest of the clan, who regarded all his learning with suspicion.

"Aye, from the medical school. I've asked him to have a look at you."

"Och, let him enjoy the day, son. There's no cure for old age."

Then he shifted uncomfortably against his pillows and closed his eyes, dismissing Si, discussion over. "Light some more of that incense you've been burning in the chapel, Morag," he mumbled with a soft smile. "Reminds me of the old days."

Mrs. Kynoch just frowned, casting them both a dark look, and bustled away.

Lying there with a blanket tucked up to his chin, Alex was practically swallowed up by the big bed which had once appeared too small to ever hold him. Si's years away hadn't seemed so very long, but neither had time stood still, he realized soberly.

And yet, his father wasn't so very old. It was just the damp and chill troubling his lungs. With proper care, he'd readjust to the mountain air and be back on his feet in no time.

"Have you seen Norval of late?" Si asked, surprised the steward wasn't hovering at his father's elbow.

"Aye?"

"And what does he say about all this?"

His father's expression clouded, telling Si all he needed to know. Norval could no more envision Silas MacKenzie as laird than he could himself. At least someone was willing to tell the truth.

Mrs. Kynoch still waited outside the chamber when Si finally left his snoring father.

"I understand the cook down at the inn will be handling everything for the day," she sniffed, doing a poor job of hiding her sore feelings.

"The Mackintoshes didn't want to be a bother to you," he said. "But I understand they've brought their cook from Inverness to help."

"So they'll be a bother to the inn instead," she laughed a little too gleefully. "Heaven help us all."

"Aye, count yourself lucky," he agreed.

"Oh, aye. My hands are full enough as it is," she replied, placated by Si's reassurance that her displacement wasn't his doing. "There's plenty to do and only wee Dorrie to help me."

"Are you asking for new staff, Mrs. Kynoch?" he asked, and she scoffed at him.

"Mmphm. With what money?" she laughed, taking herself back down to the kitchen and whatever all was keeping her so busy.

An hour later, Si paced the four corners of his library, unable to concentrate on the accounts or his correspondence. Every time he tried, he found himself drowning in a pair of bold blue eyes, as though looking up from the bottom of a well, eyes so blue God Himself couldn't have conjured them.

Even if the illness was temporary, his father was in no condition to lead. If anything, he ought to go straight back to Nice until his health improved. But the people wanted a laird, and the laird wanted Si, and the people wanted Si to marry.

And what did Si want?

His hand tingled where it had grazed Ellen's that afternoon, and he clenched his fist to try and stop it. Vivid azure eyes stared up at him. What Si wanted didn't signify.

He collapsed into a chair and, from the secret drawer in the back of his desk, retrieved a small wooden box, carved with an intricate oak tree knot pattern. Inside was a tiny painted portrait of his mother. The artist had colored her eyes a shade that nearly matched those of the Mackintosh lass, though of course Si had never seen them in person. Beneath the likeness was a piece of red jade that he'd found in the mud of a riverbank the day Laird William MacKenzie died twelve years ago, passing the lairdship to his younger brother, Alex, and forever altering the course of everyone's lives in a single breath.

There was also a lovely lace handkerchief embroidered with the initials *ICMM*—Iona Campbell Munro MacKenzie. Within its folds lay a silver Luckenbooth brooch, the one his father had given to his mother upon their betrothal. Time had tarnished the shine, but he polished it tenderly with the tail of his sark, smoothing away the years of neglect like they were tears to be wiped clean. It seemed tiny in his broad hand, but it would be the perfect size for young Ellen Mackintosh.

Even after a few weeks to adjust to the idea, the thought of a bride, *his* bride, was still too foreign to be real. But she'd been real when he skimmed her fingers that afternoon, and she was only going to get more real as the week wore on.

There didn't seem to be any getting out of it. The question was, what would he do with her?

ELLEN HAD NOT ANTICIPATED THE CELEBRATION ALREADY IN full swing at the inn. Truth be told, she'd been relieved the wedding would take place twenty miles from Inverness, far from the prying eyes of neighbors and relations. Her father was well-known and well-liked, but she hadn't expected shopkeepers or students to follow them to MacKenzie lands, and suddenly the weight of the proceedings truly hit her: she, Wee Ellen Mackintosh, would soon be the wife of a future laird.

Even the Borlum had traveled from Moy to take part in the festivities, with all her Mackintosh cousins in tow, and she'd forgotten how much her kin loved a party.

The inn was filled to bursting, along with the stable. Several families were even camped outside, all of them eating and dancing in boisterous circles, out-shouting each other over peals of raucous laughter. At least ten different kinds of cooking mingled with peat smoke and tobacco, and strangers kept grabbing her, squeezing her, shaking her, kissing her, and generally wishing her well.

It was times like these, in amongst a crowd of rowdy revelers, that Ellen realized quite how short she was compared to others. She couldn't see a thing beyond the swarming mass of bodies, and it made the air close, too thick to breathe, though her breaths came so quick and plentiful that she grew faint. Was this what it was like to be buried alive? Desperate to claw her way free?

"If you wish to leave," her cousin Logan whispered in her ear as he caught her elbow," I'll take ye anywhere you're keen to go."

Before she could offer him a grateful reply, someone grabbed her other hand and dragged her away.

"We should speak," her mother said, threading a path towards the stairs. Based on her tone, Ellen might prefer to face the crowd, and she cast a pleading look over her shoulder, but Logan and his wistful face had already been swallowed by the throng.

"Not you," her mother said to Maggie, shutting the bedchamber door in her little sister's face.

Ellen imagined Maggie sticking her tongue out at the closed door before cupping her ear against it to hear their mother's every word.

She picked nervously at a loose thread on her dress, waiting.

"I know you'd prefer the convent," her mother said.

An understatement. People seemed to know an awful lot about what Ellen wanted without caring whether she got it or not.

"And given the choice, you might have picked someone, well... prettier, more... delicate."

Ellen made a face at the assumption about her preference in men. The truth was, she'd never allowed herself to have any preference, to even entertain the notion. But if she *were* going to choose one, she certainly didn't see herself picking someone *pretty* and *delicate*. She'd have chosen someone like Finn Shaw, someone kind and generous, ready with a laugh, and braw enough to protect a lass should he need to. Sure and all, she might have picked someone a bit smaller, but one could argue there was something pretty and delicate about the lashes of Silas MacKenzie's amber eyes.

Her mother's scowl reminded her that *proper young ladies do not pull faces.*

"Whatever you might've preferred, at the end of it you'll be wed, and he's going to have certain expectations."

Oh, holy Mary, please not this. Ellen stared out the window, but the orange hues of sunset looked like the burning fires of hell.

"I won't pretend it'll be pleasant," her mother continued, staring at her own hands, twisting the wedding band with her thumb.

Ellen tried to swallow but her mouth had gone dry, and she was terribly warm.

"A dram will help. Or wine. Whatever you can get really."

She was absolutely going to faint again. Twice in one day—marriage was turning out to be such a blessing already, but at least it would end this conversation. Gripping the window frame tightly, she forced deep breaths in and out until her mother placed a cold hand on hers and led her to sit on the bed.

"If you're lucky, it will be over quickly, darling. But the main thing is, you mustn't cry."

Ellen snapped to attention. Why would she cry?

"Crying only makes it take longer for most men. Just lie back and think of the beautiful bairns you'll have because of it."

Ellen glanced sideways at her mother. Was that what she had done? Pictured the faces of her children to stop herself from crying on her wedding night and twice a week for two decades after? Was that why she sometimes seemed to resent them, Ellen and Maggie both, her two beautiful bairns?

Would Ellen's future children be small like her, or tall and broad, with golden sunbeams in their eyes?

"Now," her mother stammered, "the mechanics can be quite, well, surprising—"

That was all Ellen stayed to hear.

She had never disobeyed her mother in her entire life, but the evening of her betrothal seemed as good a time as any to begin, and with a strength she hadn't realized she possessed, she flew from the bed, threw open the chamber door, and pushed past Maggie to take her chances with the revelers below.

Logan's brother Lennox saw her and tossed her into the midst of a lively dance, and she was spun back and forth from one to another until she was dizzy and nauseated, ready to fall into the fire just to bring it to an end. Then strong arms caught her once more, only this time she was ushered away from the crowd, and when she opened her eyes in the cool, fresh air, she found her cousin Jory Shaw, standing with her husband Finn, who had performed the rescue.

"All right?" Jory asked, squeezing Ellen tight and leading her deeper into a quiet garden at the far corner of the inn.

Ellen nodded, holding onto Jory just as tightly before casting an appreciative smile at the strapping Highlander who stood guard, blocking them from the chaos and clamor.

"This one's been lost without ye," he said, leaning down to kiss her cheek. "Congratulations, Ellen. Whoever he is, he's a lucky lad."

Warmth flooded through her. Finn was the only man besides her father she'd dare let get so close, and he knew it, too, withdrawing a bit so the cousins might speak privately.

Jory took Ellen's face in both hands and peered at her intently. "How are you really?" she asked.

Tears immediately flooded Ellen's eyes, and Jory folded her into another tight embrace. "Shh, I know. Maggie said Auntie was giving you a talk."

Ellen nodded.

"If it was anything like the one she gave me, no wonder you're upset. Don't listen to a word of it."

Ellen laughed but it came out more of a sob.

"I mean it, mo chridhe. Auntie... well, it doesn't have to be that way. It can hurt, yes, especially if you're not ready, but that's the smallest part of it."

Ellen frowned, wiping away more tears. How on earth could anyone make herself ready for all that?

"There are oils you can use, and if he takes his time, you'll feel a thousand things at once. Any pain will be the least memorable of the whole lot. I know it's hard, but it helps if you..." Jory smiled sheepishly and shrugged. "It helps if you take control a bit. That way you can make sure..."

Ellen trusted Jory more than anyone else in the world, but Finn hadn't been a total stranger. They'd known each other as children and then became dear friends before saving each other from mortal peril. Finn was one of the best men Ellen had ever met. And besides, her cousin hadn't yet seen the giant of a man she was meant to marry. What did *take control a bit* even mean? When had Ellen ever controlled anything in her life?

Her skepticism must have shown on her face, because Jory said, "Maggie regaled us with stories of his height, dearest, but dinna fash, as my *wretched* husband would say. There are many different ways to enjoy the bedroom."

Ellen's cheeks burned, remembering the spark that shot down her arm when she accepted the MacKenzie's handkerchief, and the way it sizzled straight to her core.

Though smaller than Silas MacKenzie, Finn Shaw was no shrimp, and if Jory could enjoy being with him, maybe there was some hope left in the world after all.

"Have you eaten?" Jory asked, squeezing her elbow.

Ellen shook her head. She'd not been hungry, but the reminder made her weak and shaky, like her legs could give out any moment.

Never far from his wife's side for long, Finn stepped close. "I'll fix you a plate. Seems we're to be practically related on both sides now, Miss Ellen," he said.

"How so?" Jory asked.

"MacKenzie's mother was a first cousin to Alys Leask through the Campbells," he explained.

Ellen didn't really know the Leasks, but they were something like foster parents to her cousin-in-law, and she'd met the pair at Jory and Finn's own wedding eighteen months back. They'd been instrumental in helping Finn to rescue Jory from the treacherous Long Thomas Gordon at Bearradh Dearg, earning Ellen's eternal devotion.

She shuddered once more at what might have been, and Jory rubbed her arms to warm them.

"There, you see. It's practically fate. Mrs. Leask is a lovely, discerning woman. Once in her fold, you'll boast no fiercer ally."

Ellen tried to smile.

"You really must eat something, dearest. It'll be a long few days before it's over."

"I'll get it," Finn offered once more, disappearing before Ellen could protest.

"Just promise you won't try to run away," Jory said. Her tone was light and teasing, but she tilted her head, forcing Ellen to meet her gaze, and there was no laughter there.

How could she know running was exactly what Ellen had been dreaming of? She'd never run before, not even in a footrace as a child. And how could Jory forbid it, when it was exactly what she'd have done in Ellen's place?

"I mean it. There's a whole world out there. But in here," she tapped Ellen's heart, "and here," her temple, "you're stronger than you think. Give yourself a chance to prove it."

Chapter Three

Sleep had eluded Silas since he was a child, to the point that he suspected Mrs. Kynoch had told the kitchen maids he was a changeling left on a hillside by the faeries—preposterous given his size. His insomnia persisted into adulthood, and the evening of his betrothal was no different. He hardly waited for the creeping fingers of dawn to trace his windowsill before heading down to the stable, his favorite refuge as a lad. It was like stepping back in time: the smell of hay and horse, the chuffing and munching of oats, the dust filtering through the first rays of sunlight, and Gawyn the old groom running everything like clockwork.

Si breathed it all in: crisp, sweet pine and oaky tannins. Moments like this, it was good to be home.

"Madainn mhath, milord," the groom said. "Needing a horse?"

"How long have we known each other, Gawyn?" Si asked, noting for the first time that the groom's hair was no longer grey but white and wispy.

The old man looked confused and scratched his head. "Well, now, I held you in my arms the day after you were born, so you ken it's nigh on thirty years, milord."

Twenty-eight.

"Exactly," Si said, clapping the order man's shoulder. "So then call me Si. Are you well?"

"Och, aye. Fit as a fiddle. Is it Uinnseann you'll be wanting?" Gawyn picked up the saddle and tack.

"Aye, but I can manage," Si replied, taking the gear and moving to saddle his ash-grey horse himself. "My father," he began, not looking at the groom, but sensing the man still behind him. "How long has he been ill?"

Gawyn didn't answer until Si looked over his shoulder. "I think it's been some time, milord. But it's fits and starts though, ye ken?"

"How do you mean?"

Gawyn rubbed the back of his head like he was wrestling over whether to share gossip, but he finally gave in with a sigh.

"Seemed well enough the day he arrived. But in no time at all he was gripped with the lung fever."

"Coughing? Shortness of breath?"

"Aye. Then he seemed to improve before you arrived, milord."

Si tried to smile. "I always did bring out the worst in people."

"Och, never think it, milord. If anything, it was the prospect of seeing you that improved him a spell."

So it wasn't just a chest cold that had sprung up with the changing season. What else had Si overlooked or chosen not to see? "Thank you for telling me."

"I know he's overjoyed to have you back, milord. As are we all. Both of you."

Si nodded and tightened the stirrups. How many letters had his father sent in the last few years, filled with second-hand news of Bram and the clan, of who had wed and who'd gone away, but nary a word mentioning his own poor health? Would Si have returned sooner if he had? Or journeyed to France, even?

"And felicitations on your upcoming nuptials," Gawyn went on. "It's good to see the place coming alive again."

"Aye, tapadh leat," Si said, mounting up and kicking Uinnseann a little too eagerly.

"Give my regards to the young lady," Gawyn called after him.

Felicity. Was that what he should feel instead of this twisting, writhing adder in his gut?

He took the long way into the village, across misty fields of heather and gorse, past the old kirk, until finally he could avoid the inn no longer.

The lass was up early too, standing in a remote part of the garden staring off to the east, hugging her arms to her chest. Her golden hair looked like an extension of the sunrise, and the same urge to protect her which had first flared inside his chest at the kirk burned in him once more.

Si slid off his horse and ambled toward her, keeping the fence between them. "Madainn mhath," he murmured, hoping not to startle her.

She looked his way, turning those brilliant blue eyes on him, and it paused him in his tracks for a moment. He would never get used to, or tire of, those eyes.

He stooped to lean on the low wooden fence, shrinking himself down to a more palatable size. "Better today?" he asked, and she nodded once.

He nodded too. Among friends and classmates, Si was known to be a man of few words. He'd always preferred the company of horses to people, of books to peers, but he was positively verbose alongside this one.

Movement across the garden caught his attention. The sister had seen them and was making a beeline for their quiet corner. If he wanted to offer his gift in private, now was the time.

"I..." he began, but he didn't know quite how to speak to the little creature. "That is, my, ah..."

All the words in the English language seemed to have fled his brain. The faintest dusting of freckles covered the bridge of her nose, and it suddenly occurred to Si that kissing her there would be a bit like kissing the stars sprinkled across the night sky.

"Morning, Mr. MacKenzie," the sister called.

He nodded to her, then removed his mother's Luckenbooth from his sporran, the gleaming silver warm and alive to his touch. "Here," he said, shoving it at Ellen across the fence.

She practically jumped back as he thrust his arm out, and the brooch tumbled into the dirt.

"Och!" What a lumbering oaf he was. He dropped to one knee to scoop it up, but the lass reached for it too, and like the day before, his fingers brushed against hers, sending such a jolt down his arm and straight to his groin, and this time he couldn't blame the thunderstorm.

His eyes flicked to hers, still watching him, as though she knew how his body betrayed him, and they both snatched their hands back quickly, hers clasping his mother's brooch. They scrambled to their feet, but she didn't even look at the jewelry, just at him, as though seeing right down into the depths of his soul.

"I ken it's tradition for me to buy you a frock if you like," he said.

She blushed and shook her head, dropping the brooch in her apron pocket.

"She's wearing Mam's dress," the younger one answered, finally arriving at her sister's side. "Though we've had to take it up an awful lot, and I suppose we'll have to take it out again when it's to be mine."

"That's very special," Si muttered, heat flushing the back of his neck. This was all going horribly wrong. She clearly wanted nothing from him, possibly right down to his name or his hearth.

The sister tilted her head, scrutinizing him, and Si tried to shrink down even smaller under her gaze.

"Are you going to shave before the day?" she asked.

Now Ellen ripped her eyes from Si to glare at her sister.

Clearly they'd been discussing his rough and unappealing appearance, but the nice thing about facial hair was it hid his tendency to redden.

"Do you think I should, miss?" he asked the sister, forcing his voice into a friendly, teasing tone.

She tilted her head the other way. "I can't decide."

When the bride didn't comment except to grip her sister's forearm fiercely, Si searched her face for a clue to her opinion, but if there was one, he couldn't interpret it. How long before he learned to? A year? Would he have that long?

"You're hurting me," the sister whined. "Come on, Wee Ellen, it's time to finish pinning your dress. I promise not to prick you on purpose. This time," she added, grinning at Si as though they shared some secret, but the notion of her deliberately needling his bride made him feel prickly himself.

"Take care you don't," he said darkly.

Her conspiratorial smirk vanished. "I said I wouldn't. Let's go, Wee Ellen. They're all waiting," she huffed, turning her sister and tossing Si another appraising look over her shoulder. This time there was no question of her disapproval.

She'd be trouble for the lads of Inverness one day soon.

"Miss," Si nodded at her. "Milady Ellen," he said, with a bow. He knew he should call her mistress until she actually was his lady, but for some reason he didn't want to. Some long-buried part of him wanted to heft her up into the saddle and carry her off to the hot springs nestled deep in the forest.

The sister took Ellen's hand, dragging her off, and Si sagged against the fence.

Here. What an absolute charmer he was. She must have known the brooch was old, was probably disappointed by some residual tarnish he'd missed, as well as his piss poor presentation. *Here.* Honestly. He would have to do better with the ring.

To reach the smithy on the outskirts of the village, Si must pass through the green, where a market was being set up to serve the many Mackintosh and MacKenzie guests who had descended upon the town.

"Si," his cousin Cedrick acknowledged as he arranged a table full of tonics and herbs. "Beannachdan," his cousin congratulated.

"Ced."

"How long's it been?"

"Too long. You'll play the pipes on the day?"

Cedrick nodded, eyeing Si warily. "How's Himself?"

"Grand," Si lied. "Is your missus around? Wanted to ask her to pay him a visit with one of her tonics for cough."

"Not so grand, then."

Si shrugged. "Went a bit soft in France is all," and Ced laughed, though they both knew it was another lie.

"Silas MacKenzie in the flesh," a cocky voice called from across the green. "I wouldnae have recognized you were it not for the tales of Finn McCool which the folks hereabouts liken you to. You're taller than I remember, even as a gangly youth."

Turning, he saw Blair MacKenzie, the son of his father's steward, walking towards him followed by Rabbie, the farrier, and a blonde lad shooting dark glances Si's way. A good three years younger than Si himself, Blair had followed him around like a lost lamb before Si left for Aberdeen, nothing but mischief and torment.

"Blair," Si nodded. "How's your father?"

"Oh, he's braw," Blair replied, though his downturned lips suggested otherwise. "Never seen him more fit. Went to Greece last year." His lip curled up in a pained sort of way. "Brought back so many olives."

"And how did you find Greece?" Si asked, counting the minutes until he could politely continue on his way. Blair's eyes looked empty, and it unnerved him.

"If I ever find myself in that locale, I shall tell ye."

Rabbie snickered at that reply, until Blair cuffed him on the back of the head. Their third companion continued to glare at Si through narrowed eyes.

"I would ask who's the mysterious lass that finally convinced you to give up your wanderlust and settle down, but I've just been making the acquaintance of her cousin Logan," he said nodding to his glowering companion.

"Only the best for our future laird," Ced told him, but he, too, sounded a touch disingenuous, and Si couldn't decide if it was a jab at him or an acknowledgment of Bram's birthright.

"She must really be something," Blair said. "I was beginning to think we might never lure you back from the charms of Aberdeen."

Si knew better than to take the bait. His academic side was only too happy to let go all manner of sins that Blair seemed to imply. But the whole point of this charade was to convince the clan he was what they wanted and needed—at least for the next six years or so. Would the future laird just let the barb lie?

He took a breath, drawing himself up to his full height so he towered over Blair. "I certainly preferred the company of learned men in Aberdeen over a wee ankle biter like yourself," he said good-naturedly, and Cedrick roared with laughter. "And as for the lady, aye, she's special indeed, as I'm sure her cousin will attest. Flawless, like a rare gem, I think you'll find."

"Blair," a stern voice called from the direction of the alehouse. All five men turned to see Norval MacKenzie standing in the doorway. The steward doffed his hat and bowed his head deferentially at Si, who lifted a hand in recognition.

"Excuse me," Si said, tipping his own head, before making his way towards the smithy without looking back to see Blair's reaction. The tiny hairs on his neck told him Blair kept watching him all the way across the green.

"Madainn mhath, milord," the blacksmith said, glancing up from his hammering when Si entered and jerking his head at a young woman working the bellows, who made an awkward curtsy and scampered out of sight.

"Silas, please," Si said, though obviously his reputation had preceded him.

"Sam. MacPherson," the smith replied, offering his hand.

"The fellow who worked this forge when I was a lad had some talent with stones and lighter metals." Si mumbled, though looking around he saw naught but iron horseshoes, hinges, and farming equipment.

MacPherson shrugged as if to say the smith of his youth was long gone.

From his sporran, Si offered the mottled red stone.

"Jasper?" Sam asked, holding it close to one eye and then slowly extending it an arm's length away, scrutinizing the stone in a way that made Si feel inadequate. "For protection and passion."

"Aye. Can you set it in a ring?"

Sam eyed him. "Signet?"

"No. A band. Delicate enough for a lady."

Sam twisted the stone between strong fingers. "Silver?"

"If you like."

"You'll have it in time for the day." He weighed the stone in his palm. "There'll be a lot left over. Could put it in the hilt of a sgian dubh. Matched set? Every lady ought to have a wee knife. My lass Greer keeps one in each boot. I've no fear for her safety around the village lads."

Si wasn't sure about the effectiveness of a knife without proper instruction, but what harm could it really do? "Why not?" he agreed.

Sam nodded and turned back to his forge, their business apparently concluded.

"Right. Mòran taing," Si muttered, wondering what had become of the smith he'd known as a lad, the one who had accompanied his father into battle at Glen Shiel. He truly had been away far too long.

"Stand still, mo nighean," Ellen's mother chided for approximately the thirty-seventh time. And she was trying to, she truly was, but she was plagued by such a restless energy. She hadn't slept at all, replaying her mother's words about the wedding night—*You mustn't cry*—and then Jory's. *There are many ways to enjoy the bedroom*, she had said, grinning over Ellen's shoulder at her husband.

Her cousin's words had dissolved into restless dreams of the MacKenzie bathing her, of all things, in a luxurious copper tub. She hadn't felt right since waking, as if it had been real and *this* was the dream.

Heat threatened to overtake her, and Ellen shifted her weight to the other foot, then jumped into her mother with a squeak as a sharp pain pricked her hip.

Maggie grinned sheepishly up at her with a mouthful of pins. "I don't understand why we can't just tie it back with ribbons," she whined around them. "We'll have to take out all these stitches again when it's my turn."

Mother smoothed out the shoulders of the old dress fondly. "Hush, Maggie. You'll get your turn soon enough. Lennox has been looking your way."

Though fond of her cousin in a familial sort of way, Maggie groaned as though she wanted to scream into a pillow. Ellen knew the feeling well.

"Better yet," Maggie said when she'd recovered, "let the MacKenzie buy you a new one like he offered."

"Did he?" Mother asked, her eyes alight with warmth.

Ellen nodded.

"This morning," Maggie answered for her.

"How very gallant," her mother crooned. "But there's hardly time for all that. You'll look lovely in my dress, Wee Ellen."

Ellen turned toward the glass, trying to imagine herself

looking as beautiful as she'd always pictured her mother. She turned the silver brooch in her hand, running her thumb along the soft, smooth surface and pressing the sharp points of the hearts into her palm.

Here, he had said, shoving it through the fence as though someone stood behind him, prodding him in the back, but it had sparkled in the morning sunlight, and Ellen had never seen anything more lovely. She wanted to dislike the man—had in fact resolved to despise him from the very moment her father had broken the news of her betrothal.

Disliking him would make it easier to leave. But there was something about the uncertainty in his countenance that was like looking in a mirror. After years of being overlooked, it was almost comforting to watch the big man try in vain to fade into the background, when his broad shoulders and imposing height took up one's entire field of vision. It was almost endearing to think anything could make a man like him the least bit discomfited.

She wouldn't say she liked him exactly. She didn't know him. But she was drawn to the depths of his whisky-colored eyes. And she didn't hate the way he swallowed the beginnings of his words, like he had to physically force them from his mouth. When he said her name, it sounded like *'Lady 'Len*—someone strange and mysterious and bold. Someone Ellen might imagine she could be.

Lady Len wouldn't swoon because each pin in the dress closed in like one more bar on a tiny cage. Lady Len would revel in the lustrous fabric and the freedom it might afford. But Ellen was not Lady Len.

Another pin went in, too close to Ellen's ribs. The soft woosh of pierced fabric was followed by further constriction around her middle as she tried in vain to inhale.

"I'm going to faint," she whispered, but no one heard her or moved to help, so she stumbled toward the windowsill for a bit of air. Then she crumpled to her knees.

Such squealing and squawking followed as Ellen floated

outside herself, pricked by a thousand tiny claws, pushed and pulled, until she finally found herself more or less seated in a chair.

Then Maggie squeaked and shoved a wadded handkerchief in her face, almost smothering her. "You've ruined it! You've ruined Mam's dress," her sister cried.

"Nothing's ruined," Mother scolded. "Let's get her out of it quickly."

"I suppose now I shall have to have a new one," Maggie whispered triumphantly.

Ellen was lifted up and tugged at until she wore only her shift, head tilted back to stop the bloody nose. It seemed a terrible omen, blood on the wedding frock.

"Have your hives returned?" her mother asked, prodding the shoulder of her shift to get a better look at the red, blotchy skin beneath, but Ellen yanked away, pressing the sharp points of the brooch deeper into her palm, seeking strength from the pain, as well as from the former owner.

Eventually this would all have to end. Except what kind of relief was to be found when at the end there would be *expectations*?

She curled down to put her head between her knees before she could collapse again.

"What's all this?" Jory peeked inside with another woman, and just like that, calm settled over the room like a blanket.

Ellen's nostril was packed with yarrow, her dress whisked away for cleaning, and the sisters were shooed outside under orders to collect sun, fresh air, and white heather for the bridal bouquet.

"Only not too much sun, you're already beginning to freckle," her mother warned, but Jory shushed her aunt and handed Ellen a wide-brimmed bonnet with a wink.

"Do you really not wish to marry him even a little?" Maggie asked a few minutes later, as they strolled arm in arm through a field overgrown with thistles and wildflowers.

Ellen considered the question, less sure of the answer than she probably ought to have been. She'd never longed to wed the way her younger sister did, feasting on the idea like it was air. But since first meeting the MacKenzie, with his quiet, solid presence, and the way he had defended her, brooking no opposition even from her father, he had begun to intrude on her every thought. Even more surprising, she found herself wanting to know him, as she'd never cared to know anyone before.

"Is it because of the beard? I suppose one could grow used to it in time, though I imagine it'll scratch awfully when he kisses you."

Ellen's step faltered, and she stared at her sister. Maggie was far too fanciful for her own good, imagining what it would be like kissing strange men, particularly her soon-to-be brother-in-law. Holy Mary protect them all. Who would keep the child out of trouble back in Inverness?

"Och, I'm sorry, Wee Ellen, I only meant it might be, but it might not," her sister spluttered, misinterpreting Ellen's frown.

Quite the opposite in fact. Last night, when she was finally alone except for Maggie's blissful snores, Ellen had imagined the MacKenzie's whiskers to be quite soft, like a kitten. She was consumed with a desire to reach out and stroke his cheek to see for herself, and in her dream—in the bath—she'd finally abandoned restraint. In her dream she must have ceased to be Ellen and become the mighty Lady Len.

Face burning at the memory, she plucked some heather. It was purple rather than the white Jory's friend Mrs. Leask had insisted they find, but she wove the ends together into a crown, placing it atop her sister's tangled chestnut curls.

Maggie grinned, setting her own leafy crown upon Ellen's head, and then took off running across the field.

She was going to turn her ankle running like that, and then Ellen would have to go and find someone to help carry her reckless sister back to the inn. Sighing, she hitched up her skirts and hurried after her.

A time or two she nearly caught the wretched brat, causing Maggie to squeal with delight and quicken her pace until, completely winded, Ellen couldn't hope to keep up. She stood in the field, bent over with one hand on her corset and the other on her knee, gasping for breath until a prickling sensation slid down the back of her neck.

Suddenly chilled, she straightened up to see Maggie facing her with a hand up to shade the sun from her eyes. Ellen turned toward the road where stood a large, ashen horse, and on its back cutting an impressive figure in his grey and blue tartan, the MacKenzie himself: Silas.

The heat in her cheeks spread down through her loins as he watched the two of them, his left eyebrow quirked down in an air of consternation. He probably wondered how he'd become betrothed to such an unladylike specimen, traipsing through fields after her hellion sister. She wasn't lady-of-the-castle material by any means. But she forced herself to stand up straight, smoothing the wrinkles from her skirts, unwilling to wither under his gaze. She may not be the bride he wanted or needed, but she'd had no say in the matter, so why should she hide? If he didn't want her, let him speak up and end the whole farce.

After an eternity, he tilted his head and tugged his cap, then with the merest twitch of the reins, his horse walked on, and she watched them until they disappeared on the horizon.

"Well," Maggie said, sidling up to her. "Maybe the beard's not so awfully bad. Maybe if Lennox grew one, it would hide all those freckles."

Chapter Four

After handing Uinnseann off to Gawyn, Si went to check on his father. The room was dim and hot, but the Kintail appeared to be resting comfortably.

"I've asked Ced's wife to send up a tonic," he whispered to Mrs. Kynoch, and she drew back, not trying to hide her annoyance at the obvious intrusion on her nursing skills.

"My healing has been good enough with his last two spells," she huffed.

Si wanted to explain that he only meant to ease her burden, particularly with the wedding causing her so much extra work, but at her disapproving look, his tongue tangled itself into a knot. She'd be annoyed with him either way. Might as well leave it alone.

"All this fuss. I'll be right as rain tomorrow," his father muttered from bed.

"We could postpone until you are," Si offered, sitting on the edge of the bed.

"Och no. The clan needs to see you settled, lad. As do I."

"The clan doesn't care about me. They need to see you well."

"They've seen me at all sorts."

"And since you went away? Since you've returned?" Si asked.

"Aye, it was a mistake to ever leave, is that what you want me to say?" The Kintail's raised voice, no longer booming, brought on another wheezy cough, and he fell back against the pillows.

"You did what you had to and kept it going from afar."

His father scoffed and shook his head. "If you still think that, it's only because you've been away so long."

Si rubbed between his eyes and shook his head.

"They've been here," his father said softly. "You've not. They see what you cannae."

Meaning they believed their laird was dying.

"Enough of all that." Si fiddled with the bedclothes, twisting them into knots like he was nine years old.

"There's been talk that Norval should be installed as tanist," his father said.

Well, and hadn't Si thought it himself? Blair wasn't shy, he'd make an excellent second. With Alex away, Norval had made sure there were men to fight at Glen Affric and Coille Bhan, and enough money to kit them for victory. Norval alone had collected the rents in the laird's absence and taken care of everything else. His expertise was one of the reasons Si had stayed put in Aberdeen.

"He's experienced. Well traveled. Maybe he's the better choice."

"Aye, there's them that suspect he's the one really running things these last years, and they're not altogether wrong." But he didn't like the idea, Si could tell.

"Could he act as ad litem for Bram?"

"Using fancy words doesn't make that notion any less foolish. Now get on wi' ye. And ask Morag to burn some of that incense."

"All right, Da. Don't upset yourself," he said, smoothing out the blankets he'd been twisting.

Some things never changed. Si and his father had been arguing his whole life—through letters when they had to—first because Si didn't want to be sent away to school, and then because he didn't want to return. After more than half his lifetime spent away, could he even call this place home? Indeed, everything changed, and yet somehow nothing ever really changed at all.

"How's the patient?" a hushed voice asked, and Si looked up to see a familiar freckled face peeking into the chamber, her thick auburn braid hanging over one shoulder.

"Auntie Alys?" he asked, rising to kiss the cheek of the most maternal figure he'd ever known, his mother's first cousin Alys, née Campbell Hamilton, now Leask.

"Alys," his father greeted her warmly, pushing himself up on his elbows. "Where's that worthless husband of yours?" he asked, and Si's Uncle Leask peered around the door as well.

"Right here, right here," the man said.

"Then come and tell me all the news," his father said, patting the spot beside him which Si had just vacated.

Alys rolled her eyes at the pair of them. "Couple of gossipy old hounds, those two."

The old pattern of quips and jibes was grounding, and Si smiled at her.

"How is he really?" she asked.

"Who can tell?" He shrugged. "Says a wedding is the only medicine he needs. What are you doing here?"

"You'd have me miss it? And you as dear to me as one of my own?"

"Of course not, Auntie. It's good to see you looking so fine. But what have you brought? Not a christening gown?" he added with a dark look at the linen draped over her arm. He'd known there'd be pressure from all corners on that front, and he was not prepared for it.

Alys shook her head. "Small mishap down at the inn. I wanted to see if Morag could sort it."

Silas frowned. "I'm sure there's nothing that woman can't do, but what's happened?"

"It's nothing. A few spots of blood on the wedding gown."

"Blood?" he demanded, making for the door, as though he could do anything to help. "Did that brat sister stab her so hard with a pin?"

A man and woman he didn't know blocked the doorway, and Si took a step back.

"Just a bloody nose," the woman said. "Nothing to trouble yourself over."

Si wouldn't put it past Maggie, but he supposed he'd be hard pressed to blame her for that. Though if anyone could conjure such a thing, it would be she.

"Jory Mackintosh Shaw, the bride's cousin," Alys introduced her. "And my, well…"

The man raised his eyebrows in a teasing challenge.

"He's almost an impudent son to me. A bit like you. Finlay Shaw."

"Finn," Shaw corrected, shaking Si's hand.

Si nodded at the newcomers, but then turned back to Alys. "Can we not have a new frock ready in time?"

Alys laughed kindly and patted his cheek. "All that education," she tsked, and he had the sense she was being condescending. "Now, tell me everything," Alys said, leading him outside his father's chamber, her adopted son and his wife trailing behind, though Jory kept glancing back with a furrowed brow. "Have you given her your mother's Luckenbooth?"

"Is your father unwell?" Jory interrupted before he could answer.

Si expected irritation from his aunt, but her lips quirked up and she turned to him with interest.

"Repeated spells of lung fever," he explained. "He supposes he's dying."

Jory pursed her lips. "I'll leave behind some herbs," was all she said.

"You have them on you?" he asked, not sure what good it would do.

His question only made his auntie cackle. "Always," Alys assured him. "The brooch?"

"Given, aye."

"Good lad. And who's to stand up with you?"

In truth, he'd meant to ask his father, until this latest bout of illness. He glanced back towards the sickbed.

"Ah." Auntie Alys patted his arm.

"The priest suggested Bram, but the bride's sister seemed to take an immediate dislike."

"Then, if you haven't asked anyone yet, might you consider Finn here?" Alys asked, smoothing over the awkward pause. "It would look good on him given the alliance, a chance to shine before the Chattan Confederation."

She smiled benevolently, and Shaw rolled his eyes and shook his head fondly. She was good at this, Auntie Alys.

Si turned to Shaw. "I mean, if you don't mind?"

"Och, I'd be honored, if you're sure," Finn said graciously.

"It's settled, then," Alys clapped her hands, and Si showed them to his library for a dram.

"Slàinte mhath," he said, relishing the burn down the back of his throat and up his nose.

Alys and Finn then settled into comfortable conversation and Si slipped into the background, trying to order his thoughts.

When he'd seen the lass frolicking through a field of flowers like a bonnie wee butterfly, he finally understood what angels Donne wrote of. The unfettered wildness in a spirit normally so restrained had taken his breath away. Then she'd caught him watching, and such a look passed between them as threatened to set his skin on fire.

He'd have liked to take her right there in that field, even with her sister's eyes falling out of her head, and that was no good at all. He couldn't have her, not even in the marital bed, not if he cared a thing for her.

"She's truly the best person in all the world."

The words intruded on his reveries, and Si blinked away the image of those eyes, reflecting the bluebells as she laid on her back amongst them.

Finn's wife Jory, Ellen's cousin, they had said, was leaning towards him. Now she had his attention, she offered him a small, sad smile.

"Take your time with her," she said, looking him right in the eye so he couldn't pretend not to understand her meaning. "Woo her."

It wasn't a request.

Si cleared his throat. Looked away.

"She is diffident and self-effacing," Jory went on. "But if you take the time to listen, I think you'll find she has quite a lot to say."

"Does she even wish to be wed?" he asked, desperate to know the answer, but too conflicted over what he hoped the answer would be.

Jory looked at him sympathetically. "I didn't." She shrugged. "Until I did. Be patient. Make her think it's her idea to fall in love with you."

Si glanced at her husband, wondering if the other man knew some secret that he himself had never grasped, but Shaw shrugged and shook his head. "I've got nothing," he said.

Jory gave him a pointed look, but he grinned shyly at her.

"What's that look then, mistress? 'Twas you propositioned me, if ye recall."

Her lips quirked to the side, trying to hide the smile she couldn't keep off her face, but her eyes burned for her husband, and his right back at her, and suddenly Si felt like an intruder in his own library.

"The pair of ye," Auntie Alys said, shaking her head at them.

But a tiny flame inside Si's chest flared with jealousy for what they shared. Was that how it could be, if he were another man and not Silas MacKenzie, who broke everything he touched?

ELLEN COULDN'T GET THE IMAGE OF SILAS MACKENZIE ASTRIDE his ash-colored horse out of her head. They somehow matched, the horse and he. The beast was the very hue of grey within his plaid, and its black mane shone blue in the noon sun, like the navy that crisscrossed the grey. She could well imagine the MacKenzie riding into the midst of a fearsome battle, and both sides laying down arms in awe.

Like everything else, Ellen was afraid of horses, but she could admire a beautiful one from afar. And a tiny, rebellious part of her even longed to conquer that fear—to pet the beautiful creature, look it in the eye and know it, tame it—to understand what it was like to have such a creature within her power, under her thighs and under her control.

It was wicked, of course, to imagine such things, though plenty of women enjoyed riding, but it must surely be part of some deeper wickedness, the reason the Lord denied her prayers night after night, year after year.

When she was a little girl, almost all of Ellen's prayers were answered, and when she realized it, she tried very hard to wield such awesome power with only the purest of intentions. At seven years old, she watched from the corner, wrapped in Jory's arms, as her mother struggled to bring baby Maggie into the world, knowing her aunt had fought the same fight with her littlest cousin Lucy, and in the end, had not survived. And so she had prayed to God, to Mary, and to the little baby Jesus himself to bring her mother and infant sister safely through.

Four years later, when her father whisked them all away to the safety of Moy as Simon Fraser marched on Inverness, Ellen had prayed for the well-being of their neighbors and that her home would be left standing for their eventual return.

Every one of those prayers had come true.

At first it was only the forgotten prayers that haunted her. She must have forgotten to pray for the safe return of Jory's father in 1715. Or was it worse? Had she failed to do so because deep down she wanted her cousin all to herself?

Then came the matter of the kittens. That was a selfish prayer if ever there was one. She'd begged her mother and father for a little house cat, a lovely grey one with soft, folded ears to call her own. When they refused, she had stubbornly turned to God instead, promising that if her prayer were answered, she'd be ever so good and never ask for anything selfish again.

And her prayer was answered.

A mama cat belonging to none of the townsfolk had found its way into the stable and gave birth to a litter of tiny, perfect kittens. It was the best and worst day of Ellen's life. It was the day she learned the cost of selfish prayers. It was the day she learned to fear a future at the hands of men, the day she pledged herself to the Lord as a nun. When all was said and done, the kittens had been taken away, and she couldn't allow herself to consider their likely fate.

Ever since that day, Ellen's prayers had not come true. Not when she prayed for her dear friend to be spared from a fever, not when she prayed for her mother's stillborn third child, and not when she prayed to join Jory in the convent by the sea.

Oh, the Lord still *answered* them, she believed that, but unlike in her youth, the answer was a cold and resounding no. Ellen had abused her power, and now the door was firmly closed, no matter how long she pounded on it from outside.

Perhaps because, at her core, she was only ever selfish. Perhaps she merely prayed to assuage guilt, to prevent her own despair. She longed to devote her life to God and live out her days in a convent, to be sure, but she wanted it in order to avoid the brutality of the marriage bed.

And God knew it, for who else could know her heart more truly than He? She wasn't worthy of a life in His service, and if she wasn't good enough for that, then what was she good for?

"What on earth can you be thinking about, Wee Ellen?" Maggie asked, bursting into her thoughts the same way she burst into every room she entered. "Your face looks mighty fearsome."

For the past three days, the bustle of activity had constantly swarmed around Ellen, never stopping long enough to draw breath. Against the rising surge of panic, she was surprised to realize that she clung to her memory of the MacKenzie on his horse as to an anchor in a raging sea, as though the sheer weight of him might tether her in place.

Now they had all crowded into her bedchamber where she was meant to be resting.

She lifted her eyes to find Jory and Mrs. Leask looking down in concern, so she shook her head and pasted on a smile that only deceived her sister.

"What indeed," Jory murmured to shush Maggie.

"Pondering my strapping nephew, I don't doubt," Mrs. Leask added.

"Is it true what they say about the size of a man's foot?" Maggie asked, tilting her head to the side as though picturing the foot in question.

Jory and Alys Leask exchanged glances. "I can't think what you could possibly mean," Jory said.

"How it relates to the size of his—"

"Good as new," Mrs. Leask interrupted, holding up the laundered wedding gown, and Ellen was relieved on Maggie's behalf, if nothing else.

"For your hair," Maggie said, showing Ellen the crown they'd fashioned from white heather.

"And for your shoe," Jory added, holding out a sixpence piece before pressing it into Ellen's palm and closing her fingers around it.

Tears threatened to choke her, but Ellen swallowed them down, nodding her thanks.

"Oh, don't cry, Wee Ellen," Maggie whispered, close to tears herself, real ones, which made Ellen choke on more of her own. "He may yet shave that beard," her sister whispered, and Ellen burst out in a laugh that sounded more like a sob, and she wasn't sure the two weren't tangled up together.

Jory sat on the bed to her left, pulling Ellen into an embrace and rubbed her back soothingly. Maggie followed her cousin's lead, dropping down onto Ellen's other side, cooing and shushing and petting her head until she was actually sobbing.

She hardly knew Alys Leask, but the woman knelt before her, taking the hand that was still balled tightly around the Luckenbooth brooch, and her soothing presence drew Ellen's tearful gaze to hers.

"I've known Silas MacKenzie since the day he was born. His bark is worse than his bite, as they say, but I like to think it's only from lack of using his voice. He's a private, intense sort, a bit like you, but warm and soft as fresh bannocks at his core."

Ellen didn't particularly want to be barked at or bitten, nor did she think the MacKenzie looked anything like squishy dough. She wanted to ask so many questions about who he was and what he was like, this stranger she was supposed to marry in the morning. Did he prefer the taste of strawberries or rhubarb? And was there anything a man so large and strong ever feared? What was his opinion of the scent of the earth after a long hard rain? And how did he take his tea?

Her face must have shown all of it, because Alys Leask smiled sympathetically and tried again.

"You could do worse. He's not one for carousing, and he's more of a taste for books than drink."

"There, you see, Wee Ellen," Maggie said, smoothing the hair down her back. "You couldn't have found anyone more dull if you'd chosen for yourself. Even cousin Logan."

Poor Logan. Two years younger than Ellen, he'd been making eyes at her since he was six years old and got birched for putting a frog down her dress to get attention. But her father had always wanted a son-in-law called MacKenzie.

Jory snorted and shoved Maggie so she fell dramatically off the bed in a fit of giggles, and Ellen couldn't help smiling through dried up tears. A man who liked words might be reasonably persuaded with discourse and argument to send her away to France—if only she could find her voice to ask him.

Chapter Five

As usual, the night before the wedding, Si didn't sleep more than ten minutes. As a babe, if he cried too much when his father was away, Gawyn would take him down to the stables and place him in a basket where watching the horses soothed his restless spirit and none would accuse him of being a changeling child. He suspected that on his deathbed, he'd be wide awake to greet the reaper. Or perhaps he'd know that eternal rest had come for him when at last he drifted off into peaceful slumber.

This night, there was something in the lass's eyes that haunted him whenever he closed his. Not exactly fear, which he'd expect to see in the face of one so young and innocent. It was more like a knowingness. Like she wasn't fooled by his size or his rank, but somehow recognized the small person inside the large one, even as she knew that he could shatter her.

There was something in those eyes that made him imagine taking her like a beast with their hands still fasted and the whole congregation looking on, something that made him certain he must put as much distance between their two persons as possible. Galileo's Jupiter would not be far enough away.

And so, lit more by moonlight than the dawn, Si saddled Uinnseann and rode, hard and fast, with no plan or purpose. He rode into the rising sun as though he could halt its rising, until he found himself on the banks of a loch overlooking the town which had once been the lass's home.

How many times might she have stood in this spot, staring out across Loch Ness with her head full of stories about monsters and the knight who might someday vanquish them? How disappointing for her that what she got instead was not a knight at all, but the monster.

Ambling along the shore with Uinnseann, Si spotted a patch of thistles. There was something uniquely beautiful about the Inverness Caledonian Thistles as compared to their less round and prickly cousins that grew near his home.

Suddenly, ridiculously, Si was consumed with an urgency to provide one for the lass. She should have something from home on a day such as this. His father being unfit for travel, and both their fathers too eager and stubborn to wait, she'd been yanked from the bosom of all that was familiar before the first vow had been uttered. She should, at the very least, have a piece of home with her in the kirk.

Taking great care to avoid the toxic thorns, he cut several perfect flowers and wrapped them carefully in a handkerchief before placing them in his saddlebag and turning back towards home.

Si returned to Ross in time to bathe and dress. Then he stood before the looking glass regarding his dour expression and tried to force a smile he didn't feel. It looked sinister. Like someone who ate the bones of small children. He tried again, but this one made him look like he belonged in an asylum.

Downstairs, his father began to cough, but his lungs sounded

stronger at least. Si tossed his sweat-stained sark over the traitorous mirror and went downstairs to collect him.

They joined the Mackintosh brood at their inn to march to
the kirk together. There were rumblings of concern that the lass
might not possess the fortitude to walk, but Finn Shaw would be
at her side, so Si allowed the silly tradition to proceed, though he
insisted upon a carriage for the laird. Out of courtesy to his bride,
he would keep the pace achingly slow.

Ced was ready with his pipes outside the inn, and they set off
as soon as the younger sister emerged to take Si's arm. He didn't
catch more than a glimpse of golden blonde hair behind her, but
even that was enough to start his pulse racing. He'd never realized
he had a preference for blondes. He'd never allowed himself the
luxury of any preference at all where ladies were concerned.

This was all a very bad idea.

Young Maggie beamed up at him as they walked. She kept
opening her mouth to speak and then blushing and closing it
again, and Si had the sense that she'd never been quiet so long in
her life. She tossed a few sneaky glances over her shoulder at her
sister, and Si was dying to do the same, haunted by that flash of
golden hair, but some brides considered it bad luck to be seen
before they were ready, and so he kept his face forward and his
stride as short as he possibly could until at last they reached the
kirk, where he handed off the sister to Finn, and the lovely Ellen
took her place at his side.

For a moment, he was frozen in time.

Her hair, which usually had a natural wave, hung in ringlets
nearly to her waist. The pale blue dress that had caused so much
consternation the day before only deepened the hue of her
Mackintosh blue eyes. And on her head, she wore a crown of
white heather—a circle of protection, a symbol of the wearer's
wishes coming true. If only he could believe that.

The lass was handed a rosette of red plaid that clashed rather dramatically with his grey and blue, and her hand trembled as she reached up to pin it over his heart.

She fumbled, nearly dropping the pin, and winced when she pricked herself instead of his sark. And so, Si did break with tradition, reaching down to still her shaking hands. Her eyes met his, a flash of fear and determination, but he guided her hands to finish the pinning, and then raised the bleeding finger to his lips, wondering even as he kissed her, what had possessed him?

Her cheeks reddened, and he lowered her hands, releasing them so he could pin his own rosette on her shoulder. He tried to be quick. Too many people were watching them, tittering over his impromptu display, though he could sense the dagger glares of that same cousin, Logan, and three identical replicas of him, his brothers, elder and younger. But Si's hands were too large, and Ellen was so tiny, and her breasts were pushed up by her stays. It was impossible not to brush across them as he pinned her, deepening her blush. What a wretched tradition. What a softness unlike any he'd ever known.

From his sporran, Si carefully withdrew the thistles, still in remarkably good condition after being transported, and when Maggie handed over her sister's bouquet, he added the two purple flowers, safely out of reach of an errant finger, murmuring, "Careful of the thorns, milady."

She recognized them, of course, and her eyes shot back to his, brimming with unshed tears. Lord. He'd gone and made the lass cry on her wedding day, and they weren't even wed yet. That had to be some kind of record.

Father Sinclair appeared, stepping between them to enter the kirk, severing the magic spell that had surrounded them. He motioned for the bride and groom to join him just outside the door, and there, in the shade-dappled sunshine, he spoke priestly words about the purpose of marriage that brought Si back to earth—a reminder of the transaction taking place and expectation of fruitful multiplying, rather than pretty words of devotion and endless blue eyes.

And then it was time.

"Silas Michael Wolfrick Alisdair MacKenzie, will you take Ellen Elizabeth Brìghde Mackintosh, here present, to be your lawful wife according to the Rite of the Holy Mother Church?"

Elizabeth Brìghde. Had he known she had two middle names to his three?

"I will," he said. Behind his bride, young Maggie sighed.

"And Ellen Elizabeth Brìghde Mackintosh, will you take Silas Michael Wolfrick Alisdair MacKenzie, here present, to be your lawful husband according to the Rite of the Holy Mother Church?"

The lass hadn't taken her eyes off Si since he'd given her those thistles, but she licked her lips and opened her mouth.

Not a sound came out.

"Miss?" Father Sinclair urged.

She exhaled a breath, but still no words. Tears sprang to her wide, petrified eyes once more. She swallowed and glanced around in panic. This was all sorts of wrong. She didn't wish to wed and couldn't bring herself to lie.

Nearby, her father cleared his throat impatiently, and Cousin Logan looked ready to pounce.

Si took her free hand in his, rubbing his thumb lightly across her knuckles, trying to tell her not to be afraid, trying to give her the strength to offer whatever answer she would, even if her answer was no.

She licked her lips again and then they moved to form the words on another exhale of breath, and Si thought he almost heard a whispered, "I will." Or was it just his own longing to hear it playing tricks on his ears?

"Good enough," Father Sinclair murmured. "I believe you have a ring?"

Si's mind went blank. He'd forgotten to return to the smithy to collect the jasper inlaid band, distracted as he'd been by his flight to Inverness before the dawn. If she'd been unsure before, she'd despise him now. What a dolt he was. She'd be humiliated here before God and her entire family, she—

Finn Shaw stepped forward, and on his outstretched palm lay the sparkling silver ring. Finn smirked at his surprise, and Si nodded his thanks. *Best man, indeed.*

"With this ring, I thee wed." He repeated the priest's words, slipping the ring on her finger, and for the first time since they'd met at the stairs, she tore her eyes from his and studied the ring with a hint of a smile on her lips.

Then she moved her lips in the shape of words once more, and they followed Father Sinclair inside the church, hand in hand. The only sound Si could hear was the thumping of his own heart deep within his ears.

ELLEN COULDN'T COUNT THE NUMBER OF TIMES SHE HAD reminded herself to breathe this morning, from the moment she opened her eyes in the bed next to a softly snoring Maggie— where instant panic snatched her breath and turned her stomach —to the claustrophobic buttoning of her bodice, to the announcement that the big grey horse was nearing the inn carrying its big, bearded rider. She couldn't possibly remember how many times, but she kept trying to count them as though that would somehow drive the point home.

She had caught Logan's eye as she walked to the kirk, his brothers flanking him on both sides. Logan had tried to offer a sympathetic and encouraging smile, but he couldn't hide his forlorn look quickly enough.

Just get through the day, and then find a way to go to France had been her mantra, until the moment she stood alongside Silas MacKenzie on the kirk stairs. It was then she realized she might not want to go to France at all, a terrifying thought in its own right which seemed wicked after so much yearning and promising to God.

She hadn't heard a word the priest had spoken. She was far too attuned to the overwhelming everything of the man before her. He had trimmed his dark brown beard, taming it into a tidy shape, and he smelled of a bewitching combination of moss and pine that transported Ellen to a forest cave where one could be completely safe and undisturbed. His whisky eyes by turns burned with fire hot enough to sear her skin and a moment later, softened like warm honey fresh from the comb. When the heat turned down enough to really look at them full on, there was a captivating blue tinge around the edges, almost like they were reflecting her gown back to her.

And oh, the dress. He pretended not to notice, but she could still make out the telltale stains where her blood had forever merged with the fabric. Someone had done their best, a remarkable job, truly, considering the mess Ellen had made. But she saw in Maggie's downcast face and pouting lips that she'd noticed. Bad enough they'd have to take out all the stitching for her taller and more top-heavy little sister. Ellen had to go and stain the thing too.

How childish and embarrassing she must seem to a man like Silas, a worldly academic who had traveled and studied and really lived, while she had sat cloistered in her father's house, dreaming of other cloisters on other shores—a strange bird whose fondest idea of freedom was a different cage, even one of her own choosing.

Could Ellen ever possibly become an adequate wife for a laird if she had a thousand lifetimes to practice and prepare? She couldn't work out why a man such as he, who could easily command the attention of any lass he wanted, would agree to the match. She wasn't plain, but beyond her looks there was little to recommend her. She didn't play music or sing. She wasn't useful like Jory, and though her embroidery was passable, that seemed a paltry reason. Perhaps she didn't matter at all, and it was only about the Chattan alliance.

But then he'd given her Inverness thistles, symbols of bravery and luck and devotion. Had he ridden all the way to her former home and back this morning just to provide a selection so fresh for her bouquet? Just so she might have a piece of home with her, even as she left the place behind forever? Surely he wouldn't have gone to such trouble if his only concern was the alliance.

She couldn't rectify the image of the man who stood before her with the one she'd expected to find, and it left her reeling.

"You're doing very well, 'Lady 'Len," he murmured when they turned to follow the priest inside the church, swallowing his syllables as before. It reminded her to step inside the persona of Lady Len, who rode horses and swung from trees, and could swim across Loch Ness in the stark, with nary a fear of fainting.

Once the congregation followed them inside the chapel, the priest took a knife and with an apologetic shrug, he pierced both of their right palms, hers and the MacKenzie's, and then pressed their hands together, left to left, and right to right so they formed an infinite knot. The cut stung sharply, but the warmth of Silas MacKenzie's hand blunted the pain, and their pulses seemed to beat together as one.

Maggie and Finn took up bits of fine rope and strips of tartan, and with a wink from Finn and lots of giggles from Maggie, the two wound their strands around and around Ellen and the MacKenzie's clasped hands, binding them fast together.

She should have felt trapped by it, like the pinning of her dress, but Ellen focused on the MacKenzie's captivating eyes. Staring into them was a bit like she imagined standing on the edge of a cliff would be—vast with potential.

"Now you are bound, one to the other, with a tie not easy to break," the priest recited, and Ellen finally broke eye contact as a twinge of regret fluttered in her stomach.

She intended to sever this bond just as soon as possible, didn't she? To beg his leave and journey to the convent in France. Would he hold this over her, refusing to let her go? Would she blame him if he did?

"Learn what you need to know," the priest went on, "to grow in wisdom and love, that your marriage will be strong, that your love will last in this life and beyond."

She hadn't considered *beyond*. Would her soul now be bound to his for eternity? And what would her desertion mean for that timeless union? Would she damn him to an eternal life alone?

Ellen's breaths were coming too quick and shallow. The priest spoke of love, but what of convenience and alliances? This was a transaction, nothing more.

The priest slid the bindings off their hands, giving each a trailing end of the other's tartan, and together they pulled the knot tight, sealing the bond between them so that even the most nimble fingers might never untie it.

Ellen stared at the red Mackintosh plaid, no longer her own, cradled gently in his broad palm, as though he might keep it safe for her until she wanted it back, as though he understood what it was to give up her name along with everything else.

The Laird Kintail stepped slowly forward, poured a dram of whisky, and offered it first to Ellen. She took a steadying breath and then a drink, letting it burn all the way down and out her nose and ears like steam, swallowing back the urge to cough so that she wouldn't embarrass her new family any further.

After an encouraging nod, her father-in-law patted her on the shoulder and then turned to his son, proffering the same cup to him. Silas drank the remainder deeply, and it was done.

She was a MacKenzie now, though she could hardly hear the cheers for the burning whisky and the drumming of her heartbeat in rhythm with the stranger beside her.

Chapter Six

The ceremony was over much too quickly for Si's liking. All that preparation and fuss, and then no sooner had he fallen into the depths of those sapphire eyes than he was expected to heave himself back out again, shake himself off, and be sociable. He wanted to toss his bride over his shoulder and carry her away to the edge of the world, but they were swept back to the inn by an endless tide of well-wishers and Logan's scowling brothers. As soon as two revelers receded, five more flooded in to take their place, and all the while the lass clung to the crook of his arm like she was afraid of drowning. Was it wrong that he liked the weight of her fingers digging into him, holding on for dear life?

At the inn, his new mother-in-law presented Si with a dry seed cake. It crumbled, sticking in his throat, and though desperate for a dram, tradition dictated that first he must break a piece of cake gently over Ellen's head for luck. Careful not to mash it into her hair, Si memorized where each crumb landed so he might brush it all out again when no one was looking, but they were pulled apart before he had the chance, he to dance with the little sister, and she with his father.

He tried to play the attentive elder brother to young Maggie, but his gaze kept finding his bride instead, no matter where she moved. The careful, fearless way she stepped with his father, matching his pace, at ease in the old man's arms as he could not imagine her being with him. His father's eyes sparkled with delight, and Si resolved that no matter what else became of it, giving him this day had been worth it all. Besides, he already seemed much improved from a few days ago. Perhaps Mrs. Kynoch's potions were working wonders after all.

Si couldn't say when the light had gone out of his father's eyes any more than he could deny that the lass or the day or maybe just the dancing had restored it. The laird obviously regretted his years in exile, blamed himself for every failed crop and harsh winter. Now he was eager to make amends with his people by proving the Kintail would endure for years to come, serving Si's future up on a platter, complete with all the free-flowing MacKenzie whisky they could wish for.

The first dance ended, bleeding into the next, and upon releasing his sister-in-law, Si found Alys Leask in his arms, beaming up at him.

"Auntie," he said.

"You two look lovely together, Si."

"Och, like a wee goldcrest on the shoulder of a monstrous boar."

She frowned at him a little, so he kissed her cheek and guided her to the refreshment table.

"That beard of yours is as bristly as a boar. Why didn't you shave for the day?"

"And be mistaken for a wean too young to wed? Seemed best not to risk it," he teased.

She smacked at him. "You're as bad as your uncle."

He grinned. "I'm glad you came."

His aunt patted his cheek, not seeming to mind the beard, really. "I've missed a great deal more than I'd have liked, but I wouldn't have missed this for the world, Silas MacKenzie," she chided. "You know, your dear mother, God rest her, would be so proud of you."

The smile slipped from Si's face, and he tried to paste a new one back on before she noticed. Just what, exactly, was there to be proud of?

He'd visited the home of his Aunt and Uncle Leask many times during his years in Aberdeen. Their croft was more of a home to him than Castle Leod at this point, but his auntie seldom mentioned her late cousin, and Silas preferred it that way.

He searched the crowd once more and spotted Ellen dancing with Blair MacKenzie. His bride's face looked a little too dream-like. Blair was harmless enough, but he was also young and pretty and easy-going with friends and strangers alike—the very opposite of Si in every way. Never far away, Blair's sidekick Rabbie Stewart watched from the corner, where he whispered to a still glowering Logan.

Bram tugged his sleeve. "Uncle says I must ask the sister to dance, but I don't really have to, do I?"

"No," Si told him. "You must go and ask the bride."

"But she's—"

"Now," he insisted, pushing the boy towards the couple, and when the lad cut in, Blair MacKenzie stepped away with a friendly bow, but his eyes immediately sought out Si and nodded at him, a smirk tugging at his lips.

"I've never seen her looking so well—Miss Ellen, that is," Finn Shaw said, offering a dram, which Si accepted gratefully and downed in a single gulp. "Slàinte mhath," Shaw toasted, swallowing his own drink before his wife dragged him back into the midst of the ceilidh.

As the music wound down, Si made his way through the crowd to claim his own dance with the bride, but a villager stopped him before he could reach her.

"It's good to see your father out and about, milord. Is it the rheumatism ails him?"

"Och, he's grand," Si deflected. "Only keeping you lot in line wears him out."

The villager guffawed, clapping Si on the back with a wink. "Sure and it's more like keeping you out of trouble, I'll wager."

"Aye, and he'll be even more tired when the bairns start arriving," a woman agreed with a grin. "Will you be taking over the Kintail soon, then?"

"You have my oath, milord," a third cut in before Si could answer. "We've been waiting a long time for your return."

"If it's the quinsy troubles the laird, you want to stuff a fat cat with hedgehog grease and honeysuckle," an old lady piped up. "Roast the lot, and spread the drippings on his throat, but it's got to be a *fat* cat, mind, or you've wasted your time."

Si nodded at her, a bit bewildered, and hoped any fat cats in the area were taking cover.

Another young crofter looked like he had something more to say to Si than congratulations, but he kept silent.

"All right, Angus?" Blair asked the crofter, shoving an ale into his hands, and the young man nodded and took a long drink. "You were right, she's a lovely specimen, Si," Blair added with a wink that made Silas boil.

One after another they stopped him. They wished felicitations and shared their joy at his homecoming. They offered skeptical commentary on his studies and dubious medical advice for his father, wondering aloud what could have held Si's attention for so long in Aberdeen, and remarking with bawdy winks and nudges that it would be the fruitfulness of the newlyweds which would bring a more plentiful harvest to their own barren fields.

Silas kept a polite smile frozen on his lips as he nodded along, but he didn't lose sight of Lady Ellen a second time. Though he shook hands with each guest in turn, his gaze followed her around the space as she was swept up by dancers and well-wishers, never eating, but gulping every celebratory cup that was passed her way.

Several times she caught him looking, her eyes scorching his flesh from across the dance floor, taking on a more and more pained expression as the evening wore on.

Finally, she slipped away from the crowd, and Si bid a gruff excuse before following her. She stood in the same isolated patch of garden where he'd found her the day before, arms outstretched to the fence which seemed to be the only thing keeping her upright, but this time she wasn't alone.

"Say the word, and I'll take ye away from here," her sullen cousin begged.

"Logan!" one of his brothers called. "Come away now, lad. Come and have a dram."

The young man's shoulders sagged, but he stepped slowly away to rejoin the festivities, and Ellen seemed to relax.

"Milady Ellen?" Si asked, stepping out from the shadows.

She didn't answer, but he could see her chest rising and falling as though the stays were laced too tightly to draw breath, and a sudden urge to dispose of them coursed hotly in his veins.

"Are you well?"

She shook her head.

Si cast a glance behind him, where the celebration might go all night. The two of them had done their duty, surely, and could slip off without being missed. Even if they *were* missed, wouldn't everyone assume it was to make a start on the family they were all so desperately hoping for?

He stepped closer, so he might speak without being over-heard, close enough to see the beads of perspiration breaking out across her forehead.

"D'you wish to leave?"

She licked her lips as she'd done at the kirk before her whispered vows, and then nodded once.

"Give me three minutes to collect Uinnseann," he whispered,

breathing in the mingled scents of lavender and heather that intoxicated his senses more than any dram.

Even if he could not *have* her, he desired nothing more than taking her away.

FOR A BRIEF MOMENT AFTER THE HANDFASTING, ELLEN supposed she'd lived through the worst of it. Then she remembered first the feasting and later, the wedding night, were still to come.

At least she'd known a little of what to expect from having attended the celebration of Jory and Finn's nuptials. She was prepared for the dancing and looked forward to the food, but the unbridled joy for the prodigal lairdling was altogether different than the hesitant way the Chattan clans had come together to celebrate the former Shaw Wretch.

And yet, perhaps she was misreading cues as an outsider, but there seemed to be an undercurrent of discontent simmering. Also unlike at Jory and Finn's wedding, all eyes were on her every moment. No matter which way she turned, someone wanted a bit of her, until she wasn't sure there was anything left to be taken. From the time they'd left the kirk, she'd not had a moment's peace. Especially from him—from his gaze.

Ellen kept herself moving, afraid that if she stopped she might actually collapse. With every step, he watched her, marking his territory, igniting every inch of her skin. As her mother had suggested, she drank wine and then more whisky, in an effort to first cool herself, and then to burn him out of her, but it was no good. He watched, and then he followed her, and she couldn't help fearing that he found something in her to be lacking. Had he overheard Logan's ridiculously impassioned plea? Honestly, where could her cousin have taken her that she would wish to go?

She wasn't gracious enough with the guests, outgoing enough

when dancing with his family, light enough on her feet, demure enough with acquaintances. Just generally not enough.

Unlike the ring he'd given her, she was simple, plain, incapable of even imagining a band so fine as the one now resting on her fourth finger. The silver sparkled in candlelight and fairly glowed in the dark, and the red jasper stone was more exquisite than anything she'd ever seen. It truly was a ring for a lady, and she was an imposter, never intending to keep it on her hand.

She was supposed to be a nun, not the Lady Kintail of Castle Leod. What would the big MacKenzie do when he realized he'd been duped?

It all got on top of her, overwhelmed her—the merriment, the joy, the *expectation*. It had become nightmarish, as if each laugh were a taunt, each friendly face jeering at her to come clean and show her true nature.

Afraid of vomiting all over her mother's partially ruined dress, she'd escaped from the swarming, demanding crowd, to gulp in fresh, cool air.

But first Logan and then Silas had found her, each offering his own plan to escape.

And even though it would hasten the next torment, that insidious *expectation*, it was as he'd said at their first meeting *better to have it over quickly*, so she had agreed. Now she sat sideways upon the terrifying grey steed as her husband, her *husband*, held her tight against his chest to keep her from sliding off the saddle. Together they rode away from their own celebration to the site of their newly shared home.

How strange to think of a place she'd never set foot inside as her *home*, but so it must be until she managed to depart for distant shores.

Ellen had little time to dwell on the impropriety of resting so close against a man, even one who had been named her husband that very day. Nor could she contemplate the roughness of his countenance or the gentleness in his touch, or the smell of pine resin and moss. None of it stayed in her head for long, shoved aside by the sheer terror of hanging onto the horse for dear life. Horses were for admiring and fearing from afar, not for flying headlong to one's doom. Except apparently on one's wedding day.

Leod was about the size of Tordarroch, where Finn had grown up and where his brother had hosted his wedding, perhaps a little smaller than Castle Moy where Ellen had spent part of her youth. It emerged impressively from the shadows as their horse trotted up the lane.

Rather than stopping at the stable, Si rode right up to the entrance, where a young lad raced to meet him and take the reins.

He swung himself off the beast, then lifted Ellen in his arms, but instead of setting her feet squarely on the ground, he rumbled, "Believe it's customary to carry the bride inside, if you'll allow me, 'Lady 'Len," and when she didn't protest, he proceeded to do just that.

Only once inside did he let her down, steadying her with both hands on her shoulders.

Some small part of her expected him to ravish her the moment the door closed, but he leaned back against the opposite wall, trying to shrink into the shadows and asked, "Like a tour?"

Ellen nodded, dread building in her stomach. She supposed it must be a game which would end precisely when they reached his bedchamber, but he took up a torch in his right hand and held out his left for hers.

She hadn't joined hands with any but her sister or Jory in as long as she could remember, and her palm looked like a doll's alongside his, but his grip was light and comforting.

"The Hall, of course," he said, staring fiercely at the wood panels that lined the walls, as though they offended him. After sweeping the floor with his boot, he led her towards a staircase, and up to the second floor where he pointed out his father's chamber, and then an alcove next door stacked with crates and all manner of detritus, before waving dismissively.

"This was the chapel once," he muttered almost to himself, and his frown deepened. He turned that same scowl on Ellen, as though he'd read her mind, and with it, her intentions to leave him for the Church, and this time she did wither under his gaze.

"Mmphm," he growled, and turned back to the stairs, leading her down, down, down, walking quickly, as though Ellen's presence inside his home made him unhappy with it, and he was already regretting the solemn oaths of the day.

A scurrying as they entered the kitchen conjured images of dreadfully large rats, and she shuddered.

"Cold?" he asked, moving to stoke the fire, even as she shook her head, and then rummaging in a basket behind two urns of milk. "Mrs. Kynoch always keeps fresh bannocks if you know where to find them," he said, handing her one, and after the rich smells of the wedding feast, the simple roll was exactly what she wanted, but she reached for it hesitantly.

"Go on then, you've not had so much as a bite all day, I'll warrant."

She raised her eyebrow at him. After all, he hadn't been with her *all* day.

"What was it, then, a full breakfast of parritch and bacon for the bride on her day?"

That made her smile, and she hid it by taking a bite of the delicious bread.

He watched her devouring it so intently that she half wondered if he wanted to devour her, and perhaps she wanted him to, and a tension fairly crackled between them as she swallowed. Then more scuffling and sniffles from a corner of the room drew both their attention.

Silas crossed to the other corner and drew open a curtain, revealing a tiny, mouse-haired kitchen maid with red-rimmed eyes.

He knelt down so as not to tower over the girl, and she looked up at him, popping her thumb from her mouth and hiding it behind her back.

"Dorrie?" he asked.

"Yes, milord?" she answered, blinking up at him and then past his shoulder to Ellen, who took a step closer. The girl couldn't be more than five or six.

"Are you all right, lassie?" he asked, instead of the accusatory *Why are you crying?* Ellen had heard so often as a child.

"Yes, milord," she said again, smiling up at Ellen, her tears forgotten.

"Good," Silas said. "But if you weren't, would there be a reason?"

The little girl's eyes filled once more with unshed tears, and she whispered, "Nanny Morag said I was naughty and couldn't go to the party."

"Ah," he nodded, casting a conspiratorial look over his shoulder at Ellen. "Well, it was nice enough, but see? We decided to leave early."

Dorrie looked Ellen up and down as though she were a beautiful princess, and then smiled again, scrunching up her nose to show two missing front teeth.

"And d'ye know what?"

"What?" the girl whispered in awe.

"It was so chaotic, I didn't even get to dance with my bride. Now, isn't that a shame?"

"A very grave shame, milord," Dorrie whispered solemnly.

"Aye, a very grave shame, and one we must rectify. Only I'm not so good with the dancing. D'ye think you can show us what to do?"

Little Dorrie's face burst into sunshine, and she nodded shyly at her laird's big son.

He stretched out his hand to her and she scrambled out of her little hideaway bed, wrapping her tiny fist around his index finger and reaching for Ellen with her other hand. And together, without music, the three of them danced a sort of modified strathspey and amid the shadows of the flickering candlelight, somehow Silas MacKenzie didn't look quite so big and fearsome after all.

They danced with abandon, and joy bubbled up inside Ellen with surprising speed. When they staggered to a stop and little Dorrie threw herself on the ground dramatically out of breath, Ellen tried to steady her own rapid breathing, but her chest heaved up and down in the constricting bodice. Silas was panting too from the exercise, and then suddenly he raked his fingers tenderly through her hair as his eyes gleamed in the firelight.

"Crumbs," he whispered, brushing the remnants of her mother's seed cake from her scalp before dropping his hand to her face, his thumb skimming the ridge of her cheekbone which burned at his touch and did nothing to calm Ellen's breathing. Despite his beard, in the shadows of the kitchen his face looked younger, untroubled by whatever brooding usually lined it, and her legs felt a bit like jelly.

When Dorrie called, "A waltz, a waltz!" Ellen's heart echoed the little girl, for she could go on dancing like this forever.

Chapter Seven

Just as Si hoped, the impromptu dance put his bride at ease, and surprisingly lifted his own spirits too. God bless little Dorrie for offering the perfect excuse after he had failed so spectacularly at presenting the glory of Leod. It was naught but dust and decay whichever way he turned.

Ellen was a bright light in the gloom, and when they danced, with her hair flying, her face flushed with drink and exertion, he was half afraid her nose might hemorrhage again.

After the strathspey, Dorrie clapped her hands and called for a waltz, and Si was inclined to indulge her. But before they could count off the door rattled, and they all stepped back to make way for Uncle Leask and Finn Shaw, carrying the laird in between them.

"Da?" Si asked, to hell with formalities. To Shaw he added, "Is he all right?"

"Tired, I think," Shaw answered, as Si's father began to cough.

"He'll be grand. We thought to bring him through the kitchen and avoid a fuss," Uncle Leask elaborated.

"Didn't count on a welcoming party," his father choked. "Though I cannae complain about one so lovely," he added for the ladies' benefit, and both Ellen and Dorrie flushed ever deeper shades of red.

"Bannocks," Si explained. Then he moved to his father's right side, taking over from Shaw, who backed away.

"This one's always had an appetite. He'll start eating the furniture if you don't watch out," the old man whispered to Lady Ellen with a wink.

"There's a fellow back at the inn, name of Keith. A medical man," Si told Shaw.

"I'll bring him at once."

"No need," the laird complained. "Besides, I promised the lad a dram."

"Don't think I willnae make you honor it upon my return," Finn said, and then he was gone.

"Such a fuss," the old man sighed to Mr. Leask, but he allowed them to help him up the stairs to his chamber.

From the corner of his eye, Si saw the lass tucking wee Dorrie back into her trundle bed, and she looked so natural in the role it made him ache. But he couldn't worry about that right now.

"Should we not clear a room for you downstairs?" he asked when they had finally settled his father into bed.

"No, we shall not," the old man protested. Then to Leask, "Back a week, he already knows best."

Si turned away, ashamed of the disappointed tone in his father's voice, and there was his bride, standing uncertainly in the doorway.

"D'you know aught of nursing?" he whispered, not liking the note of desperation that caught in his throat or the look of pity in her crimped brow as she shook her head, so he turned away, back to his father, and sat on the edge of the bed. "You can get some rest at least, now everything's settled and over."

"Settled, ye say? Over? It certainly is not."

"I'm wed," Si reminded him, half wondering if his father's memory was going and he'd already forgotten the wedding, and half wondering whether he meant to follow them into the bedchamber and ensure it was all consummated properly.

"Aye, wed, and now we've the Gathering to prepare for."

Si froze. A Gathering had not been part of the plan—not *his* plan, at least. He'd expected to have more time. "A Gathering?"

"The sooner the men give their oaths to you, the better."

The tenuous control Si had been fighting to maintain since his return was slipping away.

"But you're getting better. You only overdid it today is all."

"It's time," his father said.

The room threatened to spin around Si. He'd come at his father's behest, agreed to participate in the sham of a wedding, and, hypocrite he may be, but he'd no notion of accepting any man's oath. The one Lady Ellen had been strong-armed into providing was already far too much.

"They should make their oaths to Bram," he said.

"Bram is a boy. And I do not have six years left in me."

"Dinnae speak so."

"Och, the sooner you see it, the better we'll all be."

Si turned his face away again, trying to mask the anguish bubbling up from his chest. He glanced back towards the door, where surely his bride must be disgusted by his display of weakness, but she was already gone. Well, who could blame her, the way Si was carrying on.

Death was a fact of life for everyone. But, though he'd been away for much of his youth and all his adulthood, there was comfort in knowing his father still trod the earth. Bad enough to become a husband, even worse a laird, but without Alex to counsel and guide him? He couldn't imagine it.

Soon footsteps fell on the flagstones in the corridor, and Keith appeared with Finn just behind.

"It was a very fine party," Keith said to him, gripping his elbow as he passed. Then with a smirk he added, "Milord," and Si rolled his eyes.

Back in Aberdeen, Silas had done his best to keep the lairdship under wraps.

Keith was a good man. A quick study of both the medical arts
and the men around him, he and Si had become quick companions thanks to his easy-going nature more than Si's.

He sat with the laird for a good long time, listening to his
chest and examining his eyes. They spoke at length in soft,
rumbling tones, and Keith took a great interest in the tinctures
and tonics prepared by Mrs. Kynoch, as well as the herbs left
behind by Jory Shaw.

At last, he patted the laird's arm and returned to Si, but the
sorrow in his eyes said all he needed to.

"I'm truly sorry," Keith whispered. "But you know the human
body can't go on forever."

Si wasn't a fool. He didn't need a physician to lecture him on
mortality. He nodded once. "Thank you for coming."

"He could have time yet," Keith consoled. "But it will be
finite."

But Si didn't hear anything else his friend had to offer. His
father wasn't dying. He was only fifty-five. Keith, he was disappointed to realize, must be a quack.

"Well now, what about that dram?" Uncle Leask asked,
breaking the strained silence that had fallen over the room.

"Aye, just so," the laird said, directing him to the whisky and
glasses in the corner. "Pour one for the doctor here, as well."

Keith and Shaw drifted over towards Leask and the Kintail.
But then Finn made his way back to Si and proffered a glass.

He looked very much as though he wanted to speak, and Si
wondered about his new friend. Alys had called him the younger
brother and heir to Tordarroch, which meant he had lost his own
father at some point in time. He was probably full of opinions on
the matter.

Si stared into the drink, unable to bring himself to do much
more than inhale its strong, peaty, bacon-laced scent.

There were other doctors. He'd heard of interesting therapies conducted on the continent the likes of which the Scots had surely never dreamed. If he allowed the men to make their oaths, perhaps his father would agree to return to the Riviera until his health was restored. Perhaps Si could accept their oaths now and still transition it all to Bram in time.

He glanced towards the doorway once more, expecting to see his cousin waiting there with Ellen. "Where's Bram?" he asked.

"Sent to bed, I think, milord."

"Do not," Si warned him. He was no one's laird.

"I apologize," Finn said, eyeing him warily.

"Do not do that either. You'll see that he gets back to the inn?" He inclined his head towards Keith.

"Of course. Whatever ye need."

"Mòran taing," Si said. He was surprised to realize that he would miss having Shaw around after he and Jory left with the rest of the Mackintoshes. Ludicrous, really, when he'd only known the man a day. "Well then, I suppose I should go and find my wife."

If Ellen were Silas MacKenzie, she would want nothing so much as privacy. And so, the minute he turned his attention to his father, she slipped back down to the kitchen where she cuddled Dorrie, humming the child a little tune, trying to drown out his desperate words, *Do you know aught of nursing?*

But his voice was etched into her memory along with the half-feral look in his eyes. He must have heard of Jory's skill and assumed it ran in the family. And it did. Ellen was just on the wrong side of Jory's family. It had been her late aunt, Jory's mother, who knew the healing arts.

Such a misconception would explain why he agreed to the match, at least. How disappointed he must be, having gone to so much trouble, and no closer to finding a nurse for his ailing father. Perhaps she could learn if she tried. She'd always been kept away from the sick because of her delicate constitution, but her husband didn't need to know all that.

Even once little Dorrie had fallen asleep, Ellen stayed in the kitchen awaiting Finn's return, presuming neither he nor the visiting physician would know the way to her father-in-law's bedchamber.

After directing them, she'd intended to observe Dr. Keith's efforts and see what she might learn, but she found herself drawn instead to the alcove next door.

Standing outside the chapel, which was piled high with gubbins and sundries, Ellen imagined what the room might once have been. Was it cozy and warm, with glowing glass windows and candles adorning every wall? Did it echo like the choirs of heaven when voices were raised in song?

There was a time when she had loved nothing more than to sing, long ago and far away, before her voice went into hiding. Some not-so-small part of her had hoped a monastic life might bring back her voice, that she might sing again in a chapel at Notre-Dame-des-Chelles. Was such self-indulgence the reason her prayers went unanswered, the reason she wasn't on a boat across the channel this very minute?

She swallowed down that line of thinking and focused her mind instead to pray for the Kintail's healing, doubting anyone heard that prayer either, and not because the room was more storage space than chapel, but because even this was selfishness born from desire to not be an immediate disappointment. Was she so flawed that she was incapable of lifting up a single wholly selfless prayer?

"There you are." The MacKenzie's tone was brusque, his brow furrowed in annoyance. "I've been looking everywhere."

"Where should I have gone?" she muttered crossly to herself.

After all, it wasn't as though he'd finished the tour. She didn't even know where she was meant to sleep.

"Ha?" he tilted his head, expecting some kind of answer, and she cast her gaze to the floor.

His father was ill, and here she was being rude. Selfish.

"You must be exhausted," he said, sounding contrite and about as tired as Ellen had ever heard a person sound, as though he hadn't properly slept in his whole life. "Come." He motioned for her to follow him up the stairs to the third floor.

Silas led her down the corridor to a chamber where some kind soul had laid a fire and blanketed every surface with daffodils. The effect was a warm, cozy glow that even brightened the groom's brooding amber eyes. There was a dressing screen in one corner, and Ellen's trunk, which she'd quite forgotten about, was already waiting for her, packed with every item she owned in all the world.

"If there's anything not to your liking, it can be changed," he said. "You've but to ask."

In a corner opposite the dressing screen stood an armchair, and draped across it, a length of plaid in deep grey and blue that matched his own. Ellen reached for it, trailing her fingers along the soft wool. She'd always found the bright reds and greens of the Mackintosh clan to be a bit too much, like a prickly holly thicket. The muted grey was much more to her liking.

"I thought," he began, having stepped up behind her very close—how did one so large move without her hearing him? He cleared his throat to start again. "It was my mother's."

Such a sentimental gesture from her new husband should have made Ellen flush with pleasure, but tears pricked her eyes. He'd lost his mother, and now here she was planning to make him lose his wife. How much could even a hard-hearted man take? And this one didn't seem so very hard at all.

She retracted her hand, unable to turn until she'd fought her face back into submission. When she finally did, he'd stepped back, out of her space, to the doorway.

"This can be barred from the inside." He showed her a heavy wooden arm that could be lowered to block entry. "There's none will harm you here, but with the Gathering in a few weeks' time, you might feel more at ease knowing..."

A Gathering? Already? Hadn't today's revelry been enough to last these people a lifetime?

Her shock must have been evident on her face because he nodded grimly.

"Aye. The Gathering was news to me as well," he said. "But the timing makes sense given how many traveled in for today. None should trouble you, but you'd be wise to bar the door all the same."

Ellen wasn't sure she had the strength to lower it on her own, let alone lift it again when she was inclined to leave, or why she would need to with a man like Silas in her bed, but she nodded her agreement.

"Through here is my library." He opened an adjoining door. You're welcome to any books that take your interest."

Tilting her head, Ellen glimpsed an empty fireplace, the corner of a desk, and another armchair with a matching footstool.

"There's no bolt for this one, I'm afraid, though I did mean to have one installed," he explained. "I'll go on through, then you can knot this bit of rope around the handle just so, and it will be impossible to open from that side."

Ellen frowned. He meant to spend tonight—his wedding night —in a cold library alone?

"I willnae trouble you."

What had Mrs. Leask said? That he preferred books to people? Maybe his aunt hadn't been exaggerating after all.

What she supposed must be relief swept over her, mixed with a fresh wave of unshed tears. He didn't intend to consummate their union tonight. Was it because of his disappointment about the nursing? Perhaps for once her prayers had been answered. She said another quick one for the Kintail just in case.

The thing was, she'd been preparing herself for this moment all day—all week. And now, what? She'd have to wait like a criminal at the end of a rope, not knowing when the floor would drop away? Would he come for her tomorrow? Or the next day? Would he wait until her defenses were completely down and surprise her?

"You've had a long day," he murmured. "And more'n a wee bit to drink. There's no reason it has to happen tonight. Or at all until you're ready. No one will know."

She tried to smile at him, but her face scrunched up tight so she nodded and turned quickly away. She didn't look back at where he'd been standing until she heard the door close softly behind him.

And that was that. Ellen Elizabeth Brìghde Mackintosh was now Lady Ellen MacKenzie, and the future Laird MacKenzie was so disgusted with her fecklessness that he would choose to spend his wedding night with books and papers, and she would spend hers all alone. It was no more than she deserved.

She was finally getting exactly what she wanted, to be left alone, and like an ungrateful wretch, she was still deeply unhappy with her situation.

"Don't forget the latch, 'Lady 'Len," he called through the door, his voice so soft it made her shiver.

She wound the knot like he'd shown her, though Lady Len most certainly would have forgotten the latch and invited him in to stay. But she was not Lady Len, no matter how much she liked hearing him say it. She was a meek Mackintosh mouse, unfit for either a man or the Church.

Chapter Eight

Silas MacKenzie was eight years old when he first learned the truth about his mother. He had snuck down to the kitchen to pilfer bannocks when he was meant to be sitting a Latin examination, and he overheard his tutor lamenting his tacit nature and poor elocution.

"I don't understand it," the young man had grumbled around spoonfuls of Mrs. Kynoch's fresh haggis. "His father speaks as clear as a bell. Was his mother a mumbler? You know, it's usually the case that when something's wrong with the pup it's to do with the bitch."

Si had flinched as Mrs. Kynoch slammed a dish down on her worktable. "I'll thank you not to speak ill of the dead, sir," she said shortly. "Iona MacKenzie was as fine a woman as ever walked the earth, no more so than when she gave her life bringing that poor wee lad into it. And there's nothing the matter with him."

A strained silence followed, and Si's ears burned, for, though he could read the numbers on the moss-covered stone in the kirk-yard, no one had ever admitted to him outright that he'd caused his mother's death.

"What's that look?" Mrs. Kynoch had demanded.

The tutor made a noncommittal sound in reply, but then decided to elaborate after all. "Can't exactly describe him as wee, though, can you?"

The cook huffed.

"The size of him, it's no wonder his mother—"

Another slammed dish, and Mrs. Kynoch's voice grew as low and steely as Si had ever heard it before or since. "I'll ask you to keep such learned opinions out of my kitchen, sir."

Si didn't stick around to hear anymore. He slipped out the cellar door and raced down to the stable to sort out his feelings on the back of a half-ton horse. He never did finish the Latin exam. From that day to this, he never told anyone what he'd overheard, and Latin still made his stomach turn.

That day, Si learned that big babies killed their mothers, and he'd spent enough time around the stables to know where babies came from.

For eight-year-old Si, it was a small thing to vow never to become a father. He'd no interest in the fairer sex. His Uncle William was laird and on the prowl, everyone said, for a lass to wed. He needed someone who could handle him, along with the rest of the rough-and-tumble clan, a Lady Kintail to provide them all with an heir. What matter was any of it to Si?

It would be a dozen years before his vow of celibacy became any kind of burden, and when it did, Si had only to think of his mother dying in the throes of labor for his grapes to wither along with the vine.

When he'd made his intentions—or rather, lack thereof—clear to his new bride, her face had fairly crumpled. It took every ounce of resolve in every muscle of his body not to lean her back onto the bed and spend the rest of the night apologizing.

Ellen's disappointment surprised him. Perhaps he'd misinterpreted her fear. Perhaps he should have worked out a proper plan to avoid an unwanted bride in the first place, rather than simply *Keep your hands to yourself* and *Stay away*. When her cousin had as good as told him she wasn't ready for the marriage bed, he'd supposed it was some Divine Providence. It had been a relief, since he'd no intention of lying with her as man and wife, whatever else they might find to get up to.

Stop thinking about it.

It had been a long while since he'd taken himself in hand. Though he ached with need, he dared not break his fast, lest it only whet his appetite for more. *Enough.* He wasn't a predatory beast to be controlled by instinct.

A rustling on the other side of the wall drew him back to the door, and he ran his hand over it as if it were some magical barrier that really could keep him out. Like every other part of this godforsaken castle, there was a crack in the wood.

He'd first noticed the dilapidation while giving the lass a tour of the place. Since returning home, he'd been aware something was off, like a shadow chilling every corner. He'd assumed it was just himself—being back after so much time, thirteen inches taller and sixteen years removed from the boy he'd left behind—not to mention the laird's illness and all the expectation hovering around Si like a swarm of bees. But seeing Leod tonight through her eyes, he realized just exactly how run down and dingy it had grown in his and his father's absence, and he burned with shame.

More rustling on the other side of that door. Without stopping to consider, Si put his eye to the crack, not to spy, only to make sure the lass was all right.

She was twisting around to undo the very many buttons that lined the back of her frock, a duty that should have been his, particularly this dress on this night. A gentleman would have offered to help instead of running away to hide in his library like a coward.

He tore his eye away, and raked a hand through his hair, but the rustling continued. What if she couldn't get it off? Would she ask for his help, or sleep in the thing?

He peeked through the crack a second time, and now she was out of the dress and working at the ribbons of her stays.

Si watched, hardly breathing, as her nimble fingers untied those ribbons and tossed the corset aside so she was down to her shift. He meant to turn away, but she whipped the garment over her head before he had a chance to move, and suddenly he was seeing all of her. Long golden hair obscured the creamy skin of her back until it ended at the curve of her bottom.

Si's cock jerked at the sight, and he finally whirled away as though he'd been caught looking. He strode to his desk to drown himself in ledgers and whisky, but the figures swam before his eyes, row after row not making any sense, though Si had always been good with numbers before now.

Turning to face the window, he was greeted by a row of six tiny potted plants along the sill. He breathed deeply, before recording the growth of each little sprout. The crofters had complained their crops weren't producing, and it was most likely due to nutrient depletion in the soil from over-sowing barley. They needed more variety, but introducing crop rotation wouldn't be easy. It would take some convincing, and if they were going to adopt any of his *newfangled university ideas*, then there would have to be excellent results the very first season.

To ensure success, he was performing a small, controlled experiment. Each pot contained soil from a different prior crop: winter wheat, oats, barley, beans. It was too soon to make a recommendation, but so far, Si's bet—the beans—were winning. Next, he would plant a variety of beans in depleted barley soil to see which of those demonstrated the best growth, too.

Studying his plants, taking down his notes, orderly and predictable, soothed him.

Next door, all was quiet. Of course it was. He'd abandoned his bride on her wedding night. Did he expect her to be giggling with her sister over tea or singing a jaunty tune? What would her voice even sound like if she did? He could hardly think how it sounded at all.

Jory Shaw had warned him her cousin was a quiet sort. What had she said? *Take the time to listen, and she'll have quite a lot to say?*

In Si's experience, inducement to speak merely required a worthy topic and an equally worthy conversant. How could he expect her to speak, when he himself had so little of note to say? As it was, he'd always expressed himself best on paper, like in his scientific journaling. He was a student who seldom raised his hand to comment in class yet could easily fill a dozen pages on whatever topic, so long as he could be alone.

Writing was just... easier. If the words tangled up, you could scratch them out and start again.

Would she find him utterly ridiculous if he wrote to her now? Would it matter if she did?

Taking up a quill and ink, he scribbled, *Milady Ellen, I hope you don't mind that I*

He crumpled the page and tossed it into the unlit fireplace.

He was pathetic. The lass had left everyone and everything she'd ever known, and here he sat, attempting to explain away his frigidness with excuses and pretty lies.

Still, he had to do something.

Milady Ellen, he began again.

When it was written, he signed it, *Your servant, Mac.*

He couldn't say why he'd done it, pretended to be some anonymous clansman, except that he'd always been a coward. The only thing better than hiding behind written words was hiding behind them anonymously.

Perhaps it was also wishful thinking, but he supposed she might be at least a little annoyed with Si MacKenzie in the morning. And she might appreciate words of support from a stranger, a member of her new, untested family.

He tipped hot wax upon the parchment, refraining from

imbedding his signet in the seal, and then he tried to settle down into the armchair and get some sleep.

What an absolutely preposterous notion.

ELLEN ELIZABETH BRÌGHDE MACKINTOSH MACKENZIE HAD FAR too many conflicting emotions to keep contained inside one wee brain. The last thing in the world she wanted was to be bedded by a man twice her size, and yet—and *yet*. She couldn't even put words to that *and yet*, only the image of a Luckenbooth brooch and brooding, golden-brown eyes, of fine lips on her pricked finger, a broad hand warm on the small of her back.

Every time he looked at her, there was something in Silas MacKenzie's gaze, like he needed to consume every inch of her, and it set her whole body alight with anticipation.

It would *hurt*, she reminded herself, so much her mother had warned her not to cry. And yet there was something in his eye that made her desperate to know the pain. Now she was all alone, and she still wanted to cry, so she might as well have done the deed.

It was mere curiosity, she assured herself. Jory's scientific nature had rubbed off on her after all these years, and she was intrigued by what the man looked like. Was there hair on his arms and his chest? As much as a wolf? And did the size of his foot reflect the size of anything else, as Maggie had wanted to know? And could it be *not horrible* as Jory had implied?

It was wrong to let her imagination bend in such a direction if she still intended to become a nun, for heaven's sake. She took out a fresh shift, one she'd altered on the inside by adding short ribbons, and from her pocket she removed a handkerchief filled with stinging nettle.

She'd found it in the herb cellar off the kitchen when she went back down to check on Dorrie, hung up but not yet dried.

Wearing gloves to keep it off her hands, Ellen tied the nettles inside her shift and then stepped into it.

Immediately her skin began to itch and burn and swell.

That would keep her mind where it ought to be, on Abbaye Notre-Dame-des-Chelles and off the tall MacKenzie with his sunbeam eyes.

He didn't want her regardless.

She'd proven herself to be ridiculously weak and childish just like everyone thought. Oh to be sure, he'd taken Wee Ellen off her father's hands for the sake of the alliance, saddling himself with a wife who could never be the lady of the castle, the nurse his father needed, or anything else to him.

Perhaps he'd already guessed her desire to leave, too. He had to know, because he saw her. He seemed to know what she needed even before she did. Would it be a relief for him to send her away, so he needn't look after both her *and* his father, and the clan, as her mother had said? Was that why he didn't touch her? Preserving her virtue so the abbey would take her off *his* hands? Would he make the arrangements before this unexpected clan Gathering so she needn't face every MacKenzie in existence before abandoning them? And if not, how would she convince him that she wanted to go, when she could barely find the words to say it?

Plagued by uncertainty, and of course the nettles, she tossed fitfully all night long. That had been the purpose, to punish herself, both for whatever deficiency had caused Silas to take his leave, and for the illicit thoughts she couldn't keep out of her mind, though somehow the nettles hadn't helped in that arena. As the fevered hives spread over her skin, what little sleep she did manage was vexed by images of him—touching her—his fingers branding her as though they were made of fire.

At some point in the night, she stripped off the whole shift, not even disciplined enough to endure her penance. Burrowing down to find what little respite she could in the cool, clean bed linens, soft against her naked skin, settled her for an hour or two.

Cross and nauseated, she dressed quickly at dawn, burying the nettle shift inside her trunk. She sat reading her Bible when Silas tapped at the door for her to unwind the rope and allow him inside.

"Breakfast?" he asked through the door, his voice harsh and raspy, as though demanding to know where his own repast waited.

He seemed angry at being denied his husbandly rights, even though it had been of his own choosing.

Irritable or not, she realized upon opening the door, he bore a tray of tea and parritch, with cream and mashed berries for the oats. "I can fetch something different if you prefer. Bacon or sausage perhaps."

She shook her head and sat down at a small table where he'd deposited the tray.

Suddenly ravenous—when had she last eaten, beyond the bannock in the castle kitchen?—Ellen studied the food, but he studied her, so her skin prickled.

"Are you ill?" he asked, his eyes lingering on the flush of her neck where the nettle rash had crept up too high.

She shook her head and pulled her shawl tighter.

"Are you sure? Keith may yet remain in the village. Or I can ride to Dingwall for the physician."

She shook her head again and poured a cup of tea for him.

"Truly, you look unwell."

"Trust me to know my own health," she muttered, barely a whisper, but his eyebrows lifted and he nodded.

Suddenly Ellen's appetite fled. He wasn't meant to hear her. No one ever heard her mutterings. Sometimes she wasn't even sure she said them outside her own head.

"A letter arrived for you," he said cautiously, nodding towards a sealed parchment nestled between the cream and fruit preserves.

Dear Mother Mary, had her own mother sent a missive with

further advice on surviving the marriage bed? For whom else could be writing to her?

"D'you not wish to read it?" he asked, looking pensive, probably supposing she was too stupid to even read. Yes, he must be having very serious buyer's remorse, though she supposed since he received her dowry, it was her father who had done the buying. Jory would have so many things to say about all of that.

She shook her head to chase away blue thoughts of her cousin and picked up the letter. The cramped, even hand was certainly not her mother's. Heavens, would it be from Logan? She'd never known him to write, but there was always a first time.

Milady Ellen,

It is my greatest hope that someone already mentioned just how lovely you looked outside the kirk this morning—like a ray of sunshine sent from heaven itself.

Truly, when the clouds parted and the sun shone down upon your hair, I was overcome, and I know I'm not alone, for I watched my laird's son closely and saw he did not draw breath. Flowers turned their petals towards you, and all the birds stopped singing just to listen for your voice upon the breeze.

Ellen blushed at this stranger's words, imagining herself as he described her, as though she were Lady Len and not dowdy Wee Ellen, the tutor's girl.

Her eyes skipped to the foot of the page to see the anonymous sender's scrawled *Mac.* Truly, how many dozens of Macs had been present at the kirk on both sides? She couldn't begin to guess. But one of them had taken the time to write to her!

> *This must be a terribly uncertain time for you. I believe it is such for the laird's son as well, for all the same reasons and perhaps more besides.*

Ellen paused. Uncertain for Silas? Because he'd not yet decided whether to send her away?

> *I hope you can look past his coarseness and not despise him. He is a man raised by men, and never learned the genteel manners to which you must surely be accustomed. To a lady such as yourself, he must seem a proper bear with a temperament to match, but you needn't fear him. Si is harmless, even to the fish in the loch and the mice in the stable, and while he has studied a great many battles, it was so he might prevent future wars rather than lead them.*
>
> *Rest assured, he means well, even if he is an intolerable prig.*

It was wrong for his kinsman to write of him in such a way, and Ellen found herself wanting to defend her new husband, even though the writer clearly held some affection for him.

Husband. She shook her head at the strangeness of this new world.

> *It seems impossible his disposition will not*

improve merely by knowing you. Indeed, we are all counting on it. You have friends among the MacKenzies, milady. Those who know would say he cannot rule without you by his side.

You'll see it's true at the Gathering. We are a proud and rowdy lot. We fought alongside Robert the Bruce—and we'll ne'er let any forget it. Our motto is to shine, not burn, and I think I've never seen one shine so bright as you, milady. You elevate Si merely by your presence, and he knows it, too. If you should want for anything, you need only ask.

Your servant,

Mac

The mysterious Mac had called him Si, as though he knew her husband well indeed, but the note might easily have been sent by any of her new family who had been in attendance yesterday.

He watched her read, and though it was surely some kind of sin, she burned with pleasure at knowing she had an ally.

"Good news?" he asked evenly.

She didn't know quite how to respond, and so she took a sip of tea.

From his sporran, Silas produced a lovely sheaf of cream-colored parchment. "Write back, if you like. Mrs. Kynoch will see it's delivered."

Ellen nodded into her tea. "Thank you," she whispered, but no words escaped for anyone to hear.

Chapter Nine

It was ridiculous. Watching the lass read the letter, her cheeks slowly pinking at the words—*his* words—the stranglehold of jealousy tightened Si's throat. On the one hand, it warmed him that she seemed delighted by the letter. On the other, he wanted to rip it from her fingers and explain that he was Mac, that they were his heartfelt compliments and fears.

Gripping the back of the chair before him, he took a moment to settle himself, counting his breaths and remembering this had been the plan, a way to comfort her, to get to know her, to study her so he might figure out what to do next.

Woo her, the cousin had said. Si had no experience wooing, had not even taken his pleasure with whores in Aberdeen, for they were still women, capable of getting with child. He didn't know the first thing about wooing, and what would be the point, when he'd no intention of consummating the relationship? It would only make her feel all the more rejected.

But he didn't want her to hate him, nor fear him, either. He sought... kinship. Companionship. He wasn't skilled at making friends, but surely they could manage it if only he could keep his clumsy paws off her. And would she accept so little from him?

Could he make her think a platonic fellowship was all she desired? He could only try, for what was the alternative? Sending her away somewhere? Never that. He'd been sent away as a child and no, being sent away from her household unto his was bad enough.

"I should like to show you the rest of the grounds today," he told her. Indeed, what else was there to do?

She blinked up at him, as though she'd quite forgotten he was standing there while she became absorbed in the blasted letter. But then she nodded her agreement and went to dress behind the screen.

That was a fresh torment all its own, so Si retreated to his adjoining chamber once more.

They merely needed to survive the Gathering. Show a united front to the clan, accept the men's oaths or convince them to swear allegiance to Bram, and then he'd have space to breathe and figure out the rest. If she wanted an annulment, he'd grant it, and send her back to Inverness, far out of temptation's reach, though something told him if he ever let her leave, he might never be whole himself.

The door opened, but she didn't so much as peek inside his sanctuary.

"Come." He lifted the bar across her door. "The day is fine, though you might need a wrap."

She picked up the knitted one she'd worn at breakfast, leaving his mother's MacKenzie plaid still draped across the chair, as though she knew he never meant to truly make her his, and it pricked at his heart as well as his conscience. But she accepted his elbow, and they proceeded side by side out of the castle and across the grounds.

Leading Ellen, Si forced himself to take exceptionally shorter strides than he was accustomed, or else risk dragging the poor lass off her feet. It became more of a saunter, and he found himself chattering like a red squirrel to fill the silence, which was most unlike him. He couldn't stand people who talked incessantly just to avoid having nothing to say.

"This was my mother's garden many years ago. It was much less wild in those days, you ken," he added, noting the weeds and thistles now choking out what had once been rose bushes, and the hydrangeas were not so much shrubs as cerulean oceans, cresting at his shoulders.

Lady Ellen looked left and right, taking it all in with wide, contented eyes. But with each step further from the castle, Si grew more ashamed of the garden's dishevelment, just as he had the state of Leod the night before. In truth he'd always relished the garden's wildness as a boy, but what had once been a controlled sort of freedom was now a veritable jungle that Si both recognized and didn't.

"You can sometimes spot a wee bunny if you're lucky, but don't let on or Mrs. Kynoch will have their hides for dinner as punishment for nibbling her herbs."

The lass smiled.

"If it's wildlife you're after," he added, turning out of the garden and down the sloping grounds towards the paddock," there's a grove of yew trees but two miles past the stables, where you can find all manner of deer, squirrels, rabbits, and more birds than I can probably name. We forbid hunting there, so it's quite safe, for you and the wee rabbits."

She smiled again. A man could get used to that smile.

Si led her down to the stable, supposing one so still would find solace in its dusty walls and gentle occupants as he always had. But she let go of his arm the moment he crossed the threshold.

Her face was as fierce as he'd ever seen it, her brow deeply furrowed, her mouth turned to the side as though trying hard to suppress a frown. The fingers of her left hand bunched up the folds of her skirt. "Milady Ellen?" he asked. "You all right?"

Her eyes snapped to his, back from wherever she'd drifted to, and she took a deep breath and stepped inside.

"Milord," Gawyn rasped, scrambling up from a low stool where he'd been dozing.

Si was glad the old groom had enjoyed himself the night before. Lord knew there weren't so many opportunities around Leod.

"I wasnae expecting ye today." Gawyn cast a shy glance at the bride.

Bugger. Everyone would be expecting the two of them to be tangled up in wedded bliss for days and days, though with the Gathering, he could ill afford it. A ready-made excuse. This once, he was grateful for his father's plotting.

"No tour of the grounds would be complete without stopping here," he answered blithely.

"Of course, milord," Gawyn agreed. Then, smiling at Ellen he explained, "Si always did have a fondness for the horses. Even as a bairn, I think he preferred four legs to two."

She chuckled at that, and it made Si's heart beat three steps too fast.

"Gawyn," he introduced the man to Ellen. "At your service any time you wish to ride."

Her face turned from cautious concern to horror, and she took a step backwards.

"D'ye ride often?" Gawyn asked her.

She shook her head vigorously. His refuge, it seemed, would not bring her the same solace. At least not yet.

"In that case, you must be introduced to Buttercup. A gentler horse you'll never meet," Si coaxed.

"In this life, or the next," Gawyn agreed.

Frowning a little, she stepped nearer to the pearl-colored horse, who chuffed a friendly greeting.

Si reached out to stroke the mare's silky nose and offered her a bit of carrot from his sporran.

Ellen watched the interaction, and he thought he heard

another tiny bubble of laughter when the horse nuzzled into his hand, searching for another morsel.

"D'you want to pet her, milady?" he asked.

Her agitation returned, but she reached out to pet Buttercup, her eyebrows shooting up, when at last she touched the velvety soft nose.

Si reached back to scratch the horse between her ears, and Buttercup bobbed and chuffed again, causing the lass to snatch her hand away. He'd never encountered anyone who feared horses, but he supposed they must be rather overwhelming to a person so much smaller than they were. Perhaps she really was a city lass through and through. Still, when Buttercup settled, she reached out hesitantly all on her own and stroked the horse's nose once more, and Si was ridiculously proud on her behalf.

Anybody could be won over by the right horse.

"You really don't ride?" he whispered close to her ear. "Have you never been taught?"

Her face fell, and she lowered her arm once more.

"Dinna fash." Si patted her shoulder. "I'll teach you."

When she continued to stare at the floor, he tipped her chin up to face him.

"Milady Ellen, 'tis no matter. I shall teach you."

She sucked in the inside of her cheek, but nodded her agreement, though her eyes looked so sad it nearly broke him. Then the sadness was gone, replaced with a piercing determination.

"Have we a sidesaddle, Gawyn?"

"Aye, milord. That is, we've..."

Si closed his eyes. "My mother's old saddle, is it?"

"Aye. 'Tis in fine condition. I've kept it oiled."

He swallowed. Decades the groom had kept his mother's saddle so that if ever the day came when Si wanted it, the thing would be ready. Had he known, he'd have told Gawyn not to bother, but now he was glad.

"Let's have it, then," he rasped.

The moment Gawyn produced the saddle and began to ready the horse, Si was drawn to its soft, supple leather. He traced his finger along the stitches, trying to picture the former owner doing the same. Had she sat there in her final days, heavy with a child too large to safely deliver? He couldn't bring himself to ask.

Before she quite knew what was happening, Ellen found herself hoisted awkwardly onto a saddle and led out into the paddock, Silas holding the reins. He spoke so softly she wasn't quite certain whether his gentle whispers were for her or the horse, but she sat rigidly to still her trembling.

Jory's father had given her cousin riding lessons in the hills surrounding Moy when they were girls. He'd meant to do the same for Ellen, but she burst into tears, far too afraid to go anywhere near the massive creatures. Her parents had discouraged him from ever trying again, and he never got the chance to teach young Maggie, though she'd have certainly been game.

From watching Jory, Ellen knew in theory how to arrange herself in the saddle. That and which end to face were about all she knew.

Secretly, she sometimes imagined asking Jory to try teaching her again, not because she cared so very much to learn, but because it bothered her knowing she'd been too frightened to try.

Fear was supposed to be evolutionary, to keep you safe from harm. But Ellen had been afraid her entire life, and honestly, she didn't see how it made her any safer. It simply made her even more afraid.

When the MacKenzie had suggested putting her on a horse, she'd expected time to make excuses, to avoid it until he gave up or forgot, to tease and evade if she had to. She certainly had no intention of ever actually mounting one, but especially not *today*.

Did her new husband suspect she'd weasel out of it given the chance, and then be bitterly disappointed with herself forever after? Was that why he insisted? Was that also why she allowed his braw arms to lift her into the saddle without complaint? Or was it simply the look in his eyes and his earnest *'Lady 'Len, I shall teach you* that did her in?

Heaven help her, Ellen wanted to be Lady Len. The fearless and bold Len would have no compunction about riding a horse so fair and sweet as Buttercup, with a big, strapping Highlander at her side. Lady Len was hardy. She was valiant. She was all the things Ellen was not.

She wobbled unsteadily in his mother's saddle. It seemed she could slip off at any moment. As Silas walked them in a slow circle, she clenched her right thigh around one pommel and gripped the other until her fingers turned white.

Ellen was never meant to witness the world from this height. It was disorienting. Up close, Silas's eyes had faint rings in them, like the age lines in an old oak tree. Did each one represent a different era of his life? And if she stared into his eyes for the next fifty years, would more rings appear? Would this time, their marriage, be a wide or narrow band?

His mouth was moving, explaining something about balance and guiding the horse, but all Ellen could hear was the rustle of wind through that wizened oak's leaves. She hadn't noticed until now, but his lips were thin and fine. If he paid attention to hers, how would they compare?

She wanted to enjoy herself as Lady Len would do, but every time she recalled where she was—far from home, high off the ground on the back of a creature who could shake her off as easily as a flea—she found herself gasping for breath, holding tighter and tighter, but still feeling as though she could slip right off her perch.

Then she'd glance at his eyes, and she was dizzy with the certain knowledge that he was rooted deep into the ground, and he alone could steady her.

"You're doing very well," he said. "Would you like to hold the reins?"

"No," she whispered.

"It's all right. Just be gentle like I showed you. Turn her head the way you want to go."

He held out one hand for hers, waiting for her to release the pommel and take the reins. When she finally did, he adjusted her grip, his large, warm hands completely enclosing hers, showing her how to let the leads drape flat against her palm and between her thumb and first finger.

"Lift your shoulder," he murmured in her ear, tapping her right shoulder to make her sit up straight. "Och, you need a whip."

"No." Ellen shook her head. She wouldn't hit the creature.

His face softened. "Aye, just to tap the saddle on whichever side so she'll know you want to go. Or I suppose you could give her a wee kick."

He patted Buttercup on the rump, and it startled Ellen, sending her mind in all manner of inappropriate directions, but of course he would never dare tap *her* rump out here for Gawyn and the whole world to see. She didn't have long to dwell on such musings, though, for the horse began trotting once more.

Their pace probably couldn't even be called a proper canter, but it was faster than Ellen expected, and she squeezed with her legs to hold on, which only seemed to encourage Buttercup to go faster.

Forgetting everything the MacKenzie had just shown her, forgetting that Lady Len would never panic, Ellen kicked the horse to try and stop. That too made Buttercup trot even faster, in a circle at first, as Silas and Gawyn shouted hurried words and lunged for the reins Ellen gripped too tightly. But after the next loop around the paddock, they careened headlong towards an old wooden fence.

She tried to yell, "Stop," but just like in every nightmare, the words strangled in her throat.

Perhaps the horse meant to jump the fence and carry her all the way to Paris on its glossy back, but somehow Ellen knew that if Buttercup did make the jump, she herself would be left behind with a mud-caked broken neck. Only a terrified exhale passed her lips, and so, right as they reached the fence, she pulled the reins back as hard as she could, not praying, but mentally shouting every foul curse in her father's and Maggie's vocabularies. Buttercup reared up, and Ellen was so certain they were both flying backwards she half expected to see a hoard of winged angels. She was surely going to die.

Landing on her left shoulder, the breath rushed from her body in a single woosh, and she tucked herself into a ball like a hedgehog before everything went black.

Her hearing was the first sense to return, ringing a loud, off-pitch tone before it cleared and she began picking up deep, guttural shouts. Then strong hands touched her back, her neck, her head.

"Catch the damn horse!"

"—the doctor, milord?"

"—breathing—"

"Go at once."

When her lungs finally filled again, she gasped fast and shallow, but she seemed to float outside her body, puffing breaths down onto herself from above.

More hands, gentle ones, swept tangled hair off her face and grazed her cheek. Finally, Ellen wrenched her eyes open to see the MacKenzie's face mere inches from her own, panting hard as relief and concern crashed against each other inside his warm, tempestuous eyes.

"Forgive me," he pleaded, resting his forehead against her own.

She'd never known such a yearning in her life, but Ellen was overcome with a desire to kiss him. To be kissed by him.

Even yesterday when he pressed her finger to his lips, even last night when he unexpectedly left her to her own devices—when she had been moved by these new and unusual stirrings—she had never thought about his lips, about the soft curve of them, about what they would feel like against her sensitive skin, about what they would taste like after his breakfast of parritch and jam.

The fall must have jangled her thinking.

Silas MacKenzie was far more dangerous than the horse.

Without concern for possible injuries, she skittered backwards, away from him, and though she ached all over, finding that everything appeared to be in working order, she pulled herself up on the paddock fence, ducked between its slats, and took off running as fast as she could towards Leod.

Chapter Ten

When Buttercup reared back, Si was certain he'd become a widow on the first full day of his marriage, beating out his father's own record of having made it a full year. With a rider leaning so far back, the mare could've easily flipped supine, pinning the lass under a ton of writhing horse flesh. But then Ellen had lost her seat and fallen off the horse completely, and Buttercup managed an odd little twist, landing mere feet from where the lass had tucked herself into a protective ball and rolled away.

It was a miracle neither horse nor rider had a broken neck.

And it was his fault such a miracle had been required.

He never should have put the lass on a horse with so little instruction. Her family had warned him she was delicate. She should be wrapped up in cotton wool and waited on like a proper lady, not coaxed into dangerous situations.

After the fall, she'd taken one look at him and fled, undoubtedly furious. She hadn't wanted to ride or even enter the stable. It had all been a terrible mistake. She was right to be angry with him, and though he wanted nothing so much as to scan every inch of her, prove to himself she was unharmed, he let her go.

Gawyn saw her running and turned back to tend the horse, presuming the physician was no longer required, but Si couldn't face him. He just kept staring at the place where she'd fallen, at the shallow impressions in the soft mud where she could have easily gasped her final breath.

He was reminded of a day, long ago, when he'd been playing with children from the village in a different muddy paddock. A little girl called Tara had brought along a toy her uncle made. Si was fascinated by the intricate gears, for one had but to turn a crank and tiny figures danced around a disk. He'd been curious to see whether they could go backwards as well as forwards. Only the gears jammed, and when Si tried to turn it, the delicate crank snapped off and fell into the mud.

Young Tara had screamed at him in fury, snatching the ruined toy away from his over-sized hands. "Och, Silas MacKenzie," she railed, "You break everything you touch!"

Her words had come back to him many times over the decades, and they rang in his ears even now. *Och, Silas MacKenzie, you break everything you touch.* Why would he have expected a fragile little wife to be any different?

Though he was in no hurry to face her and feared any apology would be rebuffed, he needed to see her, to convince himself she was all right.

He expected to find her locked up tight inside her chamber, but the door was not barred and the lass not inside. Nor was she reading in his library or visiting the larder, and he began to worry she hadn't returned to the castle at all but had in fact run to the village or all the way back home to Inverness.

"Young love," Mrs. Kynoch said in an exasperated tone after taking one look at him and shaking her head. "What've ye done?" she demanded.

Love? Sure and how could it be, when they were nearly strangers? And what had he done—where to start?

Si shook his head, unable to speak. The words, *Nothing, only nearly killed her*, got stuck in his throat like week old bread.

Then the cook's face softened. "Sit down, laddie. I'll fix you something to eat."

"Thank you, no."

She turned away, trying not to look affronted, but Si realized his mistake at once.

"Is my cooking not up to Aberdeen standards, then?"

"Dinna fash. I never ate so well in Aberdeen as I did here. Only I'm not hungry just now."

"Silas MacKenzie, not hungry? That's a first. You'll waste away like your father if you don't eat."

"Has it been sudden?" he asked, realizing she might have noticed his father's decline more than anyone else.

Now it was her turn to shake her head. "Says he was fine abroad, but I thought him mighty thin. Though he was more robust when he first graced the doorstep."

"Why did no one bother to inform me?"

Her mouth was a flat line until she said, "Himself insisted you be left alone to come back on your own like he did."

It was like a dirk directly into his side, knowing he'd been kept in the dark like a child too young to know the truth.

"Had I been here, I might have done something to help." He knew his voice sounded pitiful and small. It begged the question, *What could you have possibly done to help?* But Morag Kynoch had never been one for tears or sympathy.

"You're here now," she said simply.

It wasn't even a kindness. They both knew she meant the unasked question, *So what are you going to do about it?*

"What does he need?"

"It's not my place, milord."

"What," he said again, grabbing her mixing bowl to stop her turning away, "does he need?"

She eyed him cautiously and shook her head. "For you to do your duty."

It was another blow to the belly, and then with a right cross to the jaw she added, "And let him go in peace." Her eyes looked sad, and a little bit angry.

Si released her bowl and let her turn away, and she moved to a counter where Dorrie waited on a stool to roll the dough into new bannocks. He was in the way, taking up too much space in the small kitchen.

"I need to find my wife," he said.

Dorrie looked up at her grandmother but was shushed and instructed to keep her eyes on her work.

Thus dismissed, he returned outside to search the jungle of a garden for Ellen. He was still out there, contemplating a chain of wisteria that climbed the castle wall, as though she could be hiding in the purple flowers, when there came a little tug at his kilt. He looked down to see the child staring up at him with wide green eyes.

"Dorrie?"

"I'm to gather rosemary, milord."

"No herbs over here."

"No, milord." She looked around and then whispered, "Do you believe in ghosts?"

An oddly perceptive question to ask, when the spirit of his mother loomed over the old garden as surely as the wisteria did.

"Maybe I do. Have you seen one?"

"No milord."

"No, me neither," he said with a sigh.

"But I ken I heard one crying in the chapel earlier."

Of course. He should have searched that desolate corner straight away. It made some kind of sense the lass might hide there, the last refuge of the forsaken.

"You'd best get that rosemary, before Nanny Morag comes looking."

"Yes, milord," Dorrie agreed, scampering off to the herb garden, hopping on one leg like an off-kilter rabbit because her nan wasn't there to tell her not to.

Sure enough, he found Ellen in the chapel, wedged between crates of God-knew-what. She had folded herself onto the one visible bench seat, which had likely been cleared upon his father's return.

The lass startled when his shadow darkened the doorway.

"Only me," he said and then knelt before her, making himself as small as possible inside the tight space. "Are you injured?"

She shook her head, but she cradled her left wrist at her bosom. There were scrapes on her forehead and chin, and mud caked across one cheek, all down her dress, and in her hair.

"You couldnae find anywhere more uncomfortable to sit in the whole castle?" he teased.

She glanced around her then, as though seeing the mess for the very first time. She must think them quite heathen to have allowed the chapel to come to such ruin. And what would his mother think?

"I'm told it was her favorite—my mother's—once upon a time. She would sit in here and read for hours. Not her Bible, mind, but novels as had no business inside a chapel."

He didn't know why he was telling her all this, but when her lips quirked up in a small smile, he realized that was why.

"She'd be ashamed at the state of it. Suppose my father's the only one who's ventured in for quite some time. You can see what it came to while he was in France."

A sort of pained expression crossed Ellen's face. He hoped she wasn't hurt and refusing to tell him. The blood on her chin glistened and threatened to drip, so he took out a handkerchief.

"Will you allow me?"

She nodded, and so he dabbed gently at her face, watching every flinch and flicker. Then he took her hand to extend the arm, feeling along the bones. Her wrist was swollen, and would need to be wrapped, but the bones were intact. They'd gotten off easy. *He'd* gotten off easy.

"I've asked them to draw you a bath, Milady Ellen."

She smiled a little, but her brows knit together in a way that looked like she might cry, and he didn't think he could bear it. He eased up and out of the tiny space, offering her his hand.

She stepped gingerly on her right ankle, wincing, and he swept her into his arms and held her close against his chest as he made his way up the stairs, breathing in the scent of paddock mud and lavender. He'd always loved the smell of the paddock. But would the memories now be bittersweet, echoing with the words, *Och, Silas MacKenzie, you break everything you touch?*

ELLEN SANK DOWN INTO THE WARM ROSEWATER BATH. WHAT an absolute disaster of a day. She'd been right to fear the horse—fear was good and healthy. It kept you away from things you had no business doing. Like getting married.

And yet.

For a split second in between anxiety and terror, she had known freedom. And in the aftermath, she couldn't shake the realization that her fear had caused the whole accident to begin with. She'd been too focused on being afraid to listen carefully to the MacKenzie's instructions, and in trying to shake off her nerves and pay attention, she'd slipped and fallen into the depths of his eyes.

Then Buttercup had headed for open space, undoubtedly perturbed by her rider's anxiety, and she probably would've cleared the fence had Ellen not yanked back the reins in terror. Indeed, each successively worse moment had been Ellen's fault because, as usual, she let fear get the best of her.

When Silas found her, she was ready to face his wrath—to be chastised for not following his directions, for not trusting him implicitly, for behaving like a cotton-headed infant, for nearly costing him a good horse.

But he only looked sad and sorrowful and needy... She couldn't explain how, exactly, she recognized the need pouring off him, nor had she any idea what to do about it. But whatever his own feelings, he'd taken care of her. Now warm and relaxed, Ellen's own new sense of need spread deep in her chest and down between her legs.

Seeing him, eye to eye, first from her perch upon the horse and then lying on the ground—it was a revelation. Their height difference usually cast his features in shadow, making them appear harsher than they actually were, like cold, chiseled stone. Up close he was softer. Younger. More devastatingly vulnerable.

It did things to her that she was fair certain ought not to be done, not to a wife whose husband was avoiding her bed, not to a woman bound for the convent.

When her bath grew cold, Ellen rubbed salve on her cuts, closing her eyes to the stings, but breathing them in, accepting pain as punishment for all the trouble she'd caused and all the inexplicable emotions swirling inside her.

Then she took a seat at the small table where they'd eaten breakfast. In addition to the parchment, Silas had brought her quill and ink, and though even a simple blank page frightened her, she sat down to write, hoping it would help clear her head and order her thoughts.

My dear and noble Mac,

First, I must ask that you address me as Len.

Then perhaps we can be friends.

Thank you for your kind words. I cannot tell you how they brightened my morning. It's nice to know I have an ally. You're quite right. It has been a strange time. I feel very much like Gulliver washed ashore on

Brobdingnag, far from the home where he was safe and secure.

You seem to know my husband quite well, and I appreciate the insights you've shared, though I'm afraid I have a dozen more questions. And while I believe you are truly fond of him, I must take you to task for being too harsh on his character.

Rest assured, he has treated me better than I deserve, though I've hardly spoken two words to him, as you may have noticed during my wedding vows. It's no snub against the MacKenzies, nor even deliberate.

When I was young

Ellen paused, unsure how to continue, how much to reveal. It was odd, how easy it was to open herself to this stranger through ink. But some secrets are not easily revealed. And she must think as the wife of the future laird, not just lonely Wee Ellen. Which details were appropriate for others to know?

Her pause left a terrible blot of ink, so she pushed herself on before it bled clean through the paper.

When I was young, it was as though my voice were frightened away, never to return. It's true, I have little inclination to speak, but I'm not certain I could remember how if I tried—hardly an ideal situation for the wife of the Kintail. And I should hate for my silence to bring shame upon his head. Knowing him as you do, would he consider sending me away before that can happen?

She could think of little else to write, since she knew not to whom she was writing, so she simply added, *Do you happen to know his favorite color?* Then she signed it, *Most sincerely, Lady Len*, and had it sealed and waiting when a knock at the door was followed by the mouthwatering aroma of a dinner tray.

The food was brought in and the bath taken away, and then Silas ducked under the lintel, freshly washed and combed and trimmed to near perfection.

"May I join you for dinner, 'Lady 'Len?"

When she nodded, he pulled out a chair, angling it so he might stretch his legs out into the room instead of kicking her under the table.

The meal consisted of a sumptuous leg of lamb with roasted root vegetables in a flavorful sauce, and of course, freshly baked bannocks.

"Mrs. Kynoch's getting fancy," Silas observed, but his tone was approving. "Preparing for the Gathering, no doubt."

That reminder made a lump settle in Ellen's stomach, but she forced down every bite, hoping each morsel would shove the lump deeper out of sight. What duties would be expected of her, to be witnessed by all the clan? What missteps would she undoubtedly make to earn their pity or disdain?

After eating, he lingered, near but not quite entering his library, as though he didn't want to spend another night apart.

Ellen wasn't quite sure whether she wanted him to or not.

" 'M sorry," he finally said, an awful scowl upon his face. "For the horse."

Ellen shook her head to stop him, but he was staring angrily at some image only he could see.

"You weren't ready. I see that now. I'll not force you again."

His assurance made Ellen a little bit sad. She'd half expected him to march her trembling back to the stable first thing tomorrow and set her sternly in the saddle to try again, and next time—she had vowed—she wouldn't lose her head.

She didn't know why exactly, but some part of her yearned not merely to *not* be an embarrassment, but to make him proud. Some small part of her longed for his whispered, "Good girl," to be for her, rather than the horse.

"I'll bid you goodnight," he said after another moment's hesitation.

Then he nodded at her and shut the door between them on his way out.

"Don't forget the latch," he called, his voice sounding thick and far away.

Ellen stood at the door for a long time before she wound the length of rope around the handle, and she kept on standing there after it was done.

When he'd had the bath brought in, she'd assumed her reprieve was over.

Her belly tightened at the image of him taking her in his strong arms, laying her back on the bed, untying her ribbons one by one.

There was movement on the other side of the door, as though the MacKenzie paced back and forth like a caged cat, a distance he could easily cover in two enormous strides.

Ellen stroked the soft wood of the door idly, the way she might run her hand down his sculpted chest, and her fingers snagged on a tiny knothole. She snatched her hand away quickly and turned her back, then faced it again.

She would barely have to stoop to look through it, just to ensure Silas was all right.

The pacing stopped, but a rustling continued.

Scarcely breathing, and careful not to make a sound that would give her away, Ellen peered through the knothole.

The MacKenzie had cast aside his sark, and his back muscles rippled as he unbuckled his belt. Then his kilt dropped away, revealing only buttocks so chiseled it made Ellen ache. A moment later, his plaid unfurled, and he wrapped the whole thing around himself like a blanket and settled into his chair.

Ellen wriggled into her own shift, the freshest of the nettles still providing a little sting, as she chewed the inside of her cheek and tried to go to sleep. Instead, she lay awake, shocked by what she'd seen—or rather, by what it did to her. She'd seen Logan and his brothers splash naked in Loch Moy at all stages, but she'd never known such a thrill in her stomach or such a desire to reach out and touch.

Was this what Maggie experienced every time she spoke so openly of lads? Blessed Mother preserve her if she was becoming more like her brash little sister every day.

Chapter Eleven

Knowing him as you do, would he consider sending me away? A week after first reading them, the words the lass had written to Si's alter ego remained seared into the backs of his eyelids. There was no escaping them. She either wished to leave or feared he wished for her to go. Somehow, he wanted both and longed for neither.

He tried to push the letters aside, to focus instead on the accounts. Rents were often left unpaid and coffers were low. Norval MacKenzie had done his best in the laird's absence, but the fields wouldn't produce. And if Si's gamble on the crop rotation didn't pay off, there might not be much of a clan left to lead.

No wonder the people grew restless, while Si had been in Aberdeen avoiding his inheritance like an ungrateful wean. It was shameful. His father had been naive to think a bride would help the situation. And now that same bride wished to be rid of him as surely as his own people did.

Si pushed aside the ledgers and picked up her next missive, dreading its contents. In response to her concerns about being sent away, he, as Mac, had railed against himself as a brute, begging Ellen to confess her hopes and dreams so he might find a way to please her.

He should have known better than to ask questions he might not like the answers to. He should have asked her in person, whispered words across a shared pillow, but he was a coward.

She hadn't written back immediately, but when she did, Si understood everything and nothing at all. His marriage was just one additional catastrophe he couldn't fathom how to mend.

My dear and noble Mac,
It's not him, I assure you. It is only me. You
asked what I dream: mere foolishness. A childhood
fancy. My soul ambition was to take holy orders in a
cloister on some far-flung shore.

Even her homophonic mistake was charming, making Si smile before he frowned. She wished to be a nun. His wife, whom he would not—*could not*—bed, wished to be a bride of Christ, untouched and alone. It could not be more perfect. It could not be a greater disaster.

It has long been my suspicion that the Church
alone can be my solace and reprieve. Alas, I fear it's
not to be. You say that Silas

How far gone was he, that he liked the shape of his name when she wrote it, and traced the letters with a finger even now?

cannot rule the MacKenzies without me by his side,
but what good am I? I, who have nothing to offer
any of you? I'm not even worthy to be a nun. I

know that to be true, and I strive to accept it, but nor have I the mettle to be Lady of Leod, so what is left for me? Perhaps the former is at least something I could endeavor to deserve in time.

You say that you're my friend. As a friend, please tell me the truth—will I cause more harm by staying than if I go?

Si didn't know how to respond, either as himself or as her anonymous friend. He only knew that he didn't want her to leave, that he most fervently wished her to remain.

There was a knock at his door, and he looked up blearily. Was it still the middle of the night? "Come."

Finn Shaw entered, nodding deferentially, although their present stations were the same, both heirs to a laird unless another could be produced. Si had forgotten the Shaws were due to visit before their journey south to Edinburgh.

He rose, and Finn took in the state of the room: candles burned to nubs, empty whisky glasses, the armchair he'd very obviously been sleeping in, and the wrinkled clothes and unkempt hair which screamed that he hadn't slept at all.

"I would ask how it's going, mo bhràthair, but I fear ye wouldnae wish to answer."

The familiar way Finn spoke to him stoked a kinship he didn't wish to acknowledge at present. He didn't deserve kindness, and he shoved it away, choosing anger instead.

"My clan may soon starve, and my *wife* wishes to be a nun. *That* is how it's going."

The open concern fled the shorter man's face, replaced by something else. Guilt? Si didn't know him well enough to say.

"She told you, then?"

"You knew?"

Finn did him the courtesy of not protesting with a pretty lie. "Many young ladies wish for a different outcome than what is presented to them."

"What was to stop her from being a nun, if that was the life she desired?"

Finn shook his head. "Circumstance. And her father."

"He wished her to wed an heir?"

"He wished her to wed a MacKenzie. If it hadnae been you..."

"It would've been Blair."

"It would've been somebody."

Si's jaw tightened.

Regardless of what she might have wanted, the lass would've wed. And so would he. Faced with such inevitability, somehow there was consolation in the fact they got each other in the bargain.

"Besides which," Finn went on, "the Chattan Confederation has a healthy distrust of convents. Here and abroad. With good reason."

Si nodded. Auntie Alys had related the gossip of the Gordon clan's nefarious dealings.

"Jory believes—"

"Leave it, Shaw—"

"My *wife* believes Lady Ellen can be won over. Give her time."

"It doesn't matter. I cannot *be* what she wants. I cannot be what she deserves. I don't wish to win her over."

Finn tilted his head, scrutinizing Si. A lesser man would have told him, as Si had berated himself now many times, *Then you are not the man I thought you were.* But Finn studied him as though taking the measure of more than what stood before him, and finally he said with a shrug, "Perhaps you also need time. Like those wee sprouts there." He nodded at the windowsill, where a few of Si's plants were racing towards the sun.

Si blinked at Finn, the kinship he tried to bury forcing its way to the surface, and suddenly he felt less alone, like the brother he'd always longed for now stood before him dispensing wisdom and refusing to be kept at arm's length. He didn't quite know what to do with that.

"Oats." He pointed to one of the pots, and Finn laughed, stopping short when he realized it wasn't a jest.

"Don't imagine those pots will yield much parritch."

Si shook his head. "An experiment of sorts."

Finn nodded sagely and a slow smile crept across his face. "You and Jory are going to get on fine."

"Where is your lovely wife?"

"Lady Ellen has taken her to see your father."

"My father? Why?"

"She's a healer. It's why we reside in Edinburgh, though I've long suspected there's little the learned men can teach her that she doesn't already ken."

That explained the herbs she'd left before. Once again Si blinked back an onslaught of emotion at his young wife's thoughtfulness. He really needed to start getting more sleep before he turned into a mewling infant over every kind notion.

"Let's see what she has to say." He stood, pulling on a jacket and tucking in his rumpled sark.

Finn cast him a skeptical look. "A comb, perhaps."

WHEN A SLIGHTLY LESS DISHEVELED SI ARRIVED AT HIS FATHER'S chamber, the ladies were gathered around the bureau along with Mrs. Kynoch, where Jory instructed them in the preparation of some kind of tea.

"Perfect, Ellen," she told her cousin, who was grinding some fragrant herb beneath her pestle. To the cook she added, "This will give him the same relief without the drowsiness."

"If ye say so," Mrs. Kynoch replied, but there was a grudging respect in her voice beyond mere deference. Then she muttered something about nettles going missing before they could properly dry, and Ellen cast a fearful glance her way, no doubt concerned about her safety if there were, in fact, thieves about. Or rats.

The laird coughed, and it drew the women's attention to Si and Finn standing in the doorway.

"Silas," Jory smiled and crossed the room to take his hands in both of hers. "You look," she tried to hide a frown. "You look well, cousin."

"Well and truly trampled by a boar," Ellen muttered, and Si burst out laughing.

Everyone blinked at him in confusion, as though they hadn't heard the remark, except for Ellen herself, whose eyebrows shot up in surprise.

She'd written to Mac how her voice was frightened away, but she murmured these sharp little barbs under her breath often enough. Did she not realize she was saying them out loud? Perhaps Mac should tell her—*he* should tell her—that her voice was still inside her waiting to be set free. Except then she might grow self-conscious, stop whispering altogether, and that would be a very great shame, for when else had Si last laughed out loud?

He winked at her, then turned his attention to Jory instead of waiting for her reaction, but the tips of his ears burned as though her stare could sear his skin.

"How's the patient?" he asked.

Jory looked at his father. "Comfortable, I think."

That wasn't any kind of answer, and she knew it, leading him to the corner shelf that held his father's whisky decanter.

"He's old," she said, not unkindly, but with a helpless shrug.

"He is not." He poured himself a glass and swallowed it all in one gulp.

"Can you monitor what he eats and drinks?"

Si studied her. "You think it's poison?"

Jory cast a look around, as though making sure they weren't overheard. "None that I recognize," she admitted. "But you could at least rule it out if you're careful with what he ingests."

"He only consumes what Mrs. Kynoch prepares," Si whispered, glancing quickly at the cook, who was taking a turn with the pestle.

Jory shrugged again. "Perhaps he simply has weak lungs."

"You can't help him."

"I can ease his discomfort. With more alertness than these other draughts he's been taking. I can improve the quality of the time he has left, but no, I don't believe I can reverse the damage."

Si poured another drink but merely stared at it.

"I know it's not what you wish to hear. I'm so sorry I can't do more."

"Thank you." It was Si's voice, but he didn't remember uttering the words.

"It's hard," she said softly. "Losing someone before you're ready."

Si took another drink, willing her to stop talking. Does one ever become ready for such parting?

"But you should know he's so very proud of you."

He drained the rest of his dram. What he knew was that his father asked just one thing of him, and he was not capable of giving it.

"You're welcome here. Stay as long as you like." Then he nodded at the room as a whole and escaped back to his library, as quickly as he could without running. It was one thing to argue with Keith, to ignore his opinions and seek alternate advice. To do so twice would be foolish.

IT HAD BEEN SEVERAL DAYS SINCE ELLEN LAST RECEIVED A letter from the mysterious MacKenzie, and when she allowed herself to think of it, she feared she quite disgusted him with her talk of dreams and cloisters. She should've restricted her comments to hopes of fine weather for the shinty, to dreams of a successful Gathering and prosperity for the clan. Of course, she wanted all of those things too.

Though married, she was quite alone, and without the letters, she was lonelier than ever. She spent her days reading in the cluttered chapel or walking in the garden to avoid her new husband and her nights peeking through the knothole as he avoided her bed.

Jory's arrival brought with it a fresh wave of longing. Silas hadn't held her or petted her since carrying her up the stairs after her fall from Buttercup. Indeed, it was hard to say which of them put more distance between their two persons. Was he actually angry, as she originally feared, or still simply guilt-ridden for putting her on the horse? Or, perhaps worst of all, had the Mac told him of her desire to leave? Hadn't some part of her hoped he'd do just that?

She hadn't known what sort of reaction to expect, but she'd expected something.

For perhaps the first time in her life, Ellen didn't know what to hope for.

Like her daily prayers, her invitation to Jory and Finn hadn't been wholly selfish, either. The laird was clearly unwell, and if anyone could make him better, it would be her cousin.

But whatever news she'd shared with Silas had caused him to hide in his library the rest of the day, not even emerging to break bread with their guests, not even speaking to her through their shared door to remind her to tie up the handle. Perhaps he was angry at her meddling. She should've left well enough alone.

She wanted to knock on the door and try to comfort him. Instead, desperate for a quieter silence, Ellen crept down to the chapel. Though it was filled with the litter and dust of decades, she could envision what a beauty it had once been.

The window was shuttered with splintered boards, the walls and floor quite filthy from the refuse stored there over the years, and the bench cushions appeared moth-eaten and mildewed. But the chamber itself was salvageable, and even in its current state, it tugged at her, body and soul, begging for restoration.

That night, she donned a clean shift, and fell asleep quickly, running over a list in her mind of all the ways the chapel might be improved, and in the morning the dark cloud which had hung over Silas seemed to have lifted as well.

They took breakfast in the Hall, where Ellen watched Jory and Finn closely, noting all the little ways they touched and moved within each other's space as naturally as breathing. Jory absently stroked the back of his head when she passed his seat. He reached up to squeeze her hand. The way they would turn and smile in some shared levity known only to each other made Ellen's heart ache a little.

" 'S a hot spring near Strathpeffer, an easy distance from here," Si announced while stirring strawberry jam into his parritch.

Jory's eyes lit up immediately.

"Understand you suffer from a variety of aches and stiffness. So much travel of late can't have improved your condition. We can go today, to take your ease, if you like."

His speech was stiff and uncomfortable, as though he wasn't accustomed to making polite conversation with those he didn't know well, but it was charming to watch him try, and Jory caught Ellen's eye with a warm smile.

"I can't imagine a more pleasant way to spend our last afternoon. Will you come as well?" She directed the last to Ellen, who hadn't known a thing about it.

Seeing Silas, who was so clearly more at ease alone, embrace her family as his own, broke something inside Ellen. From what Mac had said in the letters, Si's only kin were his father, young Bram, and the Leasks—no brothers, no other close cousins or even dear friends, except perhaps the ones he left behind in Aberdeen, and she wondered if he had even allowed himself to form such bonds out there.

But here he was *trying* with the people most important to her, even as she was still dreaming of abandoning him.

How was she ever going to leave? But how could she stay, knowing that she couldn't be who he needed? Could she?

The question niggled her when she nodded her agreement to Jory. It itched while she finished her breakfast. It burned as she accepted a basket lunch from Mrs. Kynoch, heavily laden with cold meats and cheese and bannocks. She was grateful when Silas took the full basket from her for the walk down to the stables, but his chivalry only made the question weigh as heavily as the basket had.

Ellen had supposed they might take a carriage, but of course they would need to ride. She eyed Buttercup skeptically and would swear the horse eyed her back, just as unsure.

" 'Lady 'Len will ride with me," Si said, gallantly omitting the story of her disastrous first and final riding lesson. "D'you prefer a horse of your own?" he asked Jory.

She considered it, glancing at Finn, who tried to hide the smirk on his face by casting his eyes to the ground, the tips of his ears turning pink.

Ellen didn't understand what private conversation had just passed between the two of them, and yet her stomach gave a tiny flip of envy at their happy secret language.

"No need to tire an extra horse, Si," Jory answered. "We can share."

Gawyn helped them saddle Uinnseann alongside Finn's Clydesdale, Sparradh, though from his repeated glances in her direction, she knew he was wary of putting her back on a horse at all, and she quite agreed.

She sat rigidly in Si's arms as they rode out of the paddock. He whispered in her ear, his warm breath tickling her cheek, "Relax, 'Lady 'Len. I'm in complete control. I've got you, and he willnae dream of throwing me."

Ellen *wanted* to relax for him. But she feared if she released one ounce of control, he would be more insulted by her quaking.

For at least half an hour, the horses maintained an easy pace along a forest path, as Silas and Finn murmured softly to each other about matters of the clan, and Jory piped in occasionally with observations on the local flora.

"Och, she'll be wanting to stop and pick it all on the way back," Finn teased, and Jory squirmed around to try and smack him, but they were both laughing. Ellen's cousin had always vowed she would never marry, and Ellen had been shocked when they returned from their adventure and announced they were engaged, and yet somehow, they seemed a perfect match.

The former Shaw Wretch was just as tough as Jory and good natured enough to find her toughness appealing. But most of all, he made her laugh as no one else ever had.

Ellen's stomach flipped again, and, as though he could sense it, Si tightened his hold on her.

Despite her stiffness, he almost cradled her against him, holding both reins in his left hand, crossed in front of her, his right arm wrapped around her waist.

How could he be so close and so familiar, and yet still avoid the marriage bed? What did he want? What was he waiting for? And why did she care? Except that she was beginning to welcome any pain it might bring as atonement for her sins.

When they finally reached the hidden spring, Jory and Ellen turned their backs to help each other with their lacings, while the men stripped down to nothing and settled into the steaming spring. Then they joined their husbands, each wearing only her shift.

The pool was deep, the water covering Jory's shoulders when she was settled, though it only rose as high as Silas's chest. Ellen, however, had to keep her chin constantly tipped up away from the water.

"All right?" Silas asked her.

She smiled and nodded quickly, though in fact she wanted to go straight home. The heat was irritating her not-yet-healed hives, and her neck already hurt from the angle that was keeping her from drowning. But Lady Len would not run home. Lady Len would find a way to make the most of it.

"You're not," the MacKenzie said, frowning.

Ellen was ruining his kind gesture towards Jory, and she chewed the inside of her cheek hard.

"We could swap sides," Jory suggested.

"Of course," Finn agreed, though Ellen couldn't see how an altered arrangement would make enough difference to matter. She was shorter than Jory by a good few inches.

"Nae," Silas said, his alder-colored eyes piercing hers like splinters. Then he slid closer to her, put a hand on either side of her hips, and lifted her onto his lap, settling her so she straddled one broad thigh, the water now comfortably receding to her collarbone, with the added advantage that she could rest her head against his shoulder if she'd allow herself.

Jory sighed contentedly, scooting into Finn so she could lean against his broad frame too, and he draped an arm around her, pulling her close.

Ellen caught him sniffing her cousin's hair before they both closed their eyes, completely relaxed. She was, however, anything but relaxed, as her heart pounded and Silas's chest rose and fell in tandem with her breathing, his manhood periodically nudging against her thigh. The first time, it made her jump, and Silas tensed like he wanted to soothe her but was holding himself perfectly still.

Each time it happened after that, she heard and felt him swallow, but he offered no other acknowledgment of it, didn't squirm or adjust his seat. She resolved that if he could ignore it then so could she, for Jory's sake. The last thing she wanted to do was repay his kindness by embarrassing him. Only she was going to need a great deal more stinging nettle in the days to come.

Chapter Twelve

Before they even left the spring, Si was out of his mind with lust. It had been a mistake, not taking a third horse. Then at least the lass could have ridden back with her cousin instead of sitting on Uinnseann with his aching erection at her back, both of them pretending not to notice.

He'd known better when he pulled her onto his lap in the spring. He was already growing hard just from her nearness, from the way the corner of his eye caught her damp shift clinging to her bosom. It had been sweet torture.

But his lap had been the best solution, and she'd taken her seat willingly enough, not quite relaxed, but more at ease than she'd been upon the horse. At first, she'd seemed startled by his hardness, and he kept quite still, thinking of his father and flexing his thigh muscle to make it go down. It didn't help for long—how could it, with her soft bottom nestled against him, her lavender-scented head tucked perfectly under his chin?

Maybe he imagined it, but by the time they left the spring, he could swear she was purposely leaning her left knee towards him, searching out his cock, which made the thing oblige in an instant. And Lord, but it would have been so easy, even with Finn and Jory right there, to have let his fingers drift down to the hem of her shift and then back up to the sweet spot that called to him between her legs. Or better yet, to have adjusted her position on his lap so he could enter her, filling her completely, and if she was as good at being stoic as she pretended to be, bring her to completion without the others being any the wiser.

But no, based on her hushed little comments that she just couldn't keep inside, something told him she'd be deliciously noisy in bed if she could just let herself go. All of *that* was a dangerous line of thinking, so Silas turned his mind to plans, to fallow fields and seedlings on the windowsill, to science.

The lass shivered when he helped her down from the horse, her clothes soaked through after pulling them on over her sodden shift.

"We must get you warm and dry," he said, offering his hand to lead her up the stairs, leaving his guests to fend for themselves.

She nodded, her impossible blue eyes made more so by the gentle flush upon her cheeks.

Upstairs, her fingers trembled as she tried to untie her stays, and in that moment, Si came to a decision. He couldn't completely avoid her forever.

"Let me help?" His voice sounded small—a question, not a command—the only part of him, perhaps, that could ever seem small. His lips were so close that when she nodded her consent, he could practically taste her.

She sucked in her cheek as he swept her damp hair over one shoulder and unknotted the ribbons, allowing his fingers the touch they so craved, helping her out of the stays and then the skirts until at last she stood shivering, once more wearing nothing but that damp, linen shift.

The translucent garment clung to her, highlighting the curve of her breast and hip, her nipples and the soft patch of her bush on full display. Si swallowed. It was his last chance to walk away.

There were laces tied just below the hollow at her throat, and he tugged playfully on one string, not hard enough to loose it, but enough to make his intentions clear.

"This too," he whispered. "You don't want to catch a chill, milady."

Boring into him with those deep sapphire eyes, she untied the bow and allowed him to pull it off, leaving her naked and trembling before him. Instead of the creamy white skin that he'd imagined since the day they met, he found her covered in angry red hives that hurt him just to look at. Was she allergic to her bed linens or something in the water at the spring?

"Mercy! What is this? Did the water cause this?" he asked, grabbing the blue and grey tartan that had not yet moved from the back of her armchair and draping it around her.

She shook her head, pulling the edges of the plaid tighter to cover herself.

"Let me see," he said, even as he strode to a shelf and selected a small pot of dock leaf salve, which Mrs. Kynoch had given him when he'd been attacked by midges after tramping in the forest the first night of his return.

He guided Ellen—or Len as she'd called herself in her first letter to Mac—to sit back upon the bed.

"Please?" he said.

Unable to meet his gaze, she opened the plaid to show him.

Silas began at her neck, smoothing the salve into her ravaged skin with two fingers, and she closed her eyes as if in relief, so he worked his way down between her breasts and along the curve of her ribs and belly. She trembled at his touch, her breaths coming in tremulous little gasps like she was swallowing tears before she could cry them.

"Does it hurt?" he whispered.

She jerked her head once to indicate no.

"The truth, milady. You needn't fear me," he begged. She opened and closed her mouth as if trying to speak with the voice that had been frightened away. Could he coax it back with tenderness? Lord, how he wanted to try.

Si leaned forward and kissed her throat, as he had been longing to kiss her for days, the throat that worked so hard to speak.

Her breathing sped up but seemed less labored, and so he kissed her cheek and then her lips, which parted, welcoming him and sucking on his own bottom lip until he drew away. Studying her face closely for any sign of distress, he dipped his fingers into the pot of salve once more, spreading the remedy across her breast, caressing it as gently as he knew how. Though he'd never dared to touch a woman, he'd heard plenty of boastful talk and knew the mechanics of most things.

Si allowed himself to circle her cherrilet with his thumb and then smooth the salve across it as well. Her mouth fell open, breaths coming in faint whimpers, her eyes wide with wonder.

He brushed his lips across hers, then drew back and forced himself to ask in a thick, heavy voice, "D'you wish me to stop?"

Len shook her head, and he pressed his forehead to hers before kissing her again, deeply, as he continued to caress her broken skin.

He was consumed with a hunger to taste every inch of her. Would she taste like lavender and honey all the way through? He kissed along her jaw and beside her ears, then dropped to his knees upon the floor, drawing her to the edge of the bed where he could trail kisses along the inside of her thighs where the skin was unbroken, flushed from the hot water, but not marred by any rash.

Si kissed down to each knee and back up again, to the patch of skin between her belly and her fine blonde curls, while his bride squirmed deliciously upon the bed, propped up on her elbows to watch him.

"D'you wish me to stop?" he rasped again, fairly certain that to do so would cleave him in two.

"No," she gasped once above a whisper, and so Si loosed himself to apply all of his Aberdeen learning, the stuff of books and bawdy tavern talk from his most experienced classmates. He allowed himself to test the tongue which had never seemed meant for speaking but finally found its purpose between her legs as he kissed and lapped and tormented her.

It had only briefly occurred to him to try the Ancient Greek technique since their wedding night—too afraid she'd think him depraved, too afraid he'd perform poorly, too afraid he wouldn't be able to stop there. Now he pushed all of those insidious doubts from his mind and gave himself over to the sweet, salty essence of her, the soft hairs tickling his lips and nose, the wetness that flowed for him like honey, and the tiny squeaks of her voice trying to break free.

Len's panting turned to high-pitched little moans, encouraging him to continue each delicate flick, and Si smiled against her, pausing only long enough to take hold of himself, working his shaft in rhythm with her soft gasps, as he continued to pleasure her, and when finally she cried out, clenching his head between her knees as she bucked against him, Si spent himself into a corner of his plaid and then collapsed onto the bed beside her, flushed with the realization that perhaps this would be enough to live as man and wife and completely avoid the possibility of pregnancy, and the certain dread that although he would gladly prostrate himself before her day and night, she might be content with it for a time, but not forever.

HOLY MERCIFUL MOTHER. THE WALLS OF ELLEN'S CHAMBER were a shade of pink she'd never seen before, and she wondered for a moment if something inside her head had broken, seeping behind her eyes, permanently altering her vision, for surely she'd just seen stars. Her upper lip was damp, but when she dabbed at it anxiously, there was only the sheen of perspiration, not blood.

What in the name of all that was good and holy had just happened to her?

Was that what her mother had warned might hurt? For she could see how a less tender man might have made it painful, perhaps if teeth were involved. She shuddered. Or was it simply as Jory had said, about being ready?

There are many ways of enjoying your husband in the bedroom. Ellen had never imagined she could possibly be ready, but if that was what Jory referred to, she was already eager for more.

Jesus, Mary, Joseph, and the wee bloody donkey.

For once in her life, Ellen grew entirely still, her mind completely blank, afraid of nothing.

He was lying next to her with the weight of an anchor, his breaths heavy but even, and Ellen wanted to see him up close like she had that day atop Buttercup, so she rolled onto her side, wrapping the plaid around her.

The hot spring had given his dark hair a slight curl and made his skin soft, and his eyes were a calm heather honey.

"Your eyes," he whispered, like a man unraveling the mystery of the universe. "They're the most amazing hue."

Ellen curled into him to hide her smile, and he kissed her head.

"I'd say we should go meet our guests for dinner, but they'll be fine on their own, I'm sure," he said shyly, and Ellen liked watching his lips move, and his tongue behind his teeth, and a flush seized her whole body, recalling what those lips and tongue had just done.

Then his stomach gave a mighty growl, and he fought to keep his face impassive—and failed the moment Ellen burst into a fit of giggles.

"Traitor," he murmured to his stomach, casting his eyes towards the ceiling.

Then Ellen's stomach gurgled as well, and she fought to hold in another laugh.

"Is that so, 'Lady 'Len?" Silas asked, putting his ear to her belly, tickling her with his soft hair, and she pulled his face up to her own for another kiss. This time, she noted that his beard was just as soft as his hair. She supposed she'd have to write and tell Maggie. Or she could keep it all for herself...

"Can't have you starve," he said, pushing himself up. "I'll just be next door," and then he left her there to dress for dinner, when food truly was the last thing on her mind. And did she imagine the sway in his hips as he took his kilted self out of the chamber? Ellen realized with another blush that she wished she could have watched his muscled backside swagger away stark naked.

HER COUSINS WERE ALREADY AT TABLE WHEN ELLEN AND SILAS arrived, and she sat down in the chair he pulled out for her, self-consciously aware that her usually pale cheeks were still flushed a most unnatural hue.

Jory offered Finn a knowing look but said nothing, and Ellen noticed that Finn seemed particularly attentive to his wife throughout the meal, murmuring to her between bites, offering her more wine, apologizing each time they bumped elbows because they sat just a little too close together.

They all ate heartily of the fine venison stew Mrs. Kynoch had prepared, another trial run, perhaps, ahead of the Gathering.

"I should have arranged some entertainment for your visit," Silas observed aloud. "A harpist, or a storyteller perhaps. My apologies."

"Not necessary, I assure you. That hot spring..." Jory sighed contentedly. "I have never had a better host. I can hardly wait to return, and we haven't even taken our leave."

Silas smiled to himself, the tips of his ears flushing pink. Ellen loved it when the big man grew bashful like that.

"It has left me quite lazy, however," Jory went on. "Will you mind terribly if we retire early, El? We've long days coming."

Ellen shook her head. She didn't mind at all, though her stomach knotted with anticipation of how she and the MacKenzie might possibly fill the time until the Shaws' early morning departure.

While the men stayed back to talk, Ellen followed Jory to her chamber to watch her cousin pack and say goodbye for who-knew-how-long this time.

"Is he good to you, El? I mean you seem content, but I have to ask."

Ellen's cheeks burned as her face broke into yet another giddy smile.

"I see," Jory grinned, taking her hands and sitting on the edge of the bed. "Then you've come to an understanding? You no longer wish to go abroad?"

Tears sprang to Ellen's eyes at the reminder. What they'd just done was one thing, but she couldn't simply give up on her old dream. Could she? With the Gathering coming, and she certain to bungle it somehow?

"I see," Jory said again. She nodded sympathetically and pulled Ellen into a tight embrace. "Well, everyone here adores you, your husband included."

Did he? Silas was very much a caregiver, but he was also a man of duty and honor. He'd look after his wife no matter who she was or what his feelings for her.

Jory leaned back, studying Ellen's skeptical face. "Do you doubt it? El, he's the most lovesick pup I've ever laid eyes on. He took us to that hot spring today for you, though I'll gladly reap the benefit."

Perhaps her cousin was right. If marriage hadn't been quite what Ellen expected, well—she hadn't known what to expect, had she? Had hardly dared imagine it. They were still getting to know each other, still navigating uncertain terrain.

But as she headed back to her own chamber, Ellen could still feel his fingers and his kisses upon her skin, like fire. Would he consider it consummated now and forbid her leaving? Would a convent refuse to take her?

The door was open between their two chambers when she entered, and he sat at his desk, staring at a piece of correspondence. He read her face and said, "I'm sorry they're leaving, mo chridhe. You must know they're welcome any time. Your cousin's course in Edinburgh won't last forever."

He was right, but it still seemed like the final, permanent separation from Jory that she'd long known was coming and could never allow herself to prepare for.

"Come," he said. "I've something to show you."

He led her into the corridor and up a dark set of stairs until they emerged onto the windy battlements. But around the corner, the stone walls provided a shelter from the harsh, Highland wind, and when her eyes adjusted to the darkness, her jaw fell open at the vast, starry sky.

There were more stars here than she'd ever seen in Inverness. In truth, she wasn't in the habit of looking up.

Silas settled himself on the stone walkway and invited her to recline against him, throwing his plaid around her for warmth. "She may not see so many of them in Auld Reeky," he said into her hair. "But she'll be looking up at the same sky as you, no matter where each of you is."

That was a novel idea, and it made the distance feel a little bit smaller.

"That's the North Star, right there," he said, disturbing their cozy cocoon to point at the sky, sending a tiny chill through Ellen that made him pull her closer. "Find that, and you'll always know where you are. You'll always know where home is," he said into her neck, and she believed him.

She knew where she was right then in a way that she never had before.

He rubbed the goosebumps on her arms, but that just made more spring up, which was fine because she wanted him to go on touching her forever.

"See how it looks like the tip of a long handle on a small cup?"

She nodded.

"And just here, a bigger cup. The edges point right at the tip of that handle."

She nodded again.

"As long as you can find that star, and you know west from east, you can find your way home."

Strathpeffer was west of Inverness, far north of Edinburgh, and it was oddly comforting to be the corner of a triangle between her cousin and her sister. She snuggled against him as he pointed out other stars and told her all their names. And when at last he asked if she was still awake, she pretended she wasn't, afraid he'd send her to bed alone.

Instead, he placed the lightest of kisses upon the bridge of her nose, and she didn't stop smiling all night as they lay nestled together in their own private corner of the battlements, the only two people in the world, cuddled under a spectacular blanket of stars.

Chapter Thirteen

After Finn and Jory left, things between Si and Len returned to very much the way they'd been. Despite Jory's whispered, "Whatever you did, keep it up," on her departure, Si avoided Ellen as much as possible by day and his traitorous subconscious lusted after her all night long.

His excuse, being caught up in preparations for the Gathering, would soon run its course. His father had only granted him six week's delay, and every day more families arrived to set up camp on the grounds around Leod.

It was giving Si flashbacks to twelve years ago when the MacKenzies came from far and wide to offer their oaths, one after another, to his father, the second son of Kintail. Si was sixteen years old, and even then he'd known he wanted no part of it. There'd been rumblings that he should return permanently from Aberdeen, but he was set to start his course at the university, so his father granted him a reprieve.

Holding baby Bram against his broad chest, head and shoulders above men twice his age, Si had watched Alex MacKenzie take up the mantle stoically, and though they didn't speak of it, Si suspected the old man had never wanted it any more than he himself did. No wonder his father had so little sympathy. But it wasn't *his* birthright. It was Bram's.

If his cousin had been twelve when William MacKenzie died at Inverness, Alex's role would have been a temporary one until Bram came of age. Why should now be any different?

Si was meant for quieter things, for solitary pursuits and science. He was meant as counsel, right hand, and steward to the one who would actually lead his kinsmen into battle. And Bram could be that leader. The boy just needed toughening up, needed the preparation and counsel Si could provide. He wouldn't abandon his cousin, but neither would he lead men.

He was contemplating all of this when Dorrie interrupted his thoughts to bring him a letter.

A week had passed since Si spent the night on the battlements with his wife, and he hadn't replied to Ellen's last note to the anonymous Mac. Continuing to hide behind the pseudonym after such intimacy seemed worse than cowardly, but he didn't know how to reveal himself. She had shared too many secrets, asked him as a friend to tell her the truth, and he, as Mac, had promised her he would.

He was honestly surprised to see another parchment addressed in her tidy hand after her most precious confessions had gone unanswered, and it made his blood surge.

Cunning of Mrs. Kynoch to send it by way of this tiny messenger. The cook had always been good at conveying her opinion without saying a single word, and she seemed to find his letter writing naught but a childish pantomime.

My dear and noble Mac, Len began as always, and his throat constricted. If he outed himself to her, she would find him neither dear nor noble. Could he perhaps move to America never to be heard from again?

My dear and noble Mac,

I hope that my self-indulgent confession about the Church hasn't shocked you. I wouldn't have revealed it at all, had you not asked. But you've been such a kind friend, it only felt right to repay your honesty with my own. I could never have you believe milord's sullenness was a cause of any discord between us. It is only his shell—like an egg and just as thin.

And though, as I said, I'm neither worthy to serve the Lord nor the Clan MacKenzie as Lady of Leod, I think I've found a way to prove my value. Or at least keep my hands and mind busy, which may just have to suffice.

The chapel here needs a good scrubbing and a new coat of paint, and that, at least, is something I can manage. Please don't worry, if indeed you were concerned. All is quite well.

Affectionately,
Len

Needing a fresh coat of paint? That was a generous description of the chapel indeed. Si was gratified that she wouldn't reveal the true depth of Leod's disrepair to a stranger, though, soon, the entire clan would see what she was seeing—not only the chapel, but the whole of Castle Leod, as desperately tumbledown as its ailing master. If the state of the place didn't prove Si's unfitness, perhaps nothing would. A new coat of paint? Sure, and that would make the crops begin to grow.

He couldn't deny the chapel was in need of repair, but she meant to single-handedly take on the project? To what end?

Some cruel twist of logic had put the notion in her head that she wasn't worthy to become a bride of Christ. Ridiculous, of course, because she was perfect, worthy of any damn thing her heart desired. Was this project, then, some misguided form of penance by which she believed she might make herself acceptable? And then what? She'd work herself to the bone and then expect him to just let her go? He could sooner rearrange the stars in the sky.

Si had hoped that after the hot spring she might have relinquished her dreams of the convent, content to be cloistered here at Leod with him. What a fool he was. Perhaps she truly did know enough of the marital bed to realize they hadn't officially consummated their union. But if Si had to sabotage her progress every day, he would ensure the project was never complete if that was what it would take to stop her leaving. It should be easy for him, who broke everything he touched.

Before anything else, though, he knew he must come clean about his identity so that once forgiven, he might return to her bed in the Greek way, without lies hanging over him.

Taking up his pen, he wrote back without giving himself time to overthink it.

Lady Len,
It is time we should meet. I will be there during the Gathering. Please allow me to beg an audience.
Yours in service,
Mac

Clear. Concise. Direct. She couldn't possibly refuse him. Indeed, she'd probably be delighted to make his acquaintance.

Si crumpled up the invitation and cast it into the fire.

He tapped his quill on the desk until the point snapped. What he needed was to make her fall in love with him—something which a few weeks ago he could not have imagined himself wanting.

The very great problem was that without meaning to, without even wanting to, he seemed to have formed an attachment to his wife. To hell with cordial friendship. He burned with desire that might never be slaked. Based on her cousin's parting words, Ellen might not completely abhor his attentions, but she wouldn't fall in love with him. Especially upon learning the truth.

But... two years back, a Frenchman named LeBeau gave a series of lectures in Aberdeen on all things chemical: love potions, and poisons, and other dark sciences.

Si had listened, half amused but captivated by the man's ability to hold his audience in thrall. He wished now that he'd paid more attention to the content of LeBeau's lectures. It had seemed nonsense at the time, but perhaps this Frenchman would have advice on Si's domestic quandaries. Because even if he managed to make her fall in love with him, then there was the matter of what came next.

He'd read about sheaths made from the bellies of sheep, but even he was skeptical of their effectiveness. And would she agree to such prevention? She was a woman, after all, and women longed for children, didn't they? Hadn't he seen her with Dorrie that very first night, as natural as any mother could ever be?

Perhaps LeBeau could advise him on other measures that might be taken, and on his father's symptoms, as well. If there was poison involved as Jory seemed to suggest, the Frenchman would surely recognize it.

Tossing away another half-written love note, he jotted off a quick missive and addressed it to the Frenchman in Aberdeen.

Letter written, Si needed to walk, to move, to break free from the confines of this room at least. Without express intent, he found himself pacing the corridor outside his father's chamber, torn between seeing the old man in his present condition and remembering him as he was.

"Come in before you wear a hole through the floor," Alex called.

Si leaned in the doorway as instructed. His father looked a bit better, rested and with a lively spark in his eye.

"Is everything in order for the ceremony?" Alex asked. Sickness had certainly made him eager to cut to the center of every conversation.

"Mrs. Kynoch has everything under control."

The laird laughed. "I've no doubt. That woman could run a whole army with clockwork precision and brook not a single complaint."

"Aye. Perhaps she should be laird." Si said it like a joke, and his father laughed appreciatively, but they both knew he was more than half serious.

"I've been thinking. Perhaps Bram should stand alongside me for the oaths, and then when he's of age—"

"This again?" his father growled.

"Then when he's of age, I can pass the whole thing back to its rightful heir," Si finished.

"It doesnae work that way, Silas. *You* are the rightful heir, whether ye like it or not."

"If I have no sons, it will pass to him."

"Then pray ye have sons, lad. This life isnae for Bram."

"And it is for me?" Guilt over his intention to never have any children washed over him. If Bram had none either, then what would become of the Kintail? Who would Bram train in his place? The children of Blair MacKenzie?

"I ken you've no appetite for battle, but perhaps those days are behind us. James tried and failed."

"And if he tries again?"

"The men will follow you."

"Because of my size, you mean, and nothing else? No matter

what's here"—he pointed to his head—"or here," he added, pointing to his heart. "If that's so, they're a worthless lot indeed."

"Don't ever speak of your clan in such a way," his father shouted—or would have done if he'd had the breath to do it.

"My own *wife* has the good sense to want to escape from me. What makes you think the MacKenzies will be any different?"

"Take your nonsense somewhere else, boy, I've no time for it." His father huffed, folding his arms and turning away.

"It's true." His voice racked. "She wishes to leave."

"Well and why wouldn't she, when she supposed she had wed a leader of men and not a cowardly whelp?" Alex snapped, collapsing against his pillow in a brutal fit of coughing.

Si cast his eyes to the ceiling, his jaw working double time to bite back every hurtful, angry retort.

Then he poured a cup of water for his father, who drank deeply, his cough finally subsiding.

"Ye have a way with words, Silas. Could be it's only because you're so sparse with them, but when ye speak, people listen. Ye've been that way since you were a boy. Your size may make them stop, make them hear. But it's you that commands them to listen. And all that learning... all that learning means you've something to say."

Si had no response. His size alone could command a room merely by entering it, his size alone made them listen whether he had anything important to say or not. His size meant he broke everything he touched, and he would break the clan too.

"Bram can learn—"

"Bram has his head in the clouds. Och, it's more than that," his father went on. "Bram's a selfish little shit, God love him. He was coddled from birth, given every wee thing he could wish for."

"He's not a bad lad—"

"He's not. And he may well grow up to be a fine man. But his instinct is to think of himself first, and whatever he's got left after that he can spare for others. You've always had a knack for seeing what people need, even before they know it themselves. And don't say, 'what they need is Bram,' or I swear on your poor mother's grave I will get out of this bed and tan your backside. Don't think I won't. I don't care how big or how old ye are."

Si raked a hand through his hair. "All right, Da," he sighed.

"This'll be the last we say on it, aye?" his father asked, but it wasn't really a question.

"Aye. Certainly don't want you to throw your shoulder out waving your belt around," Si teased, and his father laughed at his impudence. It was good to hear him laugh. Si hadn't realized how much he'd missed the sound of it, deep and rumbling. It made him feel like a little boy.

Besides, the old man seemed better. Maybe it wouldn't be so bad, taking on the role with his father there to guide him.

"Aye, we'll say no more," he said again.

"Good. Now I dinnae ken what's happened between you and yer lass, but ye'll have a lifetime of differences so you may as well learn how to sort them out now. I hear her sometimes, humming to herself. She doesn't seem the sort to try and be unhappy."

"Aye."

"She's a good one, Silas. Don't fuck it up."

ALL HER LIFE, WEE ELLEN WAS *THE QUIET ONE*. GROWING UP, Jory spoke for both of them before Ellen was even old enough to speak. Then along came Maggie with more words than a dictionary would know what to do with, and there simply wasn't much need for Ellen to speak loudly or often.

It never seemed too great a loss when, after Boyd Gordon's brother attacked Jory in the stables, Ellen's voice had fled the way its cowardly owner had failed to do.

But now she was on her own, without Jory or Maggie, without anyone who knew her well enough to speak for her, though it sometimes seemed like Si MacKenzie could hear her voice in a way no one else ever had.

She shivered at the memory of his lips on her, trailing sweet kisses all over her body. He hadn't returned to her bed since that afternoon, though perhaps... Could it be, he was waiting for her to find the words to invite him?

Or perhaps he stayed away out of some greater disappointment. Should she have resisted his advances? Remained still as her mother had suggested? Not cried out when she came apart? Indeed, not come apart so wantonly at all? Or was her error in not returning the favor, not putting her lips to his staff as she was now so very anxious to do, as Lady Len would certainly have done? Shouldn't the Lady Kintail do as much for her laird? Could she ever be bold enough to ask the mysterious Mac how to please a man in the bedchamber?

Ellen meant what she'd told her pen friend. She would fix up the chapel, so that Si would no longer feel like his mother's shame surrounded him there, and then he'd see that she might someday be the wife a leader like him needed her to be. She needed to prove it to herself as much as to him.

The first step was to order a new stained glass window. Heaven knew what had become of the old one, before the space was boarded up.

Taking a length of ribbon, Ellen tied knots for length and width and sketched the semi-circular shape of the top on a piece of stationary, jotting down instructions and dimensions as quickly as she could, trying to ignore the raised voices next door arguing about young Bram.

Then, in a burst of bravery, she walked down to the stable where she found the horse, Buttercup. Gawyn was nowhere in sight. They eyed each other warily, she and the horse, and then she slipped a bridle over its head as she'd seen the old groom do and walked Buttercup out of the stable and down the path towards the village, after leaving a hastily penciled note explaining the mare's absence.

With no intention of riding, she merely wished to prove she wasn't completely terrified, and more than that, it was a comfort to have a companion. Quiet she might be, but Ellen wasn't accustomed to spending so much time in solitude, and even a mute companion was preferable to none at all.

Every time Buttercup made an unexpected movement, Ellen jumped, but the horse followed her willingly enough. Maybe in time they would get used to each other and she could persuade herself to try again with the riding.

THE SMITHY WAS SITUATED ON THE EDGE OF THE VILLAGE green, and the tall, dark-haired man barely looked up when he offered a gruff, "Help you?"

Ellen swallowed. Perhaps this had all been a foolish errand, but she summoned her last ounce of courage to step closer and hand him her note.

He took it in one sooty hand and studied it, then studied her and the knotted ribbon she held out. For a moment she wondered if *he* might be the Mac.

"I'm sorry, milady. I don't have the time."

Ellen frowned. She hadn't prepared herself for a rejection. Was he even allowed to refuse? Would he have turned down Silas or the laird?

The blacksmith handed the note back to her and resumed hammering whatever piece of iron he'd just withdrawn from his forge.

Dejected, Ellen turned to go back home.

She had carefully tied up Buttercup before entering the smithy, and now she struggled to undo her knot, her disappointed fingers fumbling helplessly.

"D'ye like the ring, milady?" a girl's voice asked. Behind Ellen stood a young woman that looked every bit Jory's miniature, wearing a shirt tucked into breeches, face streaked with soot and grime, her hair piled into a thick brown braid.

The girl, a few years younger than Maggie, smiled a toothy grin and nodded at Ellen's wedding band. "I helped my da make it. From Mr. Silas's own stone." She reached out as if to touch Ellen's hand and then stopped. "Some of our best work, I think. What did ye ask him for?" She nodded towards the smithy.

Intrigued by the girl and her brash demeanor, Ellen handed her the note.

"Is it a window?" the girl asked, holding it first upside down and then right side up. "Only he can't read, milady," the girl whispered. "Neither of us can."

Ellen's heart sank. How thoughtless of her to not consider that her own education had been a rare privilege not enjoyed by all members of the clan.

"It's all right, milady," the girl assured her. "You're not the one who calls it a waste of time." She rolled her eyes. "I'm Greer. What kind of window is it?"

Ellen opened her mouth to explain, but no words came out.

"Cat got your tongue?" the girl teased.

Ellen nodded, took a breath, and whispered, "Stained glass."

Greer smiled and nodded. "You don't do things by halves, do ye, milady? Tell you what. I'll make your window in exchange for reading lessons."

Ellen glanced back towards the smithy.

"Don't worry. I have time. What do you say?"

"Yes," she agreed, handing over the knotted ribbon, and she was treated to another broad grin.

"Grand. Only I want it to be a surprise for himself," she nodded towards the building once more. "Can I come up to the big house? Tomorrow? At lunch?"

Ellen smiled at her referring to Castle Leod as *the big house*, but she nodded her agreement and murmured, "Tomorrow."

Greer held out her hand to shake as gentlemen did, and Ellen accepted it, realizing once more how hungry she was for the contact. She almost didn't want to release the sweaty thing, but she untethered Buttercup and began the walk back home.

She wasn't accustomed to so much freedom. Even prior to her marriage, Ellen spent more time indoors engaged in prayer and reflection or reading or mending than out digging in the garden or foraging in the woods as Jory was wont to do. A weekly stroll down to the loch where Maggie could eat cakes and skip stones across the water was about the extent of Wee Ellen's adventures, and even then she was cautioned not to overexert herself.

But now the fresh air filled her lungs, releasing every pent-up nervous breath, and the sun shining on her face cheered her from the outside in. She was smiling and confident in her project by the time they arrived back at the stable to find something of a kerfuffle.

The old groom, along with a younger one, raced here and there, watched by Silas's elusive young cousin, but they all stopped to stare at her approach.

"Buttercup!" the young groom exclaimed, running to take the lead from Ellen.

"Milady," Gawyn said cautiously.

"Did ye ride bare?" Bram asked in awe, but Gawyn smacked him sideways.

Ellen shook her head. She hadn't meant to cause a stir. They must not have seen her message.

She followed Gawyn into the stable. "Sorry," she said softly. "For the worry."

He tsked but didn't turn around. "The horses are yours now, milady. Ye dinnae need permission to take one."

"I left a note." She picked up the paper, still lying on the shelf where she'd placed it.

"Ah. So ye did."

"I..." she tried, but the words, as usual, failed her.

"My eyes aren't what they used to be," Gawyn explained, patting her shoulder. "All's well, milady. Go and have some tea."

He was kind, the old groom. She could see why Si liked him. But she couldn't shake the sensation that she'd done something terribly wrong. She could hear her father's clear baritone berating her for going off alone, her mother's tacit agreement. *What if something happened? You as good as stole that horse.*

Even Maggie's laughter permeated her brain, teasing but demanding to know where she ever got the notion to try and spruce up the chapel. *You've never built or repaired anything in your life. Why would you think you could do it now, when no one else has managed it?*

She'd allowed it all to go to her head—the kind attention of the Mac, of Silas that solitary afternoon. They had all made her too confident, too big for her boots, too proud of the imaginary Lady Len, and now she had fallen on her face.

The smith said he didn't have time to help after she'd shamed him with her scribbled note. Perhaps he'd be angry with Greer for going behind his back, perhaps punish the girl, when it was Ellen who deserved punishing. It had been tactless to go to them, to rope them into her own selfish plan, and with that realization top of mind, Ellen passed through the herb garden on her way back inside and picked great bunches of stinging nettle to line her shift.

After changing clothes, Ellen went to torment herself with the sight of the chapel, but when she passed the laird's chamber, he called her inside. Would he yell at her for what she'd done? Rage about the noise and disruption to his peace? Could she pretend not to have heard? Make a beeline for the gardens and never show her face inside again? No, of course not, so she tiptoed anxiously inside.

"How are you finding Leod?" he asked, his voice warm if somewhat weak and reedy.

"It's lovely," she said fondly, realizing that she meant it.

"And the lad? He treats you well?"

She nodded, smiling.

"Good," he sighed, seeming to relax. "Will you sit and read to me a spell? Being old and infirm gets fearsome dull."

Nodding again, Ellen pulled over a chair and took up the book the laird indicated from his bedside table, and shutting out the nerves and the nettles, she began to read.

Chapter Fourteen

Mrs. Kynoch's usual grizzle had become a right temper over the impending Gathering, and since none of it would be occurring at all had she not conspired with his father against him, Silas took a little unchristian satisfaction in her distress. At least it meant he wasn't alone in his.

"You can eat what ye find, so long as it's not on tonight's menu," the cook growled when he stepped into the kitchen, knowing it was him without even looking up. "Between dinner and the tonics for Himself, I havenae time to see to your stomach as well. Where has that child gotten to?"

As if on cue, Dorrie scampered through the door and reached up to set a cloth on the counter. Mrs. Kynoch opened it, revealing a few measly stalks of nettle.

"That won't be enough for a week's worth of tea, girl. I told you two big handfuls."

"That's all there was, Nanny," Dorrie said with a shrug, grinning up at Si to show she'd lost a front tooth.

"All there was!" the cook shook her head, muttering, "Nettle thieves. I never in all my days. They'll be after the rosemary next."

"Thieves?" Si asked. What was going on around the place?

"What would you call it, milord? First it goes missing from me own larder, and then from the very ground it grows in, and mind ye don't say it's only my memory or my eyesight, or ye'll get not a bite to eat for a week. Speak to Norval on it, won't ye?"

Si shook his head solemnly. Had things really gotten so desperate that someone would resort to stealing plants? And what would anyone want with nettles? Unless...

"You're giving it to my father? Is it dangerous in large amounts?"

Mrs. Kynoch stiffened. "And would I be giving it to the laird if it was, Silas MacKenzie?"

"I didn't mean you," he mumbled, but he had wondered exactly that and felt like absolute shit for it.

"If there were a chance it could poison, I wouldn't give him a drop. I'd hope you'd know that, milord."

"If you expect me to call you Morag, then you must call me Silas."

"No, milord."

He huffed. "Then would you please see that this goes by messenger to Aberdeen?" he asked, handing her the letter for the Frenchman. "One of Ced's lads could take it."

The cook glanced at the address and then flicked an assessing gaze up at him. "To Ced, and not to milady?"

Si cleared his throat. "Right, of course. You're much too busy. I'll take it myself." Anything to escape from her discerning eye.

A bracing ride was exactly what he needed. Staying in his room all day made Si cross and twitchy, even when he was studying his plants. He wasn't meant to sit on a throne passing judgment, he was meant to be out in the air and the sun, turning the soil with his two broad hands. Fresh air and exercise would certainly clear his mind. Perhaps he'd take Bram along, make a day of it, practice swordplay upon their return.

He found his cousin in the garden, with his nose buried in delicate yellow flowers. Did the lad share Si's scientific passions?

"You've nae seen a nettle thief about, have you?" Si teased.

"Only Dorrie," Bram replied, squinting at the plant with one eye.

"Has St. John's Wort such a subtle scent then?"

Bram leaned back on his heels, revealing a sketch pad in his lap and a pencil behind his ear.

"It has, in point of fact." The boy eyed him warily.

Si had been away when his little cousin was born and returned for university soon after. When the Kintail went into exile, Bram had stayed at Leod with his mother. Now all these years later, bound up in each other's futures though they might be, the cousins were veritable strangers. He hadn't made enough effort with the lad since his return. His cousin skulked around the place enough to know Si meant to hand the lairdship back to him, and yet Bram seemed reluctant to spend any time in Si's presence.

For a half second, Si wondered if St. John's Wort could be toxic in large quantities, but he was seeing suspects at every turn. He needed to calm down.

"Would you like to ride into town with me, cousin? Or better yet, go and grab your sword. I'm in need of some practice."

Bram scowled at him. "I have no sword."

"Truly?"

"They're outlawed," the boy said, as though Si were the world's biggest dullard.

He scoffed. "Aye, so leave it home when you travel. You must know how to fight."

"Like you do?" the lad sneered in a tone only an adolescent boy could master.

"I certainly learned the art," Si returned. "And practice when I can."

Bram shook his head, turning back to the plants. "I'm not interested in fighting."

"And when has that ever meant the difference between two

and four? I'll go easy on you, but a lad your age should learn. You can't predict what the future will bring."

"I'm statistically much less likely to die in battle if I dinnae join one. And I'm busy."

"Looking at flowers?"

"No! I'm..."

His cousin cast around for an answer that he might deem adequate, and suddenly Si had become every bit his father, whom he'd considered quite unreasonable at Bram's age.

"I'm helping Milady Ellen," he said, raising his eyebrows at Si, knowing he'd already won. Si would never interfere in the service of his lady.

"Doing what?"

Bram rolled his eyes dramatically. "Whatever she needs."

"She has need of St. John's Wort?"

Staring at him defiantly, refusing to look away, Bram said simply, "Aye."

"Go on, then. Don't keep her waiting," Si dared, and the cheeky lad picked a handful and took it inside.

Silas sighed. His father expected the whole of Clan MacKenzie to fall into line, and he couldn't even command his cook or his twelve-year-old nephew.

THE VILLAGE WAS ABUZZ WITH AS MUCH ANTICIPATION FOR THE Gathering as it had been for Si and Ellen's wedding. Extended families who hadn't seen each other in far too long were reconnecting, and the tavern was in danger of running out of ale.

But the undercurrent of discontent flowed louder and more freely than it had a few weeks ago, as new faces and distant relations arrived by the cartload.

It was nothing new to Si. Farms weren't producing adequately and rents were too high, though judging by the ledgers, Norval had been more than generous in writing off debt. The village appeared to be thriving well enough, but off the backs of the crofters who could barely afford to buy seed. They kept planting barley season after season, except the few who repeatedly sewed oats. The yield returned smaller every year. They should be alternating wheat and field beans to restore the soil.

It was the whole point of his experiments, and the plants growing along his windowsill would help him explain it all to his father and the steward. The Kintail might be skeptical, but he was fair. He'd listen. And more importantly, he'd see with his own two eyes. And though he hadn't spoken to Norval MacKenzie about it, Si allowed himself to hope the shrewd and worldly advisor would take his side.

The steward held sway among the clan. He could take Si's ideas back to the crofts, because otherwise it would be Si himself doing all the talking.

The neck of his sark grew tight and itchy just thinking about it: weeks of bluster and swagger, of so much talk he'd be sick of the sound of the thoughts inside his head, of acting more confident than he felt even when he knew that he was right.

"Honeymoon over so soon?" a teasing voice called.

Si turned away from the barley field he'd been staring across to see Norval's son, Blair, along with his ever-present companion Rabbie Stewart, and Angus MacKenzie, the taciturn lad from the wedding, all striding towards him. A smug smile graced Blair's striking face, counterbalancing the cool disinterest of his companions.

"Tell me the bride hasn't cast you out already," Blair teased, offering a falsely sympathetic pout.

"Alas. Some business won't wait," Si replied.

Blair roared with laughter, clapping Si hard on the shoulder. "A euphemism for the lady being not yet paced if ever I heard one." He leaned in close, though if he'd had a single ounce of self-preservation, he'd have stepped far away. "Milord, if she's built too small, there's only one way to fix it. Or is it you that's too small?"

Blair looked around himself like he was holding court, though it was just the four of them, and only Rabbie was laughing.

"Lads, when I was but six years old, my father would take me round the castle to play with Silas. Hide and seek—it was always hide and seek." He turned to Si, mystified. "You'd think we'd have learned to choose a different game."

Blair shook his head and turned back to Rabbie, sweeping an arm grandly.

"If I wanted the game to be the slightest bit sporting, I had to at least *pretend* I couldn't see this big hulking lad trying to squeeze himself behind the furniture."

Rabbie guffawed and, goal complete, Blair turned to Angus with a solemn expression. "Amazing to learn his prick's too small to fill its new hiding place."

Snarling, Si meant to shove the young upstart into the nearest wall by his throat, but Angus grabbed Blair by the collar and slung him away to safety, and Rabbie stepped in between them like some kind of bodyguard.

"You'll have to excuse him, milord. Too deep in his cups, though it's only afternoon. Eejit cannae hold his drink."

Silas grunted an acknowledgment and allowed the two to drag Blair away, but he watched them out of sight, counting backwards from one hundred to still his temper.

Blair was four years his junior and though he'd followed Si about as close as a shadow, he'd always known how to get Si on his back foot, too, like it was his born mission to take the laird's big son down a peg. It galled him as much now as it had when he was ten years old. Or was it just that he danced too close to the truth? Or half of the truth, at least. Si's prick would certainly have no trouble being found.

By bracing her back against a stack of crates and pushing with her feet, Ellen managed to shift a few of the heavier ones out of the chapel. Once they were in the corridor, however, she realized she had no idea what to do with them next.

Undeterred, she added to the pile lighter bits of broken furniture and old, moth-eaten tapestries, even a tiny bellows, whose use she couldn't make out. Finally, the chapel could breathe, and she smiled, inhaling right along with it.

Straightening up and stretching her back, she surveyed her progress. It wasn't much, but it was something, and she'd done it by herself. That was a novel feeling, worth the effort. Most astounding of all, though she'd come prepared with a ratty old handkerchief, her nose had not bled a drop.

Someone cleared their throat, and she spun around to see the boy, Bram, her new cousin-in-law, offering a fistful of St. John's Wort.

"Need anything, milady?" He surveyed the mess she'd made in the corridor. "I could haul all this away for ye."

Ellen studied him skeptically for a moment. He was still a lad, and one could already see that he'd be tall, though he would never boast the stature his cousin did. But then *she* had done this much herself, so why not let the boy be useful if he wanted? She smiled and nodded, and he nodded back at her, handing her the bouquet and rolling up his sleeves to get to work.

All of the seat cushions needed replacing, but the wooden benches themselves were in fine condition, much like the bones of the old chapel. It was rough around the edges, but completely salvageable, and with Bram's help, it was soon stripped to the essentials and ready for scrubbing.

"What's next?" he asked, as if reading her mind, as she thought through her remaining tasks: scrubbing the floors, whitewashing the walls, polishing the benches. So many things were next.

She reached in her pocket, scraping her palm along the sharp edges of the Luckenbooth brooch and took a breath. "Supplies," she finally forced herself to say, and Bram's face lit up like he was eager to get out in the sunshine.

"Can I fetch them for ye?"

Ellen took her list from her pocket, and then paused. "Can you read?"

"Course," he scoffed.

Of course he could read. He was the nephew of the laird. What a ridiculous mistake to even question it. She handed him the parchment, and he took off without a backward glance.

Once he left, she looked around again, paralyzed over which task to begin next. She could scrub the floor, but Bram would soon return with whitewash, and after painting the walls, wouldn't the floor require scrubbing all over again?

A crack along the base of the wall drew her attention, where chunks of stone had tumbled out, and a small lead pipe protruded from the hole. She reached out to touch it, and gooseflesh raced down her arms, so she snatched her hand away.

Crouching, Ellen peered through the pipe. She could just make out the flicker of candlelight on the other side, in the laird's chamber. Perhaps this was how he smelled the incense that was lit inside the chapel.

A shuffle of feet in the corridor snapped her attention, and she looked up to see the laird's steward, Norval MacKenzie, watching her curiously. Ellen scrambled to her feet, dusting her palms on her apron. "Milord," she mumbled with a slight curtsy, and his brows shot up in surprise, because she, foolish girl, outranked him now.

He nodded at her and continued into the Kintail's chamber, closing the door behind him.

Why Ellen had bothered to open her mouth today, she wasn't sure. Her efforts at communicating led to one blunder after another. She really should go back to silence. Silence was easy. Still, she took herself down to the kitchen to see about a bucket of water and a hearthstone, because in for a penny, in for a pound, but even her feigned confidence wavered as the angry voice of Mrs. Kynoch carried into the Hall.

"What did I tell ye? I told ye keep yer fingers out of it, now look what ye've gone and done," she bellowed.

Ellen paused long enough that little Dorrie darted out of the kitchen and behind her skirt. Mrs. Kynoch followed with a spoon in her hand, moving faster than Ellen would've imagined possible for a woman her age. "Get back here, missy, or you'll get worse than a smack."

Spotting Ellen, the normally unflappable cook stopped and tucked her braid behind her shoulder. "Milady. Did ye need something?"

Ellen nodded, and Mrs. Kynoch waited, impatient to return to her work.

"Flannel?" Ellen began, "Water? A hearthstone?"

The creases between the cook's brows deepened. "Are the floors not clean enough for ye, milady?" she asked in a harried sort of way.

Ellen shook her head. "I want to help."

"Don't see as we need your help, begging your pardon, milady," the cook said, though there was a grudging respect in her voice. "But if you're bent on it, the child can show ye. My hands are full enough as it is. Do us a favor and take her with ye. If she gives you any lip, take a firm hand or a suitable stick to her backside." To her granddaughter she called, "Go with milady and mind yourself. Maybe you'll even learn something."

The moment Mrs. Kynoch disappeared back into the kitchen, Dorrie popped out from behind Ellen, grinning broadly, took her hand, and led her to the larder.

The little girl put Ellen to shame, pumping water into a bucket almost as big as she was, and then hoisting it up to carry inside. Knowing she'd probably struggle more than the child, Ellen took it from her, and if half of it sloshed out, then she'd try to do better when she went back for more. In the end, she only spilled a little, and Dorrie promptly produced a rag to dry it.

Safely back in the chapel, Ellen got to work while the little girl climbed all over the pews like a rambunctious kitten. She wet the stone floor with her scrap of flannel and then scrubbed it clean with the hearthstone until it shone.

Her knees hurt badly and her back ached, but she breathed in the pain, and exhaled it back out again. Same as the sting of the nettles, she offered it up as penance for all her daily transgressions—assuming incorrectly who could and couldn't read and shaming them for it, worrying old Gawyn over the silly horse, and most of all, the lustful yearning for Silas which plagued her thoughts night and day. Somehow, that lust kept a constant heat thrumming between her legs, whether she was thinking about him or not, which only made her think of him all the more.

Ellen scrubbed until sweat dripped down her back and between her breasts, making her rashy skin burn afresh, the shift clinging tightly to her form and pressing the prickly nettles deeper. She scrubbed until her knuckles cracked and bled, and little Dorrie, crying out upon seeing it, took the hearthstone from Ellen's cramped, trembling fingers to finish the last corner by herself.

When it was finally done, Ellen noticed that one of the pew racks held an old Bible, and she took it out to study. Inside, in careful ink, someone had written the history of the MacKenzie line, ending with Silas Michael Wolfrick Alisdair MacKenzie born February 19, 1699, son of Alex and Iona Campbell Munro MacKenzie, died February 20, 1699.

A prickle of familiarity tugged at Ellen's memory, but she couldn't say why, and it was soon replaced by a rush of warmth and sadness for Si. Just like her cousin Jory, it seemed, her husband had never known his mother.

He is a man raised by men, the mysterious Mac had told her, and now those words held new meaning, as did his sadness over the state of the chapel, the room which he'd been told was his mother's favorite.

Dorrie snuggled up next to her, tracing the writing with her index finger before sticking it in her mouth.

"Can you read?" Ellen asked one last time for the day.

The child giggled and shook her head.

"Then it's time you learned," Ellen whispered, resolving that when Greer arrived, the chapel would have two pupils learning their letters.

She should try to acquire a chalkboard. Perhaps there was one around Leod somewhere that Bram and Si might have used.

"Got everything," Bram grunted, tracking mud onto the clean floor and heaving a crate onto the front pew. "Quicklime, embroidery thread, all the feathers I could get for now, and twenty-one yards of linen."

Ellen's eyes widened in shock before she had a chance to school her face, and Bram's beaming confidence flattened.

"It was just about all they had. Did I get it wrong?"

"You got it just right."

Bram eyed her skeptically, then cast his gaze at the floor where he noticed the bucket and his muddy boots, and his frown deepened.

"It's fine, Bram. Thank you," Ellen whispered, jumping up to squeeze his shoulder so he wouldn't be too worried about the floor, though what she'd do with an extra nine yards of linen, she had no idea. Still, it wouldn't go to waste. "Well done."

"What did ye want it for? All that linen?"

"New cushions," she said brightly.

"Seems like a lot."

"It's the perfect amount."

He didn't believe her, but for a moment he seemed to accept the contract that they would both pretend.

"I can help with the whitewash if ye like."

"Grand," she whispered.

He offered her list back, but then stopped and stared at it. "I..." He looked back at the massive bolt of fabric. "Is that twelve or twenty-one? I thought... but..."

"It's the perfect amount," she said again, running her hand fondly over the bolt of fabric.

He nodded, but said, "I've got chores," and skulked off, whitewash forgotten.

Ellen watched him go, wondering what troubled him. Had he simply read the line too quickly? Mistakenly inverted the twelve to twenty-one? Judging by his reaction, it wasn't the first time. Perhaps she'd have three students at lunch tomorrow instead of two. Perhaps she'd found her purpose here at Leod, along with her voice, even if it only came out in whispers.

Chapter Fifteen

When Si looked in on his father before dinner, the chapel next door caught his eye. It was... empty. All of the erstwhile debris had been removed. He was honestly surprised by how much progress the lass had made. Perhaps in the interest of slowing her down, he should've forbidden Bram from helping.

Now a ridiculous notion took hold of him, and he carried all the pews two at a time downstairs to a storage room behind the larder. No benches—no finished chapel—no runaway wife. He spread bed linens over them to keep them out of sight, acknowledging that he'd never behaved more childishly, even as an actual child. What was happening to him?

He hadn't set eyes on his bride the entire day, and now she was locked in her chamber, dressing for dinner with the clan, and Si supposed he should do the same. He took greater care with his appearance than usual, battling his rather wild hair into submission and trimming up his beard. Tonight there would be feasting, and at the very least, he needed to look the part of laird if, in a few days' time, he was going to con them all into giving him their oaths.

He tapped on the door that still separated the two of them, and she opened it immediately, looking up at him through long blonde lashes. She was breathtaking in a finely spun blue that set off those Mackintosh eyes. The Borlum line was famous for their sapphire irises. Even her male cousins, Logan and his brothers, could be seen coming for miles. But Len... Si had truly never seen eyes like hers before. A man could wash out to sea and fairly drown in them—and be saved all at the same time.

"Milady Len," he rasped. "Ready?"

Her head gave the tiniest shake, echoing Si's own anxiety about the whole event, but he squeezed her arm. "Dinna fash. You'll be grand."

Then he offered his elbow and together they made their way down the stairs to the hoard of MacKenzies waiting below.

A raucous cheer went up from the assembly when they descended into the Hall, followed by a bawdy chorus about newlywed bliss that made the lass turn dark red. Si waved them to silence and guided her to a place at the table before he was pulled away by first one, then another well-wisher. It was the wedding feast all over again.

If only his father had been healthy enough to join them, he might have at least provided a buffer between Len and the prying eyes of the clan. He seemed a little better today, but still unable to leave his bed. Soon the lass moved from where Si had seated her near the head of the table to a more secluded spot amongst a group of tradesmen including Sam MacPherson the blacksmith and his daughter.

It wasn't protocol. Mrs. Kynoch would have kittens if she noticed, but the lass looked much more relaxed, smiling and nodding along with the conversation between her new companions. A pang of jealousy tickled the back of his mind like an itch he could never scratch, and he started to make his way over when an older MacKenzie stopped him.

"They say the laird's ailing." It wasn't a question.

"My father is well," Si answered with a tight smile. "A little tired perhaps—"

"He's been *a little tired*, as ye say, for quite some time, then. It's what kept him so long in France, they say, too busy to see how poor the soil has been, but he manages to collect his rents on time. Higher each year, though the farm's not producing."

"Have you complained to his steward?" Si asked, his mouth growing dry. He glanced around for Norval, but he only spotted young Angus glaring his way.

"Is the steward laird or is Alex?"

Si took a deep breath. "Have you tried rotating your crops?"

The farmer stared at him like he'd suggested planting them on the moon.

"Plant some beans next season instead of barley."

The farmer shook his head in disgust. "You've been away too long, boy. If a cow won't give milk, ye don't ask her for whisky."

The old man's argument made a sort of sense, even to Si. He was wasting his time playing at farmer. He could plant all the seedlings he wanted, record their growth from now until New Year, but if he showed the men those sprouts, they'd scratch their heads and call it witchcraft, no matter what science had to say about the soil.

Over the old farmer's head, Si noticed Blair MacKenzie had found a seat for himself next to Ellen, and he held her in rapt attention telling some boastful story, based on his broad gestures and roguish grin.

The lass smiled at Blair and laughed at his teasing. She leaned closer to hear. And the tickle in the back of Si's head began to burn. He'd assumed he understood the nature of envy ever since the day twelve years ago when he became the heir, but now he knew he'd never experienced true jealousy before in his life. He understood why it was one of Pope Gregory's seven cardinal sins, for it pushed the carnal part of him towards others on that list, beginning with wrath.

Oh, Blair could be charming sure enough, but would Len suppose he was the Mac who wrote her letters? Worse, would she be disappointed to find out he was not?

In five steps Si reached the table, put his head close enough to hers that her hair tickled his cheek, and whispered, "Milady Len, if you've finished your meal, I require your presence."

She let out a startled little gasp and it stirred a third deadly sin in Si, along with a new mission in life—to elicit that sound from her lips each and every day.

He stepped back, offering his hand to help her up from the table, glaring at Blair who smirked up at him and then winked at the lass, a gauntlet if one had ever been thrown.

Len nodded to her friends and then took Si's hand, allowing him to sweep her away, not speaking the questions in her eyes.

But she *could* speak, damn it. For hadn't she repeatedly told him not to stop as he buried his face between her legs?

A jolt shot straight to his groin at the memory.

"Would you be willing to address the clan for me?" he whispered. "To show a united front and get them on my side?"

She stared up at him with such abject horror, he immediately regretted the petty request. But he pressed on. "They'll like you, milady. And what's more, they'll expect it."

Shaking her head ever so slightly, the lass looked around at the assembly, opening and closing her mouth, unable to even object. Si should leave it alone, of course he should, but his own roving gaze landed on Blair laughing with Rabbie Stewart over some shared joke and he added, "You must speak, lass, or after that display they'll expect you to cuckold me with Blair MacKenzie." The words sounded much more cruel and pathetic to his ears than they had in his head.

When he looked down at her, all color had drained from her face and her eyes darted around the room like a trapped animal. She surveyed the Hall, filled with dozens of rowdy MacKenzies who may recognize her from the wedding but many of whom were essentially strangers to them both. He shouldn't have asked even if she did seem to possess a voice just begging to be set free.

"A quick welcome would suffice," he offered, squeezing her cold hands and searching the depths of her stormy eyes, knowing it was mean, but hadn't she told the Mac she couldn't be what he needed? And didn't he owe it to her to prove such notions incorrect?

"They don't understand me," he tried to explain. "I've been away too long. They think I abandoned them. But you came here. You're the reason I returned. They'll love you. They already do."

Her eyes widened and a flash of anger replaced the fear. "I'm to be your pawn too?" she whispered. "Clean up your own mess, Silas MacKenzie."

Then she yanked her hands away and marched off towards the stairs, and Si just watched her go, grinning like a fool. He couldn't explain it, but he liked the way his name spilled from her lips even when she was angry. There was fire buried inside her, a willingness to stand up to him in a way that almost no one ever did. It delighted him, and it made him rock hard for more.

He was tempted to follow her right up to her chamber, except who knew what the clan might get up to in his absence?

Instead, he waited until the last reveler went to bed, and then returned to the solitude of his library determined to tell her the truth about the letters. She might be angry, but, he smirked to himself, maybe a tongue lashing from her wouldn't be the *worst* thing. Regardless, he couldn't have her supposing the Mac was Sam MacPherson, or worse—Blair MacKenzie.

And he couldn't be with her in any way with such a huge lie standing between them. Len and Mac must finally meet. But not tonight. He needed a few more hours to prepare for, and worry himself sick about, her reaction. Tomorrow would be soon enough.

. . .

He barely slept all night. Between the ripples of anxiety that made his blood boil and sing, and an urgent desire to lie beside his wife to ease those same emotions, Si tossed and turned and paced the floor rehearsing all the different speeches he needed to make in the coming days, not only to his wife, but to his father, to Bram, and to the clan. It was almost a mercy when dawn finally showed its face.

During the morning hours, Si walked among the people, listening but not trying to change any minds about new farming techniques. He'd learned that lesson the night before. He was simply out there because he needed to remain in constant motion or he might explode. It was a relief when Cedrick and some others started organizing a shinty match, so Si went in search of Bram to join in.

Wee Dorrie's voice alerted him to activity in the chapel. "W, X, Y, Z," the little girl recited, to a small round of applause and murmured praise from Len.

When he crept close enough to peer inside, he found letters being painted on the dingy walls in whitewash. The blacksmith's daughter was copying out her own row above Dorrie's, and in the near corner, Ellen stood with Bram, who wasn't drawing letters but simply covering the wall in perfect, even stripes of white.

"Reading's all right," Bram told her in a low voice. "It's just the numbers that seem to play tricks. I dinnae ken how, but they... move around. Don't tell Si or Himself. They already think me worthless."

Stung by his cousin's words, Si took a step back. Bram was young and unprepared, but Si hadn't really given him much thought beyond that. Certainly not that the boy was worthless, except perhaps in unguarded, frustrated moments.

"The very opposite," Len assured Bram. "He wants you to be laird, like your father. He wouldn't ask that of someone he found worthless, would he?"

Again Si was stunned—first to hear her voice, soft yet strong and unwavering—but also because she raised that lovely voice in his defense, even after he tried to pressure her into speaking last night. And how was she so keenly attuned to his own intentions, when he'd never expressed them outright to her?

"My father's dead," Bram said forcefully.

"Still your birthright."

Why was it that she could speak so freely to the boy, loud enough for Si to hear from his hiding place, and then have so few whispered words left over for him?

"I don't *want* to be laird," Bram yelled, his voice echoing Si's own words every day for the last twelve years, though it had never occurred to him his cousin might have the same reticence.

"What *do* you want?" Len asked the lad.

And how different would their lives be if anyone had ever asked her that? Or Si?

A long silence passed before Bram answered, "To paint."

Paint? Was that what the Kintail meant when he said Bram's head was in the clouds?

The boy glanced his way, so he stormed into the chapel, the others turning to him with varying degrees of unease, except for Dorrie, who grinned toothily.

"What's going on here?"

"School," the little girl proclaimed proudly.

"Modern education calls for writing on walls, does it?"

"Aye, milord," she giggled.

"Bram," Si said, not looking at any of them but Dorrie, who continued to grin her big, gap-toothed smile. "You're needed for the shinty."

"Don't like shinty," Bram whined.

"Too bad. Family honor and all that."

The boy sighed. "Yes, cousin."

"We have class," Len protested, stepping closer and scowling up at him, and Si breathed in the sweet scent of lavender and something else. Rosewater and dock leaf salve?

"Not today. The lad can read and write well enough," he said, and she snorted her displeasure.

It put the devil in Si, and he leaned down so his lips almost brushed her ear and whispered, "You've had a letter."

He delighted in the immediate flush that spread across her cheeks, but his enjoyment was short-lived, quickly replaced with a smoldering jealousy that one spark would ignite into a raging blaze. Jealous of himself as much as a phantom, it was madness!

Withdrawing the letter from his sporran and handing it over, he searched her face for some clue of how she'd react to learning the writer's identity, but she crossed her arms, waiting for him to leave, so he did, Bram shuffling along behind him.

ELLEN GLARED AT THE BACK OF SI'S HEAD UNTIL IT WAS LONG out of sight. She'd wanted to show him the pipe in the wall, to ask where they kept the incense her father-in-law liked so well. But then he stormed in all brooding and bossy, like he was determined to prevent her from doing anything helpful, like he was still angry at her for refusing to do her wifely duty and speak on his behalf the night before.

She didn't know quite what had gotten into her, only that she'd been surprised and frightened and angry. None of those were new emotions, but she usually kept them locked inside. It was as if Silas had somehow unleashed everything she'd been afraid to feel.

"Can *we* go and watch the shinty, milady?" Dorrie asked.

Ellen nodded. "Don't get underfoot," she said as the two girls hurried past her, their lessons quite forgotten.

Silas MacKenzie had a way of getting under her skin as badly as a bunch of fresh nettles. He seemed to sneer at the idea of her teaching the children to read, and yet he was one of the most educated men she'd ever met. He was bitter at being made to take on a role he didn't want but turned around and tried to bully her and Bram into the exact same position. He acted jealous of her pen friendship, yet he handed over the letter all the same, when he could just as easily have kept it for himself or tossed it into the fire.

She didn't know what to make of him. Were all men so confounding? That was the sort of information her mother and Jory should have shared, rather than advice on performing the marital act. Little help that had been.

With shaking hands, she tore open the parchment from Mac. Maybe she could ask *him* to explain the male species.

> Lady Len,
> You looked radiant at dinner last evening, but I was too ashamed to speak. Please will you meet me this afternoon? There's a forest glade beyond the stable. I'll be waiting.
> Your humble servant,
> Mac

Ellen sat heavily on the floor, the benches having gone missing overnight. Her eyes flew to the bare spot on the wall where the crucifix used to hang, its pale outline still staring back at her in judgment.

Her mysterious friend wanted to meet. There was nothing wrong in that, was there? How could there be, when he already knew who she was and she was meeting new people left and right these days? He was a cousin, no different than Finn or Bram.

Though, from the angry heat wafting off Si when he handed her the letter, she wasn't sure he'd agree. Perhaps she should meet this mysterious writer and then give him up for her husband's sake. Why did that notion make her so desperately sad?

There was yelling outside, but the chapel window was still boarded up, so she followed the noise out to the grounds behind the garden, where two dozen burly MacKenzies and Bram chased a ball around. They were playing shirts and skins, and Si was easy to spot, standing a head above the rest, his broad, glistening back sculpted like a drawing in one of Jory's anatomy books.

A bigger boy slammed sideways into Bram, and Ellen started forward, but Si whirled around with a look of warning in his eyes. She froze in place, as if physically pinned down like a moth to a board by the stern expression in his eye. Or was it the defined shape of his chest? The dark, curly hair trailing like an arrow down into his kilt, muscles rippling under his skin as he reached a hand down to help Bram to his feet.

Ellen shook herself and backed away. Shinty was a blood-thirsty game with a lot of running and falling down into the mud and altogether too many crunches of wood connecting with bone, or bone connecting with bone for her liking.

Si seemed to shadow Blair, preventing his every scoring opportunity, frustrating him, and knocking the smaller man brutally to the ground every chance he got. He seemed to have it in for the fairer man. In fact, she couldn't see that Silas actually tried to score even once. He would simply toss the ball to another player and slam Blair to the ground for the fun of it.

When at last the match was over, Bram limped back inside with Greer's help, and Silas pranced around the field gloating like a victor as though personally responsible for every point scored. The rest of the MacKenzies hollered and cheered and passed dram after dram, so perhaps his bravado was working, but Ellen had seen enough. She slipped off towards the stable, then kept on going into the forest beyond.

The glade Mac had described was easily found, verdant and carpeted in bluebells. Sunlight filtered through the trees to make a shadowy faerie den, and Ellen sat down on a rock to wait, to reconsider all the reasons why she ought not have come. Chief among them: it was disloyal to Silas, even though her own feelings were nothing more than friendship. How could they be anything else, when she was married? And as frustrating as Silas was proving to be, he was also gentle and kind, and devilishly handsome.

Soft footsteps at last alerted her to someone's approach, and Ellen jumped up to see—none other than Blair MacKenzie? Her breath caught. He was a bit worse for wear after the shinty.

When considering the options, she'd been unable to believe it could be him. He seemed too boastful, too proud, and there was a hardness underneath his jocular demeanor that she hadn't discerned on paper.

A bruise was already setting in around one eye, lending it a dark, dangerous edge that made her shiver.

"Saw you sneaking off," he said.

She swallowed, meaning to reply that she certainly was not sneaking, that it was merely a lovely spot, but the words couldn't find their way past her throat. Could she pretend the letters had been intercepted and weren't written by her? A fresh wave of panic hit her lungs.

"Ye must be lonely out here," he said, a wolfish hunger creeping into his eyes and lacing his voice with danger.

Ellen shook her head.

He stepped closer. "No one at Leod but that bloody great oaf to tend ye?" He laughed and shook his head. "There was a time, not so long ago, when I thought he hung the moon. But then I grew up and realized size isnae all that matters. You and I both know that's true, don't we?"

Ellen could only shake her head.

"You don't have to pretend. I know what it is to be lonely. Silas left, and the Kintail left, and my father left, but I stayed. I know all the castle's secrets, all the best hiding places where no one would ever find us. And I could teach you so many things. Things I'll bet Silas, with all his book learning, doesn't know."

Unable to reconcile his manner of speaking with the correspondence she had treasured, Ellen swallowed once, twice, and tried to conjure the right words to send him away.

"I could've gone to school like Silas. Or traveled the world with my father: India, Africa, Japan. But I was content right here. That counts for something, doesn't it?"

Unsure what he meant, she nodded her agreement, always the safest course of action for a woman. Men liked to be agreed with.

Blair reached for her face and she stepped quickly back, tripping over the rock she'd been sitting on, and scrambling to keep her balance. He took hold of her elbow to steady her, but then he didn't let go, and she all but stopped breathing.

"Come, now," he said, eyeing her lips and then dropping his gaze to her bosom peeking above the stays. "Is it even consummated, or does he still hide from girls like he did at the age of eleven? I can show you how a lady ought to be treated. Silas never needs to know."

"Please leave," Ellen whispered, trying to yank her arm from his grasp, but he held on tighter.

"Please, is it?" He smirked, pretending not to hear the rejection in her reply.

"Please," she whimpered once more.

"Ye don't have to beg."

Ellen struggled harder against his hold, but it only made him grasp her more tightly.

Then he grinned a sick, wolfish grin. "Unless you like that sort of thing."

Ellen froze, unable to move or even breathe. How, after so many years of keeping her guard up, how had she put herself in this situation? And how could she have been so wrong about the Mac? She'd assumed she would know instantly when she met him, believed him good and kind and noble, a worthy friend to Si. Not this, not a snake luring her to an empty forest glade.

"If anyone should be next in line, it's my father. Everything he did was for the good of clan, while Alex hid like a coward in France. And d'ye know what that makes me? The proper heir." Blair sidled closer, his face inches from hers, and she shut her eyes tight and twisted away.

And then there came an almighty roar and a crunching thud, and Ellen was flung backwards against a willow tree, as her eyes flew open to see Silas landing punch after punch on Blair MacKenzie's once pretty face.

"Jesus, Si, I found her here alone. I was only trying to convince her to come back for her own safety," Blair gasped, but Silas didn't relent.

At first, the younger man tried to fight back, clawing and grappling, and landing a blow here or there, but he was no match for an outraged husband.

"You know I would never..." Blair fell to his knees, trying ineffectually to block his face, but Silas held him up by his shirt collar, continuing to pummel him, his knuckles slick with blood.

And some small, wicked part of Ellen was relieved. Some dark part of her soul wanted Si to beat Blair until there was nothing left that could grab her arm or sidle up to women in a forest glade. But the rational part of her mind knew she had to intervene.

"Stop," she finally cried, for if Si didn't, he'd surely kill the man and if he did that, he'd be hanged—by the law or the Watch or Norval and the clan. Even if he wasn't hanged, at the very least he'd lose the favor of the MacKenzies, Ellen's whole reason for being there.

Si looked at her in shock, blinking as if only just realizing what he'd done.

"Mercy," Ellen whispered. "Show him mercy."

And he nodded, tossing Blair to the ground in disgust. "Can you walk?" he growled.

"Fuck you," Blair spat, which appeared to be good enough for Si.

Without a second glance, he scooped Ellen onto his horse and rode back to Leod, not loosening his hold around her waist until they reached her chamber.

"I'll have them draw a bath," he said, his voice hoarse with restrained fury.

She shook her head. She was dirty and coarse, and she longed to be scrubbed clean until all her skin peeled off, but she'd no desire to disrobe, and she didn't deserve the comforts of a bath, in any case. She deserved to stew in her own filth for flirting with disaster. He had warned her last night of how it must look, and she'd treated his warnings as ridiculous, but now she was the fool after all.

"Bed," she whispered, though it wasn't even late enough for dinner.

Silas scowled at her, searching her face, her neck, her arms for marks, she suspected, that would grant him leave to go back and finish murdering Blair.

"Did he hurt you?"

She shook her head and chewed the inside of her cheek to keep from crying.

He nodded and stepped away from her, but returned a moment later, holding out a little knife, a sgian dubh like Jory's, but finer, with a stone of red jade that matched her wedding band in the hilt.

"I should have given it to you sooner," he rasped. "But I was afraid..." he cut himself off.

Ellen reached out hesitantly to accept the gift, knowing full-well what such a thing was capable of.

"I'll teach you how to use it," he promised.

Ellen could only nod, still gazing at the weapon in her hand.

Then Si nodded too and stepped back into his library, adding, "Knot the door," over his shoulder as he went, and when she was alone, Ellen crumpled to the floor and wept.

Chapter Sixteen

What kind of pitiful excuse for a husband would promise to protect and instead lie about his identity and lure his wife off to the forest only to be attacked by a sniveling weasel of a man? Len appeared physically unharmed, but every shudder and every tear was Si's fault, all because he'd been too weak and cowardly to speak to his own wife since the day they wed.

Thank Christ she stopped him before he took his retribution too far. What a terror he must have seemed, rage made flesh, beating the lad bloody with every barb and insult ever flung his way, every moment of inadequacy, every second of despair in his eight and twenty years.

He wasn't a man of violence. He abhorred it, which was one of the reasons he didn't return to life at Leod after the prior Kintail's death. He could fight as well as any man and better than most, but his heart wasn't in it, and usually, thanks to his size, he didn't have to. Until today. Now the lass had borne witness to his temper unleashed, seen just what he was capable of, and she would fear him more than ever. She would absolutely insist on leaving Leod now.

He pulled himself together in time to go down to dinner alone and ordered a tray taken up to her room, to be left covered in his library if she didn't answer. Working the Hall as he had done the evening before, he smiled and nodded at the slaps on the back praising his shinty skills and the teasing, "We'll make a man of young Bram yet." He allowed the taunts about his father's absence to roll off his back like so much water, putting on the mask of his most charming self and never rising to the bait. It was easy, because his mind wasn't there in the Hall with the clan. It was with Len—only Len.

"D'ye have Old Kintail stuffed in a coffin upstairs?" one of Cedric's brothers asked.

"Well now, if I did that, the old bastard'd be haunting the place, wouldn't he? Throwing food, spilling wine. Pinching you when nobody's looking."

"He would at that," Gawyn agreed, patting Si's shoulder so he'd know he wasn't alone.

Si would be completely lost without the groom.

"But really, where is the laird?" another asked. "Is he so poorly he cannae even show his face? Or is he not sick at all, and merely preferred exile?"

"Ashamed, more like," chimed a third, Angus, the one who held his tongue at the wedding and interceded for Blair in the street. "Ashamed of how high he's raised the rents these last two years, and how little to show for it."

"Or maybe he's just tired of your bellyaching, Angus MacKenzie," came the Kintail's voice from across the Hall—stronger than Si had heard it in days, but controlled to hide the wheezing. "Maybe 'tis not for you to decide what rent is proper, but what amount would make you happy? None at all, for it goes against human nature. I could cut it down by half and half again and you lot would still be complaining."

Angus, perhaps all of twenty years old, immediately studied the ground and backed away muttering, "Aye, milord."

"Alex, you're looking well," Norval greeted, moving to his side to assist him, though the laird shook him off, determined that the clan should not suspect any weakness.

"And why shouldn't I be? I'm not the one who got his tail kicked from here to next Tuesday on the shinty pitch." There was a twinkle in the old man's eye when he said it, but Si heard reproach for letting the game get out of hand. If anyone else did, though, they masked it with teasing and laughter. "Now, who's going to fetch me a dram?" the old man asked.

All eyes turned to Si, who poured the drink and took it to his father.

"Good to see you," he said softly, handing it over.

"There's some saying you were too hard on the lad at shinty," his father said before taking a swig.

"Bram? He probably was a might small to join in the game, but he's fine."

"Not Bram," his father said, nodding toward the doorway where Blair and Rabbie had just slunk inside, searching the room nervously. He looked like hell, and Silas's mouth tasted of iron.

"Ah," was all Si said.

"Shinty can be an unforgiving sport," Gawyn added, sliding his own glance over Blair, who was now assembling a plate of food.

Si relaxed his hand, which had balled into a fist at the sight of the younger man. "Aye, especially the way we play."

"Suppose that's true," the Kintail agreed, watching Si watch Blair. "Did he deserve it?"

"He did indeed."

Alex nodded. "Only remember, son, start as you mean to go on."

He was suggesting, of course, that Si must rein in his temper unless he wanted to rule the clan by violence from start to finish, and he knew well enough Si had no stomach for that.

Well, and wasn't ruthlessness what was expected of him on account of his size?

"I have," he told his father, because if anyone else tried to force themselves on his wife, he would probably kill them. He should check on her. "Since you've everything under control, I should see to my wife."

"Where is she?" the laird asked, looking around. "Not under the weather, I hope."

"Most likely overexerted herself on her project. She'll be well by morning." Why was he lying? Why not admit, loudly and publicly, what Blair had tried to do to her, the reason he'd earned all those bruises? Except it wasn't Si's story to tell.

"Project? What project? Is that what's been going on in the chapel? I dreamed I heard singing."

"Singing?" Silas scoffed. When she refused to speak above a whisper? "It's nothing. A hobby. I'll go and see she's all right."

"Ask her to come and read to me again tomorrow."

Si turned, again unable to cover his surprise. "Read?"

"Aye. She spends more time with a poor, sick old man than his own son does. Ye can barely hear her, but then I suppose that's why it's so soothing. I have to concentrate on listening and it makes me forget my worries."

"How long's this been going on?" he couldn't help asking.

The old man shrugged. "I cannae tell time anymore. Ask her to come tomorrow?"

Si nodded to his father and cast Gawyn a *please keep an eye on him* look, which he knew the old groom understood.

As he crossed to the back staircase, Cedrick yelled, "Where's your bride, Si?"

He forced himself to laugh. "She's had enough of you rowdy lot for one day," he replied, earning a hearty guffaw in return.

Upstairs, not a sound came from her chamber, so Si took up his quill and hastily scribbled a note, lest she actually believe Blair was the MacKenzie behind his letters.

Dearest Lady Len,

I offer my sincere apologies for being unable to meet with you today. I was unexpectedly called away, but the loss was entirely mine. I only hope you wasted no time in looking for me.
Your humble servant,
Mac

Then, to take his mind off his self-loathing, he measured his sprouts and carefully recorded the changes in each—their size and the vibrancy of color, which he graded on a scale from one to ten. Next, he reviewed the ledgers until his eyes began to cross, trying to make sense of Angus MacKenzie's accusations, searching for ways to lower the rents which were already so low as to be almost nonexistent. Finally, he gave up and settled into his chair with only a dram and a guilty conscience for company. There was little point in even attempting to sleep, but he drifted in and out of haunted dreams.

His father had seemed better, then worse, then better again. Si was no physician, but he'd never seen the like. Tonight a new symptom plagued him. The old man tried to hide a slight tremor in his hand, but Si caught it. He shouldn't have retired, he should've been a more attentive son, but Alex couldn't stand him worrying *like an old hen*, as he liked to say.

Jory Shaw had suggested monitoring what the laird ate and drank, and he'd been lax there, too, for Mrs. Kynoch had final authority over such matters, and she treated both the laird and Si like her own sons. Perhaps more deferentially than her own son, who died at Coille Bhan. For, though she'd threatened to box Si's ears and withhold his dinner, she'd never taken a birch to keep him in line, and Si well remembered Marcus Kynoch being forever on the receiving end of a swat. Gawyn told him that she had grieved fiercely after he died in the battle which, as heir to the exiled laird, Si should've fought shoulder to shoulder in.

A chilly prickle ran down the back of his neck. Surely the cook didn't hold the Kintail responsible for the deeds of the bloody English?

His grim ruminations were interrupted by screaming. Si's heart pounded in his throat and in his ears. Had Blair somehow forced his way into Len's room? But the door off the corridor was barred from the inside, as was the one he reminded her to tie off.

He slammed his shoulder into it once—twice—three times until it gave way and he realized the keening had stopped and the lass was alone.

Si rushed to her window, just to be certain, but it must have been nightmares plaguing her.

Her breaths were coming short and shallow now, and he wasn't sure how to approach without looming over the bed and frightening her all the more.

"Shh," he whispered, approaching slowly as he would a skittish horse. "Shh, mo nighean bhàn, 'twas only a dream."

THE DARKNESS WAS CONSUMING ELLEN, STEALING HER BREATHS, threatening to suffocate her. She tried to blink it away, gasped desperately for air, but she was half afraid the darkness was going to win and she'd never see daylight again.

It had been a dream. Nothing more. It was only a dream.

Like always, she had tried to scream, and like always, even in her waking hours, no sounds escaped her throat. Except this time perhaps they had, for Silas sat on the edge of her bed, whispering soothing words to her, and she found herself wishing he would smooth her hair back from her sweaty face.

He must have noticed her fevered flush, because he put a cool hand to her forehead, and then rose and came back with a damp cloth. Gently he wiped her cheeks and neck, pushing away the sticky hair just as she'd wished.

"I'm sorry," he murmured. "I'm so sorry. Please forgive me, mo chridhe."

The cool cloth was like heaven, but she was still restless and unable to settle. After having sat huddled in the corner for an eternity, Ellen had eventually changed into a shift lined with every last bit of nettle she'd pilfered, and now she itched and burned like nothing she'd ever experienced before in her life.

"You're on fire, mo chridhe. Your shift is soaked through. Let me help you change?"

"No," she gasped, shaking her head, and he stopped, his hand on her hip, but the damage was already done. He'd noticed the nettles.

"What's wrong?" he asked.

Please go, she wanted to say, but she just closed her eyes on his sorrowful, moonlit face, and even the tears that leaked out itched and burned.

"What is it?" he asked, an edge of fear creeping into his voice, and she hated hearing that fear and knowing she alone had caused it.

He was big and brave and strong, and she put fear into his voice.

"Show me," he whispered, but it sounded more like a request than an order. "Please?"

Goading, demanding Silas made her strong and angry, but tender, vulnerable Silas was dangerous. She'd do anything, reveal anything he asked when his voice turned plaintive like that. She let him help her out of the shift, and he gasped at the state of her before inspecting the plants tied into her clothing. When he finally lifted his gaze to hers once more, he looked stricken.

"Don't touch," she cautioned him in case he didn't recognize the nettles for what they were.

"What have you done?" he whispered.

She closed her eyes again, more tears leaking out, trickling into her ears, but still she could see that look upon his face.

"Shh," he said, smoothing her hair once more. "Dinnae cry." Then he took the damp cloth, rinsed it again in cool water, and returned to kneel alongside the bed to sponge the weeping sores that so much contact with the nettles had wrought.

His ministrations brought such relief that she began to cry harder. She'd missed Jory's companionship, but also her touch and the sense of being cared for. She ached for friendship and for connection, even for Maggie's mindless, dreamy prattling as she brushed out Ellen's hair. She had longed for it, and yet she didn't deserve this compassion. She had accidentally developed feelings of a sort for the mysterious letter writer. She'd gone to meet him on her own—she, a married woman, and to this impossibly gentle man who would have killed Blair to protect her, if she'd allowed him to. She'd done that to him.

Her skin washed clean, he took the rest of the burn out with the pot of salve he'd used before, kissing her as he went, as though he could kiss the rash away and murmuring, "Never again," over and over like a benediction. "Promise me," he whispered, touching his forehead to hers and she could only nod.

Silas eased her onto one side so he could reach her back, and under his sure and steady touch, she began to doze, but her dreams came in fretful bursts, images of fire and prickly thorns. She jerked awake the moment he rose to leave.

"Don't go," she whispered, and he immediately sat back down, placing the pot of salve on the floor.

Ellen remained on her side, her back facing him, but she heard him pull his sark off over his head, and she realized that was all he'd been wearing in his haste to reach her.

Then he slid under the bedclothes, not quite touching her, lying flat on his back, one arm crooked under his head, so still, like he was afraid to move, afraid to brush up against her.

Even so, his presence was a comfort, solid and warm beside her, and she found herself leaning backwards into him.

Si nuzzled into her neck, then rolled onto his side to meet her, cradling her close. He lifted the tangled, damp hair away from her neck and kissed her behind the ear, feather-light, but lingering, and for some reason, she began to cry a third time.

Immediately, he backed away, but Ellen caught his hand in hers and cradled it around her, burrowing into him. He held her tight and whispered, "You're safe now."

She tried to still the tiny spasms that crying caused, knowing he felt each one, and he spread his fingers wide across her belly as though trying to catch them for her.

He kissed her neck once more, her ear, her temple, breathing deeply into her hair, and she turned her head back to catch his lips, wanting him, needing him to consume her and to allow himself to be consumed. She kissed him hungrily, greedily, sucking his bottom lip until he groaned, until she had to stop to catch her own breath.

She could feel him hard against her, and her first instinct was to shy away—but why? Because a nice girl ought to? Because it might hurt? Lady Len wouldn't shy away, not from her own husband. And so, tentatively, curiously she reached behind her, but all she found was his stomach, the angular bone of his hip, rough, curly hair. She shifted a little and then reached between her own legs and found the tip of him, softer and wetter than she would have imagined for something that had seemed so solid digging into her from behind.

His breath came in short, hot gasps when she stroked his manhood, and it jerked as if alive and responding to her touch all on its own.

Then he reached down to take her hand away, kissing her cheek to distract her.

"Let me?" she asked in a strong, unmistakable whisper, the voice of Lady Len, and his hand fell away instantly, landing instead on her center, which responded to his touch much as he had to hers.

They held each other like that for a moment, and Ellen was certain that she needed more. As if reading her mind, Si kissed her shoulder, his right hand reaching up to make lazy circles around her breast.

It was dizzying. Maddening. Her nerve endings exploded and distracted her when what she wanted was to concentrate on exploring and performing the same dark magic on him. She ran her thumb around his silky tip and he jerked again, and Ellen slid down lower in the bed so his member was poised right where he was touching her between her legs.

"Are you sure?" he whispered, not removing his hand from her breast.

"Please?" she begged, and he chuckled, tipping her head back to kiss her lips, distracting her so she forgot to brace herself against the pain, and then he entered her with another surge of heat that filled her up, and yes, it hurt, deliciously.

He paused for a moment, and her awareness skittered through time and space alighting on everything at once, on his breaths shallow against her cheek right before he swirled his tongue around hers, on his salty, mossy scent, and the softness of his skin. Then he began to pump in and out while teasing higher up with his fingers.

She moved with him, like a dance they were only just learning the steps to, and she saw music in flashes and sparks, and she heard moonlight, and she whimpered though she was anything but sad, and when she turned back to gaze at him in wonder, she became a caterpillar trapped inside the amber fossils of his eyes, about to burst out as a butterfly all shiny and newly formed.

Chapter Seventeen

In the wee hours before dawn, Si reflected on the exact moment when his resolve had crumbled. With Len still cuddled close against him, sensual flashes of the night before played through his mind, making him grow hard all over again. He buried his face in the back of her neck, drinking in the scents of lavender and delicate perspiration blended with dock leaf salve.

There'd been no ulterior motives when he'd gone to treat her hive-ridden skin. But then she had begged him to stay, and for a moment he'd forgotten his reluctance. And then she had touched him, and he'd chosen to forget everything else.

All night he had pictured the moment when, caught up in the emotion and the ecstasy, he had chosen not to pull out because he couldn't bear to be parted from her yet. He consoled himself with the scientific fact that it was an imperfect prevention, little consolation though science was.

With the damage already done, he had swept fear aside and allowed it to happen twice more throughout the night, each time Len had grown restless and needy and reaching, each time tearing deeper at his conscience until only the throes of passion allowed him to ignore it.

She'd been upset and vulnerable, and like a barbarian, he'd taken advantage of her to satisfy his carnal lusts. In the moment, it was nothing short of miraculous, but now... he splayed his fingers over the soft skin of her belly. What if, already, his seed was taking root within her womb? How could one so small possibly survive the child of a Goliath monster of a man, bigger even than his father had once been?

He slid out of bed, snatched up his sark, and stalked back to his empty library. All those years of abstinence and self-control, all for nothing. A whispered, *Don't go*, and his common sense fled along with his restraint. A warm hand and urgent, *Let me*, and his resolve had crumbled into dust.

If anything happened to her because of him, he couldn't possibly forgive himself. He swore never to return to her bed even as he lay beside her. Let her loathe him if she must, but let her live.

He ordered a bath to be drawn and breakfast sent up alongside the apology letter from Mac, and then he went out to ride—anywhere, it didn't matter. He just needed to be away.

It was cowardly to run, but he had long since established himself as a coward where she was concerned, and nothing cleared his head like riding. How else could he begin to sort out his emotions—the constant fluttering in his stomach, half ecstasy and half dread at the thought of his bride? The blind jealousy that gripped him in its iron clench, threatening to destroy his self-control? The niggling worry in the back of his mind which refused to be ignored, whispering louder and louder that his father's time was running out?

Si couldn't bear to think about any of it, though ignoring it would only cause it to fester. For now, he chose the fester and the back of a horse.

Riding would bring a clarity found nowhere else except

perhaps swimming in the ocean, and with no ocean at hand, a horse would have to do.

Before reaching the stable, however, he was approached by young Angus MacKenzie, still looking shame-faced after last night's dressing down by the laird. For half a moment, he wondered if the lad could have found a way to poison his father, but that was absurd. Si was seeing villains in every shadowed corner.

He didn't have the energy to hold the lad's shame alongside his own, so he pretended not to hear him call, but Angus fell into step at his side, the determined whelp.

"I want to apologize, milord."

"There's no need." Si didn't slow his stride, but the lad was undeterred.

"My sister's always telling me I cannae hold my ale. Seems she may be right."

"Och." Si clapped the younger man on the shoulder. "You didnae say a thing a dozen others weren't thinking."

"Still, I... I should've addressed such grievances in private."

Si was intrigued by the man, by his willingness to speak truth to power, even if he now regretted it. The excuse of intoxication was an easy way to smooth over an awkward encounter, though he hadn't seemed deep in his cups last night to Si.

"Angus, isn't it?" Si swept one arm towards the stable. "Ride with me?"

Angus squinted, confused, then nodded his agreement.

With Gawyn's help, they saddled Uinnseann and a darker mount, and under the auspices of checking the Leod boundaries, they set off, Angus watching Si warily as they went, probably aware of the not-so-secret beating he'd given Blair, perhaps fearing the laird's son would lead him somewhere remote and give him a taste of the same. *Start as you mean to go on*, his father's words rang in his ears, and Si winced.

"Be honest," he said, relieved to have something to focus on besides the woman in his bed. "How bad is it? The plight of the crofters?"

Angus didn't answer for a moment, considering his words more carefully than he had last night. "It's bad, milord," he finally said. "Most of the farms aren't producing. What they do scrape out of the ground is barely enough for the families to eat. The crofts are crumbling, children are cold and hungry. Some have ambition to try and graze sheep, but they havenae the funds to start. And still the rents climb higher every year."

It was all as Si had feared, but it was another thing entirely to hear it said. And his father hadn't raised rents in a decade, though Si couldn't admit it to Angus.

"Surely the worst debts have been forgiven."

Angus tilted his head. "They've been offered reprieve, milord, with a promise to repay thrice over next year. A few were desperate enough to accept such terms, more fool they. The children wear moth-eaten tatters to pay for Norval's fine new tog."

Si's head snapped up at the mention of the steward and a sour, sinking sensation writhed within his gut.

"You did ask me to speak plainly, milord," Angus said, frowning.

"I did at that. Thank you for doing so. I trust you've held nothing back?"

Angus shook his head, still frowning. He didn't relish speaking so forthrightly. He was a young man, and keen. Would he be more open to the ideas Si wanted to share?

"What will you do about it?" Angus asked.

What indeed?

"Our coffers are not so full as they should be, but we may be able to help purchase a handful of sheep."

Angus's eyebrows shot up in surprise, but he nodded. "It's a start."

"It's the barley that's ruined the soil. You might as well be planting in stone. Or planting stones themselves."

"The barley?" Angus looked doubtful, but Si had to try and explain it again.

"Every plant requires certain minerals to grow. Planting the same thing, year after year, it leaches all the minerals from the soil until there's nothing left."

His companion's brow was creased in concentration, but Angus was listening. "You learned all that in Aberdeen?"

"Aye."

"Must we leave Ross?"

Si shook his head. "The solution is to rotate the crops. Plant beans one year and oats the next. They'll take different minerals and replenish what's been lost."

"I suppose grazing for a season would help as well?"

"Exactly!" It was delightful watching the other man catch on instead of having to go another round defending the science.

"Sort of like changing up a cow's diet when she won't milk?"

It was a brilliant analogy, such a simple and obvious answer to the old crofter's challenge about cows and whisky. "Exactly," Si agreed again.

Angus nodded thoughtfully. "It's a change. So. They willnae like it."

"No." They would hate it, and there were none so hard-headed as the MacKenzies of Ross-shire.

"Perhaps if the Kintail provided incentive. Gifts of seed or debts forgiven free and clear."

Si liked the way Angus's mind worked through the problem out loud, unabashed and unapologetic.

"Do you think that would be enough to convince them to try?"

"Some. Others'll need to see the outcome for themselves before they'll change."

Si nodded. Some would be better than nothing to start, and surely Angus could persuade them more easily than he. "D'you want a job?"

Now Angus looked away, ashamed, as though Si were having a laugh at his expense.

"I have a job, milord," he said softly but clearly. Angus MacKenzie didn't mince words or speak with a mouth full of stones. "I'm a farmer. And a carpenter to pick up the slack."

"I ken what you are, but if I'm to be laird, I'll need my own steward. One who knows the people, the land."

"Blair MacKenzie will take over for his father. Everyone says so."

"Not at Leod, he won't," Si answered darkly.

Angus sighed and pulled his horse to a stop, turning to face Si head on. "You're serious?"

"Quite."

"I'm flattered, milord. But if I've presented myself as more educated than I am—you want someone who understands—"

"I want," Si interrupted him, "someone honest. Someone who *understands* what it is to be a crofter. Someone with good instincts who's not afraid to speak his mind, particularly to me, or where injustice is concerned. The rest can be learned."

Angus scratched his horse between the ears, considering his answer.

"Well, I've never had a problem speaking my mind," he finally said.

"Then you'll do it?"

"Aye. But it's you'll have to explain to my sister that it wasn't my idea to reach above my station."

"Then your first assignment as steward is to help me reconcile what you've just said with the story told in my ledgers."

The younger man's mouth formed a solid line, realizing the gravity with which Si was treating his accusations against Norval, and he nodded once, grim and determined.

. . .

They entered Leod through the kitchen so that Si could pilfer a few bannocks. Mrs. Kynoch was just passing through with an armload of linens. Her face lit up with mischief when she saw him.

"Well. Finally," she exclaimed, hefting the pile of bedclothes with a wink. "Might actually get some wee bairns around here," she practically sang, disappearing into the scullery.

The half-chewed bannock stuck in Si's throat like mud. His conversation with Angus had just about taken his mind off things.

Had there really been so much blood that Mrs. Kynoch had noticed? Had he hurt the lass? Len had seemed wet and wanting last night, so for him to have drawn blood was just further evidence it could never work between them. He had no business going anywhere near her ever again.

Angus clapped a hand on his shoulder. "All right, milord?" he asked without a trace of teasing or lechery.

Si forced a smile that felt more like a grimace. "Grand," he lied.

Jory was right. Last night Ellen had felt a thousand different ways all at once. At first there had been residual fear, brought on by the nightmarish specter that infiltrated her sleep. Then relief, because Si had come to her and chased the dream away. There was shame, too, when he found out her secret with the nettles, and deep uncertainty that she'd be able to honor his request not to punish herself again. Even now the insidious urge reared up, to bear the itching and burning without allowing herself to scratch or wriggle.

Even so, she couldn't help smiling when she remembered what had come next—the comfort Silas had offered with his salve, the care, and then after... surprisingly *those* memories held no shame at all, only a heady, urgent desire to do it all again.

Silas had seen a portion of her shame and instead of sitting in judgment, he'd shown her tenderness.

She'd been perplexed to find him gone when she awoke, but then a bath arrived for her, and as Ellen soaked comfortably in the lavender-infused water, she realized such decadence would definitely not be possible in a convent. Would they even have jam for her parritch? Did they eat parritch in France?

Whatever else happened, it was done now. No hiding behind annulments and cloister walls, even if she wanted to. She was married in every sense. It was time to focus on the ways she could help her new clan, like the chapel. There was much to complete. That would be enough.

Though she feared another encounter with Blair MacKenzie, Ellen steeled herself for a journey into the village. Greer had invited her to examine the progress on their window, and she didn't want to let the girl down. After all, Lady Len wouldn't be afraid, nor would she let any man hinder her own ambition, so Ellen stood as straight and tall as she could, and made up her mind to go.

In the chapel, Bram had removed the old rotted wood that covered the window, and he knelt on the floor in the sunshine sketching with charcoal on a piece of parchment. He scrambled up to hide his work when Ellen peeked in.

"May I?" she asked.

Hanging his head, the lad stepped aside to reveal a stunning portrait of his cousin. "Don't tell Si," he begged.

For a moment, Ellen could only stare at the breathtaking likeness of her husband, frozen in a look of perplexed fondness that she'd seen so many times, so real she could almost lean down and kiss it, knowing the skin would be warm to her touch.

"Tell him what?" she whispered. "That you've an immense talent to be nurtured?"

Bram turned scarlet from his throat to his ears. "He wouldn't understand."

"Do you want to go away and study?" she asked, kneeling before the parchment and reaching out to stroke Si's face, stopping herself before she could smudge it.

Bram shrugged, then slouched against the wall.

"You should tell him."

"He wants me to be laird."

"You should tell him," she said again. "May I have this?"

"It isn't finished."

"When it is, then," she said, getting to her feet.

He nodded then. "Are you off somewhere?"

"To visit Greer and see the window." The anticipation made her pleasantly warm, or was it simply the morning sunshine pouring through the window? "Can you finish off the whitewash?"

"I'll make a muck of it," he mumbled.

"Nonsense. There's no one I'd trust more."

The boy grinned. "Can't be held accountable should Dorrie come charging in," he said, and Ellen laughed in agreement.

But when she passed through the kitchen to snag a carrot for Buttercup, the little girl was drawing her letters in the flour where they'd been preparing the day's bannocks, while her grandmother looked on in amazement. Catching Ellen's eye, Morag pressed a piece of bread and cheese into her hands alongside the carrot, and then turned back to watch wee Dorrie and her writing.

"Thank you, Morag," Ellen said, relieved by the cook's reaction. Then she skipped down to the stable, breathing deeply of the fresh morning air.

Inside, Gawyn bent low over a shirt he was mending, which gave Ellen an idea. All that remained to be done for the chapel besides the whitewash and the window was sewing new cushions for the pews.

"May I?" Ellen nodded towards his shirt, and he handed it over for her inspection. "Very fine stitching," she said, and the groom blushed and tsked and tucked his work out of sight.

"Did you want a bridle and saddle, milady? For your walk?" he asked, looking desperate for her to say no.

But she nodded. "Looks silly without," she explained.

"I'll just fetch the former Lady Kintail's—"

Ellen stopped him, not wishing to be a bother nor wanting an added reminder of the day she was thrown. "That one's fine," she said, pointing to the closest saddle on a nearby shelf.

Gawyn's lips pressed into a thin line, but he readied the horse without argument.

"Milady," he said when he finally handed over the reins. "I wanted to ask—that is—I understand ye've been giving lessons to the weans up at the house."

"Yes," she exclaimed, realizing she was quite proud to admit to something so useful.

"Only I wondered," the groom stammered, "well, my eyes aren't so young as they used to be, but I always wished to learn to read. D'ye reckon ye could teach an old dog like me? Before it's too late, I mean?"

Ellen squeezed his hand. "I'd be delighted. In return, could you help me with some needlework?"

His brow creased, but he nodded, perplexed, and Ellen set off with Buttercup, more content than she'd been in quite a long time.

When she stopped to search for a woodpecker that was hammering away in one of the pine trees, Buttercup nuzzled against her neck, reminding her once more of Silas burying his face in her shoulder, as if she needed any reminding, and it sent a warming thrill through her whole body, even as she gently pushed the horse away.

"Trying to make up for throwing me?" she asked, stroking Buttercup's velvet soft nose, which didn't help her efforts to forget stroking other velvety soft things.

"I know," she told the horse. "It was mostly my fault. I was afraid of you. I was afraid of everything, really." And her own use of the past tense made her pause.

She'd been afraid last night. Foolish, really. When had a dream ever hurt anybody?

But then, in Si's arms, she'd stopped being afraid. When she asked him to stay, and he slipped into bed beside her, she should've been terrified—of his nearness and his nakedness, of his power and strength, of his anger over finding the nettle-laced shift. She should have been afraid of eternal damnation for her sins, and how she could ever live up to the role of lady of the castle. The window would be a disaster and the whitewash would turn grotty, and her project would make a mockery of the chapel the late Lady Kintail held so dear.

But as Si's heart beat fast against her shoulder and she curved perfectly into his long, hard body, she had finally been unafraid for maybe the first time in her entire life. She knew only safety and protection and... calm.

Si made her still in a way that not even Jory had ever been able to do. In his arms, she became the fierce and brave Lady Len, cherished wife of the future Kintail. She became... whole?

The woodpecker stopped hammering and hopped to a new branch, drawing her eye, and Ellen marveled at it. This wilderness was so much slower and more magical than Inverness. The town had its own charms, of course, but Ellen realized with a deep exhale that she could breathe here. And wasn't that some special sort of magic?

Buttercup nuzzled her hand, hoping for a carrot, and she reached in her pocket for one, remembering too late the unopened letter she'd placed there after breakfast when she discovered it nestled between the tea and toast.

She should've thrown it straight into the fire. She didn't want to read Blair's excuses. It would be disloyal to Si to even open it. Especially now.

Having finished the carrot, Buttercup tried to eat the parchment too.

"Oh, all right," Ellen muttered, snatching it out of reach and opening it to skim the brief message inside.

Relief washed over her to learn that her mysterious Mac was not Blair after all, and then guilt twisted her stomach over her relief—for not wanting the memory of a man she didn't know to be stained by yesterday's events, and why? That she might continue to care for him? It was just as well he'd been detained. Silas might easily have beaten him senseless, too.

She resolved not to send any more letters, but a sad uneasiness spread through her. He had become a friend.

Offering Buttercup another piece of carrot, Ellen looked the horse in the eye. "What do you say? Should I give this riding thing another try?"

The horse jerked its head as if nodding to say, *Yes, we're friends now, too.*

Taking a deep breath, Ellen put one foot into the stirrup and then dragged herself up onto the horse, with her belly on the saddle and her bottom in the air.

"I may be stuck," she told Buttercup, but, though the horse nickered, it stood perfectly still.

Ellen rocked herself back and forth until she managed to get the other leg over the animal, and then wriggled into the saddle so she could sit up, both feet in the stirrups, her skirts in great disarray. She hadn't thought this through.

She looked around from her new height. Even the woodpecker stopped searching for its luncheon to observe her. Ellen trembled, but she tried to tell herself it was merely the shiver of delicious anticipation, and this time, her fright didn't outweigh the thrill.

Instead of helpless, sitting astride like a man was exhilarating, powerful even. She became every bit the embodiment of Lady Len MacKenzie. Perhaps if she was capable of this one thing, she was capable of anything.

"Walk on, then," she whispered to Buttercup, pointing the horse's head towards the village. "I know better than to kick you this time."

As though in answer, Buttercup ambled off at the same plodding pace as before, and though it had been quite reasonable while walking herself, astride the beast it seemed unbearably slow.

"Well done," she encouraged the horse. "You may go a tiny bit faster, if you like."

Buttercup sped up just enough that Ellen began to bounce in the saddle, and it was deliciously painful. Somehow it chafed the same places Si had touched, and she felt a bit warm and a bit naughty. She nudged the horse to go a little faster, making her bounce harder still, imagining it was Si beneath her instead of the saddle, and oh, now she understood the allure of riding.

She was most likely going to Hell either way, but would there be horses in Hell?

Chapter Eighteen

A letter arrived from the Frenchman, LeBeau, whose reply omitted love potions but detailed many signs of potential poisoning. LeBeau described arsenic's effect on the intestines, as well as arrhythmia and sore throat. He described hemlock induced vomiting, tachycardia, tremors, and paralysis.

If your father has been poisoned, given the waxing and waning symptoms, it is likely some long-term exposure at the lowest possible dose, a few drops, perhaps a vapor, and I would urge you to take the utmost care of yourself as well. Trust no one.

Si remembered the aromatic plasters Mrs. Kynoch insisted on preparing for the laird's chest, but if they contained nefarious substances, wouldn't she have grown ill as well, with the exposure of preparing them?

There is one powerful toxin made from the seeds of the otherwise innocuous castor plant, which has been known to cause difficulties in the lungs when inhaled. At a low enough dose, the lucky individual can recover in time. Though the plant isn't native to Britain, it is, on occasion, imported from India and Africa, where it may be found in abundance.

Si's head was spinning, but he knew what he must do. It was time to stop fighting his father and put him on a boat back to France with all due haste. There, at least, he'd be safe from potential assassins. In two days, Si would accept the clansmen's oaths as the Kintail wished, drink a dram, and send him on his way.

As for the other issue, a small dose of pennyroyal and a diet rich in figs if they can be gotten, or Queen Anne's Lace if they cannot, should fix your lady right up and prevent any unwanted visits from the stork.

Si rubbed his aching temples and tossed the letter onto a pile of half a dozen he'd tried writing to Len.

Pennyroyal and Queen Anne's Lace? He knew not whether they could be found in his mother's garden, and what if she ingested the wrong dose? It would all be so unnecessary, if he'd just kept himself to himself as he'd intended. But then she had cried out in terror from her nightmare, and he'd discovered her skin even more damaged than before, ravaged by near constant exposure to Mrs. Kynoch's missing nettles, and he needed to make everything better.

And then she asked him to stay.

Given her recent history with herbs, it seemed unwise to introduce more plants into their relationship.

And so, coward that he was, he kept his distance from his wife the next two days and nights. Twice she had knocked upon the door that separated them, and twice he held his breath, waiting for her to go away, disappointed when she didn't burst inside to have it out with him.

He had focused instead on his oats and beanstalks, on how to save the clan. Though his father had made an appearance at dinner the evening of the shinty, it seemed to have come at a great cost. He'd barely risen from his bed since. Clearly skeptical of Si's choice for steward and plans for the crofts, he brooked no resistance to the scheme, which Si suspected was more about the old man's health than his confidence in his son.

The Kintail hadn't argued, though he strongly suggested that Norval should take young Angus under his wing, but the idea made Si twitchy. He couldn't prove Norval had falsified the ledgers, but something didn't seem to add up. Angus had been there, while he had not, and might find something in the ledgers that Si was missing. The question was, between Norval and Angus, which man was the right one to trust?

Unable to sit still, Si wandered through the garden, searching the plants but desperate not to find one that matched LeBeau's description and crude sketch. Searching and not finding, however, relaxed him, and he'd almost given up the game to pilfer warm bannocks instead, when large, green, eight-pronged leaves caught his eye in the bed just outside the kitchen. With feathery white flowers and prickly red pods, the castor plant was unmistakable, and Si gagged up bile. Surely there was a reasonable explanation. He would figure it out, just as soon as his father was safely away.

Bypassing the kitchen, he re-entered Leod through the front door instead, heading straight for his father's chamber, but he was drawn to the bloody chapel as to his mother's knee. The walls were pure white, the crucifix rehung, and the pews had been discovered and returned from the larder.

Even now, the lass was holding court with Bram, Dorrie, the MacPherson girl, and—Gawyn? All of them, stitching cushions and reciting and spelling words.

"Let's see it, Gawyn," Len said, and the old groom flipped around the square he'd been sewing. "Luceo non uro," he said, showing the fiery mountain he'd stitched, along with the clan motto in both Latin and English. "To shine, not burn."

"Perfect," she crooned, and the old man's chest swelled with pride, but for some reason Si grew small and hollow as the outsider looking in.

"Dorrie?" Len prompted next.

The little girl grinned, and showed off her crooked stitching, as crooked as the new tooth that was starting to poke through her gums. "As the Lord has forgiven you," she read haltingly, "so you also must forgive."

"Excellent. Greer?"

The MacPherson girl glanced shyly at Bram and then turned her cushion around. "And they shall forge their swords into plowshares, and their spears into pruning knives: nation shall not lift up sword against nation, neither shall they learn war anymore."

"Sounds like Si, that," Bram said, and Len nodded approvingly.

"Let's see yours, then," the girl asked him, and Si craned his neck to get a glimpse as well.

His cousin sighed. "I just did..."

"Go on," Len encouraged him, and he turned it around to show a sun dappled holly tree straight from the forest glade, except made in a hundred shades of green and golden thread. Si hadn't known a cushion could be a work of art, but it was as fine as any tapestry in a kingly palace.

The lad looked to Len for approval.

"Oh, Bram, it's lovely," she breathed, and he beamed at her, completely besotted.

Si knew exactly how he felt.

"There's heather and horsehair to stuff them when you're ready," she said, then glanced towards the door and startled to see Si, catching him in the process of being completely undone, and he was raw as he scrambled to mask his emotion.

"What are you playing at?" he growled, his voice cracking a second time, as it hadn't really done in a dozen years or more.

She opened her mouth and closed it again, still unable to speak to him, and he lifted his shoulder in mocking question.

Then he stepped inside the chapel, inches from her, close enough to smell the lavender that should have soothed him, but it only stirred his blood. He looked around the perfect room, so beautiful that it made him angry, because she'd have loved it—his mother—but she would never get to see it. Because of him.

"Who asked you for this?" he ground out between clenched teeth.

Gawyn and the smith's girl had stood when he entered. Both now hung their heads, but when he added, "What's the point?" the groom shot him a disgusted look.

Len's face crumpled and her mouth opened and closed a few more times, but still, no words for *him*.

"The point is because why not?" Bram spoke up. "They wanted to learn to read. And we all wanted to help milady."

"Didn't ask you," Si snapped, hating himself for it as much as Bram did.

"To be useful," she finally whispered.

"It was useful as storage." Si stepped even closer, invading her space, daring her to back away, but she didn't. She tipped her head further back to look up at him. "What use have we for God here?" he asked, the question he had wondered his whole life and never dared to say out loud before. "What use have they for reading?" he added, just to goad her.

Because he wanted her to say something cutting and cruel. He wanted her to fight back. Why could she speak under her breath, speak out loud to Bram and Dorrie and Gawyn, why to strangers like the blacksmith and his daughter, but not to him? Never to him.

"Class dismissed," she told the motley group, and they all dropped their sewing to scuttle away, the MacPherson girl leading Dorrie by the hand and Gawyn shoving Bram ahead of him. When they'd gone, he'd expected an angry rebuttal. Instead she coldly informed him, "There's a pipe buried in the wall just here to let incense pass through to the laird's bedside. There was a bellows, too, before. I'm sorry, I think we threw it out."

It was the longest speech he'd ever heard her give, and then she brushed past him and out the door, leaving a trail of lavender and honeysuckle in her wake.

Si breathed it in, closing his eyes to imagine, for a moment, that they weren't fighting. Then he stormed after her, determined to make those blue eyes flash at him, to make her mutter some cutting remark for his ears alone. "I asked you a question."

She kept walking towards the stairs.

He glanced back at the pipe, chilly intuition prickling, fighting for attention he didn't have to spare. "Do not walk away from me."

Ellen climbed the stairs two at a time, Si's preferred gait, but a bit steep for her. On the landing he caught her elbow, and she whirled around to face him.

"Tell me why," he asked again.

She scowled at him. "Why I want to be useful?" she scoffed, her face red with the effort of holding back tears. She jerked free from his grasp and continued towards her chamber door.

Her tears almost made him stop. Why did it seem like she had warm words for everyone else, but only tears and sarcastic mutterings for him? Had he somehow broken her kindness the same way he destroyed everything else?

"Why is it that you seem perfectly capable of conversing with everyone but me?" He held up his arms in surrender. "Am I *so* abhorrent?"

Her shoulders slumped, but she didn't look back, so he followed her into the room.

"Why is it you'll rebuild an entire chapel just to get away from me? Give yourself *hives* rather than ask for whatever you need? What are you hiding, Len? Tell me, for I know you're not mute."

"Fine," she whispered. Just one word, raw and chilling, but it took the fight right out of him.

She collapsed on the foot of the bed and covered her face with her hands, and he wanted to go to her and take it all back and somehow make it right, but he stood frozen in the doorway.

"Fine," she said again. "When I was a lass of twelve," she began, holding her elbows, one in each hand. "Their names were Boyd and Thomas Gordon," she tried again. "Jory and I were playing in the stable with my kittens."

A sick dread filled Silas's stomach, her hesitance about entering the Leod stable suddenly making sense. He was scum. He didn't want to hear anymore. "It's all right, lass. I can guess what happened."

She pierced him with such a stare. "You demanded I speak. You will listen to what I have to say."

Something flared deep within his chest, and he shut the door to keep it between the two of them, then leaned back, against the wall, chastened, trying to shrink into it and disappear.

"It was Jory they wanted. I suppose they thought they could get away with doing it to an orphan girl of uncertain origin. I should have run for help."

She shook her head, staring off into nothing.

"I should have stopped them. But I was frozen. I couldn't move. Even if I could have, the younger brother grabbed hold of me and wouldn't let me go. I tried to call for help. But it was like a nightmare. I screamed and screamed but nothing came out. Jory, she—" The lass shook her head again, a mirthless smile crinkling her eyes. "She had to save herself like always. And me, too."

Si stared at her in horror and slid down the wall to sit on the floor, regretting every time he'd touched her, every time he'd kissed her, everything he'd done that must surely have added to her trauma.

Len touched her throat. "My voice got scared away," she said. "And everyone let it go. *Poor Wee Ellen. Always so quiet.*"

She opened and closed her mouth a few more times before adding, "It isn't an easy thing to speak freely."

"I'm sorry," he whispered, knowing it would never be enough.

"For what?" she snapped. "Jory and I hid under the bed until my mother found us. She put me in a bath that was nearly scalding. Scrubbed me until I bled. They hadn't even touched me, I…" she closed her eyes. "I was stained by intention, ruined by what almost happened, by what might have happened."

That was why she wanted to live a cloistered life away from men. That was why she assuaged her need for purification. Si deserved to have every last ounce of stinging nettles formed into a birch rod for lashing him the rest of his days.

"Did you even want to marry?" he asked, echoing the question he'd asked her cousin before all this began. How differently things might have turned out if someone had simply told him the truth. "Len? Tell me what you want."

He caught her gaze and held it while her eyes filled up with tears. Then she shook her head. "No. All my life, I wanted to be a nun."

Si blinked rapidly, almost as rapid as his breathing.

At least if she was with child, she might be safer in a French hospital surrounded by nurses than here, in the mountains, surrounded by coarse men and sheep.

He nodded. "Then," he said with every last ounce of his strength, "that is what you should do."

ELLEN'S HEART STOPPED BEATING. HE WOULD SEND HER AWAY? Now? After everything? After she'd surrendered herself, body and soul? After they'd finally consummated their wedding vows before God?

"Is that what you wish, milord?"

He stared at her, his hard amber eyes as cold and sharp as the sword he might as well have run through her belly. "Aye," he said. "It may be best." Then almost as an afterthought he added, "It's what you want still?"

After so much truth, Ellen had almost forgotten how to lie, but if he didn't want her here then this was her chance to go, and she found herself nodding. "Yes."

He nodded too, no longer looking at her. "I'll make the arrangements. You may leave tonight."

Her stomach dropped, or maybe her stomach stayed in place and it was the world dropping away.

"After the ceremony?"

He shook his head. "Why wait? My father shall accompany you."

"He's well enough to travel?"

"He's well enough."

Was it all preplanned, then? And the laird himself in on it? How long had her husband been plotting to send her away? And had the other night been a claiming, knowing she would go?

"I shall pack," she whispered.

Without another word, Si turned on his heel and left, and Ellen buried her face in her arms and wept.

EVERYTHING WHICH FOLLOWED HAPPENED SO QUICKLY, ELLEN hardly had a moment to reflect, not that she was keen to. They would travel by carriage to Aberdeen. Instructions for their passage to France, along with a letter to the convent, were being sent on ahead.

Dear Gawyn refused to drive them, claiming his vision was not reliable in the late evening light and a storm was on the way.

Si offered a stopover for a few days in Inverness to see her family, but Ellen declined. It wasn't fair to the laird. If France would heal him, then best get him there quickly, and besides, she couldn't bear her family's disappointment. The only thing she'd ever been good for, a strategic marriage, had failed almost before it began. Si was a good man. He'd honor the alliance even as she disgraced him before his whole clan, but her father would never allow himself to live down the shame.

After packing her trunk and a smaller valise, she crept into Si's library to pick out a book for her journey. Somehow after all these years, her Bible offered little solace. What business had she becoming a nun?

The room smelled of him, of moss and earth and sweaty musk, and for a moment she just closed her eyes and breathed. Years from now, when walking alone near a forest stream, would she catch a whiff of rich damp soil and think of him with fondness or with an empty sort of longing?

There was a volume on the shelf called *Paradise Lost*, and Ellen couldn't think of a more apt description of her current circumstance, so she added it to her valise, almost certain he wouldn't begrudge the theft, but realizing how little she actually knew him.

Seedlings lined his window ledge, and she studied them, as though she could glean insight into his inner life. She imagined the careful way he must have tended them, his big, sure hands pouring measured water and tenderly caressing the leaves. She couldn't help comparing them to his own seed, which he would never have the chance to nurture and watch grow into a child.

Returning to her chamber, Ellen noticed the MacKenzie plaid draped across the back of the chair, and fresh tears sprang to her eyes. She added it to her valise as well, though she'd no right to wear it now. Then she went down to the chapel to wait.

The room might not be much, but she was pleased with how it had turned out. It was like a bright, calm center in the bustling, chilly castle. Si might pretend to miss the point, but she was happy knowing it would be there for him when she was gone—a place to rest and clear his head in this new world which he would now face alone.

She was still sitting there in the quiet stillness, trying to remember how to speak to God, and how to listen, when there came a clamber in the corridor, followed by a surprised, "Oh! Milady!"

Greer looked in, gestured for someone to wait, and then came in to sit beside her.

"Why d'ye look as though you're going on a journey?" she asked.

Ellen plastered on a smile. "Because I am." It didn't even sound like her voice.

Greer looked at her hard and saw right through her smile, reading the despair in the depths of her eyes. "Because of all this? He was that angry?"

Ellen shook her head. "No," she whispered. "Some things just don't work out."

The girl didn't seem to know how to respond. "The window's ready. We came to install it," she explained, picking at a spot on her shawl.

At her words, Sam MacPherson entered with the patchwork stained glass, and Ellen gasped. Seeing the design and the frame and the bits of colored glass hadn't prepared her for the work of art before her now. Dozens of tiny squares in reds and golds, blues and purples, and every shade in between, fitted neatly together in a whimsical non-pattern within the black iron frame.

"It's perfect," she whispered.

Greer and her father beamed with pride, and the girl pushed a pew close to the window and stepped up onto the bench.

Sam handed her the plate of glass and then left, presumably to help from the outside.

Ellen watched in awe as they placed and sealed the window, the bright rays of afternoon light filtering into rainbows upon the wall, and she smiled. At least the chapel was complete before she left.

"Magnificent," a scratchy voice breathed, and Ellen looked up to see the Kintail in his traveling cloak staring gleefully around at the soft colors.

Greer scrambled down from the bench to offer a little curtsy, and then she and Ellen helped the old man to a seat. "Just magnificent," he sighed again, studying Bram's incredible cushion before taking his ease.

"Thank you for everything," Greer whispered, kissing Ellen's cheek before scurrying away, leaving her alone with her father-in-law, who still hadn't stopped smiling.

"This was my dear Iona's favorite place in the world," he said.

Ellen still wasn't certain the laird was well enough to travel, but she was glad he got to see the chapel complete before they departed.

She offered a small, sad smile, and he nodded sympathetically and patted her knee. "Nothing's ever as dark as it seems," he said.

Ellen chewed the inside of her cheek to keep a fresh wave of tears at bay.

"Ye've proven that." He gestured around the chapel. "Ye've transformed all this. Ye've transformed my son."

"I'm not so sure," she whispered, blinking and struggling to swallow.

"I am. Dinnae argue with your laird, now."

That made her chuckle. She'd miss reading to the old man once they parted on the continent. Perhaps she could visit him from time to time if he remained there instead of coming back to help Silas. "Will they pledge to him?" she asked.

The Kintail sighed and shrugged. "I hope they will."

They sat in silence as the light around them grew dim. Ellen wasn't ready to leave. She wanted to see this room at every hour of the day and night.

"Whatever he's done," the laird finally said, "it'll eat away at him the rest of his life. That's how he holds on to things, tight and festering, while everyone else moves on."

"He hasn't done anything," she assured him.

"No?" he asked, frowning. "I thought maybe this time he finally had."

Ellen didn't understand quite what her father-in-law meant, but the sound of a gathering crowd filtered from the Hall into their sanctuary. It was time for them to go. She leaned over to kiss the laird's cheek, and he squeezed her hand tightly.

"You can tell me all about it on our journey. He's sending us both. For our own good, he's sure."

And Ellen finally understood that Alex couldn't hand over the title of Kintail and still tell his son what to do.

Chapter Nineteen

The junior groom, Fraser, loaded their trunks onto the carriage that would take Len and the laird away, and all Si could do was watch. He had the sense of being powerless to prevent disaster while knowing he was the only one who could stop it. Knowing he was the cause. None of it seemed real. To avoid a scene, Fraser had brought the carriage to Leod's rear door, off the garden, typically reserved for hauling supplies straight into the larder.

"It's been raining for days, milord," Gawyn implored softly at his elbow.

"How astute," Silas bit out.

Gawyn shifted, unaccustomed to Si's sharp tone, and the sickness in his belly grew. "Fraser's a good lad, but he's green, and the roads'll be naught but muck."

"Are you telling me I employ a groom who's incapable of handling a pair of horses in some mud? Because if so, perhaps we should employ a new groom. Or two," he added, because he hated himself, and something inside him wanted everyone else to hate him too.

The grooms exchanged uncertain looks, and Gawyn dropped

his voice. "He's inexperienced, milord. And he's been at the ale. Give it a day or two for the roads to dry," Gawyn urged, his tone cold and deferential.

But Si didn't have a day or two. If he allowed her to stay another hour, he would lock her in her chamber and never let her leave, and besides that, his father could well be dead. "I asked you to drive them, did I not?" he snapped.

"I told ye, my eyes. The dark."

"Yes, you said." Another reminder that everyone he held dear was growing older, and they too would move on without him. One day soon, Silas would find himself completely alone.

"I could take them in the morning," the old groom relented, clearly distressed.

"They leave tonight," Si said in his lordliest tone, knowing Gawyn wouldn't argue further.

Trunks secured, Si glowered toward the kitchen doorway, where Len embraced young Bram, whispering something in the wee bugger's ear as envy slithered up Si's throat. Bram handed her a parchment, and she kissed his cheek before tucking it away in her valise.

Dorrie clung to the lass's skirts, and Mrs. Kynoch pressed a wrapped parcel of food into her arms, while giving Si the evil eye. It was enough food to feed them seven times over. Si hadn't realized the cook had warmed to his bride, but now she was as pained as the rest of them to see her go. They would all make sure her departure was a living torment for him.

And he deserved it.

He destroyed everything he touched, so it was little wonder his marriage was in shambles. If the men gave their oaths tonight, in a year there'd probably be nothing left of the clan at all, though he'd do his damnedest to pull them through the worst of it.

Her goodbyes complete, the lass led the Kintail out the door and over to the carriage, but she waited with the horses, petting Buttercup on the nose, to give the two of them a private moment.

They stared at each other—bleak, silent reflections.

Si half expected a parting, *I hope ye know what you're doing, laddie*, from his father. But the old man studied him long and hard before saying, "Ye've always found your own way of doing things. Just remember that ye'll never be wrong, so long as you can learn and change based on yer learning."

Si rubbed his temple to try and keep the tears at bay.

"Fail fast, so ye can win," the old man added, cupping Si's elbow in his frail grip.

Then he turned and reached out for Ellen to help him into the carriage. She took extra care settling him in, spreading a warm blanket over his lap and another around his shoulders. Then she glanced back at Si but turned and embraced old Gawyn instead.

"Proud of you. Keep at it," she whispered, and Si watched the groom blush a deep shade of crimson. She kissed his cheek and squeezed his hands, and then finally turned to Si, though she seemed unable to look up into his face. He was cutting out a piece of himself to give her the freedom she'd always craved, and she couldn't even meet his eye while he did it.

He cleared his throat. "If you'd rather wait—"

"For what?" she interrupted him quickly.

Si licked his lips and looked around. What was the point of dragging it out? He shrugged. "For the rain to stop. For the roads to dry. For Gawyn to drive you."

Now Ellen stared hard at him, and he shriveled beneath her gaze.

For you to change your mind, he wanted to say.

"Best to have done with it quickly," she said, parroting his earlier words back to him.

Funny how easily she seemed to speak to him now that he'd given her what she wanted. His gut twisted. Perhaps her silence had been a ploy all along.

And what of the Mac? She hadn't written him a letter for several days, but would she have left one with Mrs. Kynoch now, explaining her sudden departure? And how would she explain it? Did she plan to continue writing him from her convent across the sea? He hoped not, but Christ he hoped so, too.

Best to have done with it quickly, advice he should have heeded in confessing to her about those letters. But those words were for doing things you dread. This was her heart's desire. Wasn't it?

"Aye, it's best," he repeated. "Because you want to leave. You long to be a nun in France."

Her brows knit painfully together, but she nodded in agreement. "Yes," she whispered. "I want to leave."

"Safe journey, then," he told her stiffly, clasping his hands behind his back to keep from grabbing hold of her and never letting go. There was no use holding on. It was the best thing for her, for both of them.

He was a fool and a coward for not telling her the truth, and yet this moment was the bravest thing he'd ever done because letting her go might actually kill him.

She stood on tiptoe and reached up her hand to cup his face, stroking his cheek lightly with her thumb, then threw her arms around him, and he buried his face in her neck one last time. He would never be able to stand the scent of lavender after this. He would have every bit ripped out of the garden down to the roots and set ablaze.

"You're a good man, Silas MacKenzie," she murmured to his collarbone. "Trust yourself to be a good laird. And if you can't trust yourself, then trust the people who trust you. They can't all be clotheids."

His eyes welled up once more. Some laird he'd be, sniveling like a wean all the time. "Pray for me?" he whispered.

The lass nodded, then swallowed and took a breath like she wanted to say more, but she sucked in her cheek and chomped down.

When he was a lonely lad in Aberdeen, Si often recalled his departure from Leod. His strongest memory of his father had been upon his leaving—of the look in his eye that young Si had interpreted as disappointment, which he now realized might have been disappointment in himself rather than his son—his frown, perhaps caused by the iron taste of regret.

At the time, Si had wanted to beg to stay, but his pride wouldn't allow it even then. Now he wanted to beg her not to go, but his pride had only deepened over the years. He'd grown accustomed to his new life. In time, the lass would too. And so would he. Somehow. The difference was, she wanted to go. He couldn't get in the way of that.

It was all for the best.

He would endure it, just as he'd endured the loss of his mother and his own banishment to the coast, just as he would endure losing his father all over again, along with whatever choice the clan made here tonight. Si would endure, broken heart and all, because what else was there for him to do?

Fraser, the young groom, was fiddling with a bit of string, waiting for her to board, so Gawyn stepped forward to assist her, just as Si did.

She looked at Si's outstretched hand for a moment, and then accepted it, and when she touched his skin it practically burned him, as though she herself were made of stinging nettle.

When she let go, he clenched his fist at his side, certain her touch would haunt him for the rest of his days. He rather hoped it would.

Si watched the carriage until the road curved out of sight, Gawyn and Mrs. Kynoch studying him silently.

He wanted to demand just what they had to say, but he also knew well enough he didn't want to hear it.

"Milord?" Gawyn asked, reading Si the same way he read the horses.

"Will they give me their oaths, d'you think?" he asked instead.

"Dinnae ken," Gawyn said shortly. "I don't really want to after that, and ye'll pardon my saying."

Neither would I.

ELLEN ROCKED WITH THE RHYTHM OF THE CARRIAGE AS IT pulled away from Leod, biting her cheek as hard as she could to try and stave off tears while her father-in-law dozed on the seat beside her.

For half a moment, she'd thought Si might ask her to stay. And for half a moment, she'd thought she might agree, beg his forgiveness for every transgression, find a way to start afresh as man and the wife he needed by his side.

But he had looked at her so sternly, repeated her words back to her, that she wanted to leave, and she remembered it would be best for him if she got out of the way. Perhaps in time he would tell them all she died, find a new wife among the bonny lasses of Ross-shire, one who wouldn't be afraid to take matters in hand like a true Lady Kintail.

Part of her wanted to rage at him for ever agreeing to the match in the first place. She'd had no authority to turn him down, but one look at her should have told him all he needed to know about her. And if he'd said no, even her father would've been forced to listen.

Why in Heaven's name hadn't he said no?

Her lip trembled, and she bit down hard, reminding herself if he had declined the match, her father would've only found someone else to take her off his hands. Someone less gentle and understanding. At least this way she was finally getting the life she'd always wanted. It was only the deepest, most Catholic sense of irony that she wasn't sure she wanted it anymore.

Though she'd spent so many years yearning for it, some part of her had always believed the Church was out of reach. She had tried so hard to be *good, perfect Wee Ellen*, as Maggie used to tease her, hoping and praying that she could make herself pure enough and deserving enough to find a home in a convent. After all, what better purpose could one have in life?

Why, then, was her heart so heavy? Perhaps fixing the chapel had finally proven her worthy to have her prayers answered. The Lord had finally said yes.

And yet, she was no more deserving of being a nun than she was of being the Lady Kintail. Somehow, after all this time, that's what stung the most. She'd fixed up the chapel for all the MacKenzies and for herself, not for Jesus. It was a way to settle into the lot she'd been given, to carve out a place within her new family and her new life. And now she was somehow finally worthy? Now that she'd accepted things as they were? Now that she wanted to stay?

It seemed more like a punishment. Because she'd been weak in her dealings with the mysterious Mac, who might not even *be* a MacKenzie. She'd allowed herself to form a friendship with a man who wasn't her husband, and, if that wasn't enough, there had been her behavior towards Silas: first stiff and cold, and then craving and demanding. She'd allowed him to see her as wanton. Perhaps her boldness had even misled him to think she was experienced in the marital act. Perhaps all those years ago she'd been ruined by intent after all.

Whatever her sins, she was being sent away for them now, and there was nothing to do but atone.

The MacKenzies had welcomed her with open hearts and open arms. They'd delighted in her, just for being there. No one expected her to be better, no one asked her to change. Si's one request was to hear her voice, and she used it to lash out at him. Ellen had known welcome there in the bosom of her new family —from her first dance with the Kintail, to her later one with Si and Dorrie, to the letters from Mac, to Bram's confiding in her, and Gawyn's request for tutoring.

No one called her *poor Wee Ellen* here or shouted about good handkerchiefs. Other than Silas, no one seemed to mind whether she spoke, and she suspected he wouldn't have been bothered, if only she hadn't had an easier time with the others. She couldn't even say why she'd done it. Only she could be easy around them, whereas with Si, she had far too much to lose. More irony, now she'd lost it all.

As the horses carried them further and further from Leod, she realized that maybe for the first time in all her life, she had started to become herself, the self she was meant to be, independent of fear and guilt and pity and expectation.

Would that all change in the cloister? Would she be forced to hide Lady Len away, to become meek, sorrowful Wee Ellen all over again?

The sorrowful part, at least, wouldn't be an act.

She was leaving more than just the castle behind. She was leaving a large part of herself.

Perhaps she should have asked to stay.

Ellen tried to recall the last time she'd asked for anything. Before asking Si to stay the night with her, she'd written impassioned letters to persuade her father to send her to the abbey, begged God fervently for the same. One request granted, so many others ignored. And it was Si who granted it, Si who knew without asking what it was she needed, when she was hungry, or cold, or lonesome.

He would have let her stay if she'd asked him to.

If he didn't love her, didn't want her, could she have led a happy life learning to farm a croft? Or could they have stayed married in name but led separate lives as they had nearly done so far?

No, of course not. He would have needs, desires. It had happened so quickly, but Ellen knew that if she couldn't have all of him, then going far away to the convent on the continent was the only possible answer. Even now, he would haunt her there, him and his amber-fossil eyes.

She had snuck one last glance at those eyes right before they parted, and she had seen only distance and determination. A tear rolled down her cheek before she could force it back by sheer will because the thing was, tears were like a bleeding nose. One drop would lead to a torrent. In the safety of the carriage, though, and with her father-in-law dozing on the seat beside her, Ellen put her face in her hands for the second time that day and wept.

Chapter Twenty

A proper laird wouldn't be found moping in his father's bedchamber. That was probably rule number one in the book of lairdship, but Si had never claimed to be a proper laird. Instead of joining the clan at table or outright accusing his cook of attempted murder, he was staring down a decanter of whisky in his absent father's chamber. Dinner would be over soon, and then there would be the oaths, but still he sat in a corner near the empty bed, staring at a blank parchment.

He'd sat down intending to write the truth about the letters from Mac, though he didn't know quite what he hoped to accomplish. Len was already gone. Admitting his deceit would hardly bring her running back.

For a brief moment, as a clamor came from the corridor, he allowed himself to hope she *had* come running back. Then the door was thrown open and in trooped his Aunt and Uncle Leask, with Bram on their heels.

"What the devil's going on around here?" his auntie demanded.

"Could ask you the same," Si said, not hiding his shock at seeing them again so soon.

"We came for your ceremony of course," Auntie Alys said, crossing the room to take his hands and frowning at the empty bed.

"Wish you wouldn't've. I'm honestly not sure which way it'll go."

"And I can see why. What's this I hear about Himself and Ellen Mackintosh leaving," she asked in a loud whisper.

Si shot a look at his uncle, who closed the door. "Ellen Mackintosh MacKenzie," he corrected her quietly.

"Oh, so you do remember that particular vow, do ye?"

"Auntie—"

"You know the match was my idea? And I'm never wrong. She's perfect for you. Now what did you do, hmm?"

Si sagged into his chair and poured himself another dram. "She wanted to be a nun," he said, twisting the glass to watch the candlelight sparkle in the amber liquid.

"And I wanted to be a fishmonger's wife."

"Did ye, now?" Leask asked in surprise, and Bram snickered.

"Yes, of course, darling, but never mind." She pulled up a chair across from Si. "What happened?"

He scowled at her, his eyes welling with tears at just being asked. He was so tired. He hadn't slept since that night, with her in his arms.

"It's only me, dear boy. Tell me everything."

He rocked back and forth, rubbing his temples, but he couldn't find the words. "You proposed the match?"

"Aye, and as I said, I'm never wrong."

"Well, this time you were," Si rasped. "And I wish you'd stayed out of it."

Auntie Alys looked at Bram and jerked her head towards the door.

"Why do I have to go? He's the one who's been a complete eejit."

She lifted her eyebrows at him, and Bram dragged himself out.

Alys topped up Si's whisky and poured one out for herself. "Tell me."

"He's just outside."

"I am not," Bram protested.

Alys gave her husband a look and another jerk of her head, and Leask followed Bram into the corridor.

Then she turned back to Si with a penetrating stare. "No more excuses."

She wasn't going to let it go, or probably let him out of his chair until he told her. Between her and the hoard below, he wasn't sure which fate was worse.

"She's too small," he said finally.

Alys looked at him like he'd said she was a kelpie.

"Too small for what, Silas MacKenzie? To reach the top shelf of your library?"

He made a face at her, and she caught on that he meant more intimate interactions.

"Jesus, Si, is your prick so massive you can't find any way to use it without hurting her? Thought you were more creative—"

"I can use it fine," he said through gritted teeth. "But if I get her with child—*my* child—it'll kill her as surely as it did my own mam."

"What?"

He lifted his eyebrows at her. Did she really need it spelled out? "Big men beget big sons," he said, nodding towards his father's empty bed.

"Jesus, Mary, and Joseph," she breathed. "You're tall now, I'll grant ye—"

"Always been tall." He stood a head above his peers, even as a toddler.

"Maybe so, lad, but yer mam didn't give birth to all six feet of yeh."

"She died all the same."

"Now you listen to me, Silas Michael Wolfrick Alisdair

MacKenzie, and you listen good. I dinnae ken what you've grown up believing, but I was there. You were born a babe, same as any other bairn. No bigger than the rest, certainly not the biggest I've ever held in my arms."

"She died, Auntie. The day after I was born. You can't try and say it wasn't me that killed her."

"What is it about men that ye think nothing happens in the world except by your own action? Yer mam had a fever. She was sickly for days before you finally graced us with your wee presence. She held on long enough to see you into this world so she could press her lips to your head and give you her blessing."

Eyes burning with unshed tears, throat bursting with unwept agony, Si shook his head as he struggled to take apart and rebuild the image of himself that he'd spent decades believing to be true. Was it really possible the fault could not lie with him?

Was it true that his mother's name would have been carved into stone whether or not he'd existed? He glanced at the window recalling his seedlings—all starting out the same small size before some grew into robust plants and others withered.

"My sweet boy," Auntie Alys said, reading his face and pressing her forehead to his. "My darling, darling boy, how I've failed you."

"No, Auntie."

"I certainly failed you if you've carried this around your whole life. Your mam was my cousin and my dearest friend. She'd be devastated and downright irate with me to hear ye blamed yourself all this time."

He couldn't think, could scarcely even breathe. After so many years, he didn't know how to be if not guilt-ridden.

"You're a man of science. You know women die in childbirth. But they also get fevers and suffer accidents. People die for all sorts of reasons, you know that."

He looked at her skeptically and she shrugged.

"They get thrown from horses, and they drown on ships that sink in the ocean."

"So you're saying I may have sent her away to her death, anyhow," he said helplessly.

"I'm saying you don't get to decide who lives and who dies. Even as laird."

Si's heart beat so quickly it was surely going in reverse, and his thoughts along with it. "She willnae wish to come back."

"I forgot ye knew everything," she chided. "How terribly inconvenient that must be."

"She didn't wish to marry at all," he said sadly.

"D'ye want to know why I chose her for ye?"

He nodded.

"When I met her, she was a sickly wee thing, stifled by those around her into believing she was incapable of anything at all. She couldn't walk down the street without someone worrying she'd faint dead away. But it takes real strength of character not to break under all that condescension and contempt, to just keep trying to do better. And she managed it with such kindness. You could tell by watching her, she was meant for more. She had a servant's heart, same as you do Silas. And I knew you were battered. I didnae ken why, and I'll surely regret that until my last breath. But I saw in her, in that deep goodness, a partner who could protect your heart even from yourself."

Tears ran down Si's cheeks. His hand still tingled where he'd held hers to assist her into the carriage.

"I'm such a fool," he whispered.

His aunt reached for him and he crumpled against her chest like the nine-year-old lad he was inside.

"No such thing," she murmured into his hair. She stroked his head and shushed him softly before pulling back to look him in the eye. "Your mother was the most precious person in the world to me. I should have done a better job of remembering her to you."

"You had your own life, Auntie."

"And what is that, where family's concerned?" She smiled sadly at him. "Wee Ellen Mackintosh may have believed she wished to be a nun. But I saw the way she looked at ye in the kirk on your wedding day, and I saw what she did in that chapel next door. Who d'ye think she did that for? It was for you. And Himself. And the whole of Clan MacKenzie. She's not Wee Ellen Mackintosh anymore. The two of you just make sense. And, as I said, I'm never wrong," she reminded him again, and somehow he knew she was right.

But what did it matter, except to prove what a dolt he was?

"It's too late."

"Bah," she said. "It's never too late. How long's she been gone?"

"Hours. They're stopping at an inn tonight. I suppose I could ride out, beg her to forgive me. Tell her I…"

Alys covered his hand with hers. "Telling her you love her would be a start."

He looked up at her sharply. Love? But then he supposed that must be what this shattered feeling in his chest amounted to.

A LIGHT RAIN BEGAN TO FALL ON THE ROAD THAT LED AWAY from Castle Leod, the town of Strathpeffer, and the County Ross. Ellen envied the driver. Sitting alone in the rain as he did would afford her plenty of cover to weep the bitter tears banging against her ribcage without giving her away.

In the end, she had been selfish, trying to be the Lady of Leod in the way she wished to, instead of being whatever it was that Si needed her to be. She had hoped fixing up the chapel and educating those around her would help in some small way to elevate his station and ensure the loyalty of the clan. But the one thing he'd asked of her, to speak to the assembled men, that single thing she had flatly refused to do.

And now he was sending her away. Not because of what he

needed. She understood well that her absence could only hurt his chances with his kin. But he sent her away to protect her, because it was what he supposed she wanted and needed, for hadn't she told him as much? And perhaps the Mac from her letters had too. Her mysterious correspondent had promised whatever she wanted. Perhaps he'd gone to Silas on her behalf and broached the idea of the convent, perhaps begged her reprieve.

Si was sending her away to take care of her, the same way he tried to take care of everyone: to save his dying father, against all hope and reason, to restore to Bram a title he believed he'd otherwise be stealing, to replenish his people's fallow fields.

At his core, Silas was the central support stone trying to hold up the entire castle on his own. He was the roof offering shelter, the earth offering sustenance, and the sky offering rain. He was trying to be all things to all the people, to nurture them, and give them care. But who gave care to the carer? She knew well enough from observing Jory the last few years the toll it could take. Without someone to look out for him, Silas would burn out like an overused candle wick.

In the end, that was what he'd needed from her, and she'd been too self-absorbed to see it. Instead of standing strong by his side, she'd hidden herself away in the chapel. Instead of ministering to his needs, she'd allowed him to push her aside, remaining ensconced in the bedchamber each night while he slept in a cold library. Her mother had prepared her to be the wife of a merchant or a scholar, not of a laird, but a wife nonetheless, and Ellen hadn't learned that lesson well enough.

Silas had tried to tell her what he needed.

He'd asked her to speak to the clan, and she had yelled at him. Belittled him. Refused.

He had asked her to trust him when he put her on the back of a horse, and she'd pulled back and gotten herself thrown.

He had begged her to stop lining her shift with nettles.

Ellen fidgeted with the seam of her dress and dug her

fingernails into the fabric. She had honored that request at least, and only partially because she'd already used up all the available nettles. It might be the hardest thing she ever did, but she'd keep that promise better than she'd kept her wedding vows.

She had supposed she wasn't the same person she'd been a month ago, but that wasn't true. She was still the same selfish Ellen. She deserved to be sent away for spending her time learning about him through letters from a stranger instead of just speaking to him. Still and all, accepting her banishment, however deserved, somehow seemed like running away. She was leaving him alone right when he needed her most. Maybe he was pushing her out of fear, the same way she'd been pushing him.

If only someone could tell her the right thing to do.

Poor Wee Ellen, she imagined Maggie saying from a seat on the bench beside her. *I'd have never imagined you had the courage to run away.*

"I'm not running away," she muttered, but even imaginary Maggie didn't hear her.

And what will the Borlum say? Her father's voice boomed like the thunder outside. *How will I ever show my face at Moy again after this?*

Ellen sighed. They didn't have to remind her she was letting not only her family down, but the whole of Clan Mackintosh, and indeed all the clans of Chattan as well.

Is it a deficiency in the MacKenzie? her mother would have prompted. *Were things not... in working order?*

That must be it, her father would agree over Ellen's protests. *Not man enough even for our poor Wee Ellen. Say the word, my girl, and we'll have it annulled. We can try again with another clan. No one will think the worse of you for it.*

"Stop," Ellen tried to scream, at the voices in her head and the driver outside the carriage, but the word came out barely more than a whisper.

Are they wrong? another voice asked, a strong voice with a hint of laughter in it.

Ellen opened her eyes to see Lady Len as she imagined her, long golden hair twisted into a loose knot to keep it out of the way, never mind what was or wasn't fashionable. Instead of skirts she wore breeches like Jory would sometimes do, and one of Silas's shirts, and most of all she looked relaxed and happy. Ellen hardly recognized herself.

Are they wrong? Len asked again.

"I don't know how to be you," Ellen said.

Len smiled. *Do you want to be?*

"You don't have to be me, lass," the laird said, patting her knee. "You're enough as ye are."

"I don't know."

Ellen picked at a loose thread in her dress. Never mind the convent, would they lock her away in a hospital if they knew she was talking to herself this way?

I think you do know, Len said matter-of-factly.

Ellen shook her head. "What would you do if he didn't want you?" she whispered.

Len quirked a smile. *I wouldn't believe him.*

"Och, don't believe him," the Kintail murmured. "Men are stubborn, lass, and none more so than the MacKenzies."

Then Ellen's mind flooded with memories—of thistles on her wedding day and being whisked away on a horse by her knight in shining armor, of his forehead against hers and the yearning in his eyes, of his body curled around her keeping her safe and warm.

Men are stubborn, Len agreed. *How many times have we heard our mother say it?*

We. Not I, not you, but we, because Ellen was Len. Len was a part of her even still.

Why did you want to go to the convent? she prodded.

"I wanted to be safe," Ellen whispered, remembering again how safe she had felt in Si's arms.

Len shook her head in exasperation, but the old laird just nodded.

"In a convent I wouldn't have to worry about men or the world outside those walls."

Those predictable, orderly walls. Alluring, I'll grant you. Len sighed. *Admit it. You wanted to join the convent years before the Gordons arrived in Inverness. You promised yourself to God when you were seven years old.*

"A convent was the only way for me to be useful."

"Pish-tosh," the laird scoffed.

Seven-year-olds with bloody noses and fainting spells aren't very useful, are they?

"I didn't have the stamina for housework or a steady hand for stitching. I didn't have the voice of a songbird or the attention for cooking."

"It's all right, lass."

Len frowned sympathetically. *Because they told us we didn't.*

"No." Ellen shook her head.

Och, Wee Ellen, don't exert yourself with that sweeping. Your nose will bleed, and I'll have to scrub the floors all over. Len's imitation of her mother was spot on. *Burned the bannocks again, have ye? Don't let this one near the fire, dear oh dear.*

Ellen swallowed but refused to cry.

Stop that infernal racket! Len chided, mimicking Ellen's father now. *It's a good thing she's pretty. This one won't be winning any suitors off her cookery or her singing. Och, poor Wee Ellen.* Len even patted her cheek the way her father used to do when he said it.

But then she took Ellen's face in both hands. *They were wrong. You proved them all wrong.*

A tear streaked down Ellen's cheek and was lost in the corner of her mouth.

"There now, don't cry, lassie. I heard ye singing in the chapel. So lovely, it reminded me of my dear Iona."

Do you still want to be a nun?

Ellen shook her head and said, "No," at the same time her

imaginary Len did, and she wasn't sure which voice was actually her own.

She looked at her father-in-law. "I don't want to be a nun."

Then you know what you have to do.

Ellen leaned her head back and stared at the ceiling, swallowing down the nausea and anxiety caused by the jostling carriage.

"Stop," she called out, but the same word was yelled from outside the carriage, along with other shouting, some of the voices familiar, as the vehicle rattled faster and harder, just like the disquietude raging within her, and then suddenly she was thrown against the opposite wall, and then the ceiling, as they tumbled and tumbled, and her face grew wet with more than tears, and she was engulfed by darkness.

Chapter Twenty-One

S i stared at his father's empty bed, while Alys stared at him.

"Was it wise?" she finally asked. "Sending him away with her?"

"I think," he said slowly, "someone may be trying to poison him."

The expression on his aunt's face turned to such sympathy. "Alex is old and sick, my dear," she said gently.

He nodded. It was a strange, unsettling thing to hope that someone had indeed been hurting his father, even if it was Mrs. Kynoch, because that would mean he'd saved the old man, rather than the alternative.

Alys wrinkled her nose. "D'ye smell that?"

"Incense," he whispered, grabbing her hand and racing from the room, shutting the door silently behind them.

He put a finger to his lips and crept next door to the chapel, where he was surprised to find Norval MacKenzie kneeling beneath the crucifix, a kerchief tied around his nose and mouth, using a tiny bellows to waft incense through the pipe Ellen had discovered.

Holding his sark up to cover his nose and mouth, Silas took one step into the chapel, catching Norval's attention. The steward closed off the censer and rose.

He didn't try to make an excuse. He just stood there, staring Silas down. He obviously didn't know the laird had left the castle, and any accusation Si might have made died in his throat. He'd done enough accusing for today. There would be time enough to deal with Norval once he prostrated himself in apology before Len.

"Si," Bram called from the stairwell. "Angus MacKenzie's looking for ye. I think it's time."

Time? For the oaths. He'd completely forgotten.

"Later," he said, shaking his head, turning his back on Norval and guiding Bram and the Leasks away. "We'll have to do it later," he said, and they all bobbed their heads, seeming to understand he had a higher calling at the moment.

Si crept down the back stairs so as not to be seen, but there was no slipping past Mrs. Kynoch. "It's about time," she said. "They're getting restless, and we've nearly run out of food."

"Ye found him?" Angus asked, joining the party.

"Everything's ready. Best get out there." Mrs. Kynoch nudged him towards the Hall.

"It'll have to wait," Si said. "They'll all have to wait."

Angus raised his brows in concern, casting the question from Si to the cook and back again.

"I need to go get my wife."

If eyes carried heat that could burn, Si could not have sensed Mrs. Kynoch's gaze more fiercely, a look that said, *It was you that sent her away.*

"Milord, there's been talk all week. Someone's stirring up unrest. Blair, if I had to guess. If you disappear now, whatever the reason, I'm afraid he'll put them to a vote."

"And?" Si asked, the reality hitting him that Blair and Norval had been working to similar ends. Were they working together, then?

Angus studied his feet. "Ye've been hiding yourself away. They don't trust what they cannae see."

It was an impossible choice: let them go—the father he could only hope to protect, the bride he hadn't known he wanted—in exchange for the lairdship he'd never sought, or forsake the house of Kintail and hand it over to Blair and Norval, who'd almost certainly tried to destroy his father and the entire clan, as well. Could he allow Clan MacKenzie fall in order to chase a fool's errand of his own making? To go after a lass who wished most fervently to be a nun?

He glared at Angus and the lad glared back, searching his eyes for some sign of which he would choose. "I could go in your place," the younger man offered. "Try and persuade her?"

Si nodded, even knowing that it had to be him. "A note perhaps," he rasped, withdrawing the apology he'd scribed that evening.

Angus accepted it with a nod. "I'll leave at once."

"Angus," Si stopped him. "The laird is with her. He must be protected at all costs."

Angus frowned in puzzlement but nodded.

"What's this about the laird?" Mrs. Kynoch asked.

"Your castor plant."

She blinked at the abrupt change in topic. "Aye, what about it?"

"How did you come by it?"

"Norval MacKenzie brought it back from his travels. You're not falling ill now too, are ye, milord?"

"No."

"Then what d'ye mean to say?" Mrs. Kynoch asked, fussing over him and straightening his shirt.

"That I'm a fool who couldn't see what was right in front of me."

"To the clan, Silas."

Si blinked. "Ah." He'd prepared a little, but now his mind was blank of anything but Ellen and his father.

The cook rolled her eyes. "Just ask them for their allegiance and have done with it."

"Here he is lads!" a ruddy-faced MacKenzie called, spotting Si and dragging him out into an ebbing sea of cousins. "Hiding wherever there's fresh bannocks. And not much changes under the sun, does it, Si?" he guffawed, slapping Silas on the back as others yelled and laughed and he was surrounded and shoved towards the front of the Hall.

"Well, I..." Si began, but no one could hear his stammering over the general rabble of the clan.

"Where's your father, Silas?" Blair called, stepping away from the wall he'd been leaning against with crossed arms, his eye still a mess of bruise and swelling. "Shouldn't he be present on a night like this?"

"As should yours," Si replied, noticing that Blair stood alone, without either Norval or Rabbie Stewart to flank him.

Blair shrugged. "Everyone knows my father washed his hands of me years ago. Besides, it's not *my* special night, it's yours."

"Let's get on with it, then." Si made his way to the top of the Hall like a salmon persevering upstream.

"I notice your wife is absent as well. Neither of the people who're supposed to love you best are here to bear witness on your momentous day. What does it mean, I wonder?"

A rumble went up from the men surrounding Blair, while those supporting Silas fell uncomfortably silent.

Then Ced the piper stepped forward. "You always did like the sound of your own voice, Blair. Every man here knows the Kintail chose Si."

"Way I heard it," one on Blair's side piped up, "the Kintail hasn't been fit to choose much of anything for quite some time."

"Maybe we should go and ask him," Blair said with a grin. "Or at least ask the bride. Now, where could she be hiding? With a stranger in the forest glade perhaps?"

Si was two seconds from ripping off Blair's lips and shoving them up his arsehole. Then a stramash turned his attention back to the kitchen door where a soaking wet Angus was pushing his way inside, his face white as a ghost, and Si's stomach fell.

Intellectually he knew it couldn't possibly be to do with Ellen or his father, for Angus wouldn't have reached them yet, but still he was afraid.

Si forced his way back towards his newly appointed steward, but there were too many blasted MacKenzies in the way and none of them inclined to move.

"I beg a word, milord," Angus called, and Si started shoving men out of his way, ignoring their yelps of surprise and grumbles of dismay.

"What?" he asked, and Angus jerked his head back towards the kitchen, away from prying ears. "What can be more important than delivering that letter to my—" they pressed into the kitchen to find a sodden messenger warming himself by the fire.

"Tell him," Angus ordered.

"McInnes, sir. Of the Sheep's Head Inn."

Si's stomach would have emptied itself there on the kitchen floor if he'd remembered to eat since breakfast.

"Say your piece," Angus urged.

"They send word. Well, here." The boy handed Si a note, which he unfolded with trembling hands.

"What's it say?" Mrs. Kynoch asked, peering over his elbow.

Si read the words three times before they began to sink into his brain.

"The coach never made it," Angus told them. "They fear it must have crashed. Gone over a rim in the rain."

"Did ye see any signs of such a thing on your way here?" Mrs. Kynoch interrogated the messenger. Her voice sounded far away.

Si had to remind himself to inhale and exhale or he would stop breathing all together. And honestly, maybe that would be the best thing for everyone.

He was forced into a seat, a dram placed in his hand.

The next thing he knew, he looked up into the faces of Alys and Leask, Bram, Sam MacPherson and his daughter, Angus and Gawyn and Mrs. Kynoch, all watching him with concerned faces.

"What d'ye want us to do, lad?" Mr. Leask nudged his shoulder.

He looked around at all of them, waiting to follow his lead. He didn't deserve such allegiance. "Organize a search," he rasped. "Only those we know are loyal to the Kintail and not to Norval or Blair."

It would be dangerous, going out to search the roads in the rain and the dark.

"We'll need food for the searchers," he added to the cook. "Strong tea and parritch if that's all we've got." She nodded.

"And the oaths?" Leask asked.

"None of that matters."

"I should have gone with them instead of Fraser," Gawyn muttered. "I knew, I felt it in my bones, but I thought—"

"Stop," Si interrupted him, shaking his head. "Blame'll do no good. I need you, Gawyn. No one knows these hills better than you. I need you to direct the search parties to places where they'd be most likely to..." He cut himself off, unable to say it.

"Aye, of course."

"Bram?"

"Yes, cousin?" the boy asked in a creaky voice.

"Fetch every lantern you can find. Quickly. Take them from the campsites. From the nearer crofts, if you have to."

The boy nodded and ran out of the kitchen with the smith's girl on his heels.

"We'll find her," Leask said, and for the first time in his life, Silas prayed he was right.

"Has something happened?" Blair called from the doorway. "Your wife finally take the measure of you and run away?"

Angus and Mr. Leask stepped between Blair and Si. "Leave off, you," came Ced's deep growl.

Si had to find her. He couldn't possibly lose them both. He couldn't bear the guilt of killing both his parents and his wife. He'd be forced to stand before God and answer for ending it all in a desperate attempt to join them.

THIS COLD, DARK WEIGHTLESSNESS WAS NOT HOW ELLEN HAD ever pictured heaven. And, she realized with a bitter laugh, it was far too damp and chilled to be hell. Perhaps Purgatory then, a great black screaming nothingness, had swallowed her whole.

But no. That wasn't right either. The screaming was only a creaking sound, and she registered the rhythmic drip, drip, drip of water on her face. There was water all around her, in her ears, and in her dress, and nearby, a ragged sort of wheezing.

They'd been riding in a carriage. And then there was shouting and the crack of a rifle shot, and then a scream that might have been her own.

She forced her eyes open, but it was still blackness and everything ached. A shiver ran through her, bone deep, and the air smelled brackish and musky. Something rocked her, gently, like a boat anchored in a current.

The laird coughed.

Ellen turned her face towards the sound. Her head throbbed, her neck burned, but she was relieved that it turned, submerging her cheek in icy water that made her splutter. "Milord?" she whispered.

She tried to reach for him, but her wrist! Oh, her wrist was numb with pain that shot up to her shoulder and down to the tips of her fingers.

"Milord?" she whimpered, trying not to voice her panic, and when he didn't answer, she surrendered to the darkness once more.

When she next awoke, Ellen was shivering so hard her teeth hurt. Some clouds had finally cleared, and stars peeked through the upside-down carriage window.

Si had told her once that even tucked up far away in Edinburgh, Jory would look up at the very same stars. Was he doing that tonight too?

There was a cough, but this time it came from outside somewhere, and she froze. Had the laird managed to drag himself free? But no, she could still hear his wheezing breath nearby. The groom, perhaps?

"Mr. Fraser?" she called, but it came out barely a whisper. "Mr. Fraser?" she tried again.

"Aye," his voice came back strained but not too far away. "All right, milady?"

"I'm..." she began, but she wasn't sure. She'd forgotten how to try to move. "I'm... not dead," she finally answered, and he snorted. He must be hurt himself, if he hadn't come to check on her. "I think I'm well," she decided, ignoring the pain in her wrist. "And the laird is breathing. How are you, Fraser?"

"Pinned. And should be most obliged to pass out again. With your permission, if I may have it."

"Absolutely not."

Si would come for her, just like he had that day in the glade. He would come and find her and take her home. She knew it, the same way she knew that grass was green and that his smile was like the sunlight when the clouds first parted. The same way she knew that she couldn't let him come. Tonight was meant to be the oath ceremony. The last thing he needed was to have to mount a rescue as well. He didn't even know where she was.

"There were voices. A gunshot." Ellen remembered flying and closed her eyes against the sensation. "The horses? Are they...?"

"One may be all right. Managed to loose it before the whole thing flipped over. The other..."

It didn't bear saying.

"If I can get out of the carriage," she called, "am I in danger of falling off the side of a cliff?"

"No, milady. We've done that already."

"But are we at the bottom?"

"We've landed in the deepest bowels of Hell, you ask me," he said. But she hadn't asked, and she wouldn't ask either.

"Hell wouldn't be this wet," she told him, repeating her earlier thought.

"My granny was Greek, and she'd beg to differ, milady. Dinnae ken if it's Styx, but we've landed in a river."

Pushing herself gingerly, Ellen found she could sit up without rocking the carriage too badly. The laird slouched beside her, perhaps frail enough that if she could get the door upon, she might just be able to drag him out. Except she didn't know how to swim.

"Milord?" she whispered, and his eyes fluttered open. "Are you hurt?"

He looked around without moving his head and laughed once, setting off another round of coughing. Ellen had to get him warm and dry. There was no one else to do it.

Slowly, she pulled herself to the nearest door and tried the handle. It was stuck fast. She kicked it weakly, and the carriage rocked.

Both Fraser and the Kintail moaned.

"Is that hurting you, Fraser?" she called.

"No, milady," he gasped through gritted teeth, but she wasn't sure she could believe him.

Biting her lip, she repositioned herself, bracing her back against the basket that normally held blankets beneath the seat. It might hurt Fraser, but it was this or they all die, so she dug deep, imagining she was an angry donkey, and she kicked hard with both feet.

The door released, more water rushing inside.

"Sorry, milord," she grunted, grabbing him under the arms and sliding him under the water just enough to escape the cabin.

Outside the carriage, a swift current tried to drag them away, but Ellen's dress caught on a bit of debris and she managed to grab hold of the side with her bad hand, clinging tight to the laird with the other, helping him float on his back so his face stayed out of the frigid water.

"Fraser?" she called again.

"Still here, milady," his voice answered from the other side of the carriage.

A breath at her shoulder startled her, but then a velvet soft nose nuzzled into Ellen's shoulder. "Buttercup," she sighed, tears stinging her eyes as she buried her face in the silky neck.

The water came up to the horse's shoulder, which explained why Ellen couldn't find purchase with her feet. With one arm around Buttercup's neck, she managed to splash herself and the laird to the riverbank and drag him onto the silty shore.

Buttercup nosed Ellen's hand in search of carrots. "Sorry, girl," she cried, stroking the horse before diving back into the water to help Fraser.

His boot appeared to be wedged awkwardly under the carriage wheel, his other leg tangled in the spokes, his kilt knotted around the brake shaft. Almost completely underwater, it was a miracle he hadn't drowned, but his head was tilted awkwardly back to keep his nose and mouth dry. His eyes were closed, but his teeth chattered loud enough to wake the dead.

"Quite pinned, indeed," she said.

"I'm sorry, milady," he gasped through the pain.

"It was an accident."

"It wasn't."

"What?" she asked absently, trying to figure out how to free him.

"Rabbie Stewart and his mates. They came out of nowhere like the devil himself, yelling and carrying on. Spooked the horses. I tried to scare them off wi' my rifle. Just spooked the horses more."

"What did they want?" Ellen asked, wondering if Si could have changed his mind and sent them to bring her back home.

"This, I suppose," Fraser gasped.

"Then we must make sure they don't get away with it. If I could give you an inch, Fraser, could you pull yourself free?"

The groom forced a bitter laugh. "That carriage must weigh five times what you do, milady."

Still, Ellen had surprised herself these past weeks working on the chapel. She'd seen new definition in the shape of her arms and her legs, and a new energy in herself too. Maggie would probably bemoan her shape as less than ladylike, but Ellen's recent work had made her stronger than she'd ever been before, and that was worth more than being a lady.

"An inch. Could you do it?"

"My right arm's useless," he gasped.

"I'll be right back. Don't move," she teased. Then she brought over Buttercup and, ripping the hem of her dress, fashioned a lead which she wrapped around Fraser's fist and tied to the horse's bridle.

Then she used the sgian dubh Si had given her to slice the groom's kilt free of its entanglement. Taking the deepest breath she could, Ellen pulled herself down under the water and along the carriage until she could set her heels into the sticky mud. Her back and shoulder against the carriage, she heaved with all of her might, lifting it the tiniest fraction.

It was almost peaceful under the water. She couldn't hear anything, and it was so cold that it numbed her pain. But the force of the water buffeted her as Fraser tried to kick himself free, just as her feet began to lose purchase in the mud. She bent her knees lower and bellowed an air bubble, which must've produced the most unladylike sound, as she tried again, digging deeper into herself than she ever had before. Buttercup splashed and Fraser kicked and then he was gone just as the mud at her feet gave way, and she dropped the carriage and plunged to the surface for air.

Chapter Twenty-Two

Whilst everyone around Si leaped into action, he felt as though he was moving slowly, backwards, through a bog that threatened to drown him. It filled his ears and brain with sludge so he could no longer think what to do.

"Is the Kintail truly too sick to join us?" Ced asked. "Blair and the lads say either he comes down or they'll go up."

"You'd better go and speak to them," Mrs. Kynoch said.

As though an external force controlled his body, Si managed to drag himself back to the Hall.

"Are ye avoiding us?" a young cousin of Blair's called out.

"Avoiding responsibility, more like," the lad's father added.

Around the edges of the Hall, the men known to be most loyal to Si stepped away to join the search parties, but he knew what it would look like to the rest: abandonment. He had to address them—now, before everything completely fell apart. Before *he* completely fell apart.

"There ye are, ye bloody great giant. Thought maybe ye'd run away to Aberdeen again."

"Where *is* that lovely wee bride of yours, Si?" another heckled. "I'd rather see her face than your backside."

"I thank you all for coming out to this Gathering," Si began with some hesitation. "And I apologize, but I must humbly beg a delay."

"A delay? Ye've delayed for years already. What delay were we given when rents were due?"

"Aye, d'ye want our oaths or not?"

"We left our lands for this, our farms—"

"And our women!"

Si rubbed his sweaty palm along his kilt.

"Peace," Norval said, stepping out of the shadows and holding up a hand. "Let the lad speak."

"Aye," Blair jumped in. "For we all know how long it takes to get his words out."

"You seek a delay?" Norval asked gently, like he was on Silas's side, and it made Si's skin crawl.

"He's been away too long," Blair told them, his voice echoing through the Hall. "He doesn't know ye. He doesn't know what it costs ye to be here."

"I ken well enough," Si growled.

"Yet you *humbly* beg another delay," Blair said, his voice filled with challenge.

"And for that I apologize, but there is an emergency that requires my—"

"An emergency? More important than the well-being of your entire clan?" a man interrupted.

Sweat broke out across Si's forehead, burning his eyes.

"I—" he began, but Norval took another step forward.

"He's young. Inexperienced with handling the many complex demands that face a laird."

"I can manage very well. I only seek a delay. My wife is missing. Even now, search parties—"

"Missing is it?" Blair asked, a glimmer of mischief in his smirk which made Si's blood run cold. "Or has she run off?"

Si lunged towards him. "Have you done something with her?" he growled through clenched teeth, but strong arms held him back. A brief look of terror crossed Blair's face before he simply laughed.

"Steady, milord," Angus said.

Si shook the steward off him. "Why are you still here?" he demanded in a barely controlled whisper.

"Making sure you don't do something ye very much regret."

"How can he expect to control a clan if he can't even control one wee wife?" Blair asked the crowd with a smirk.

"What is it, Si? Cannae get a bairn in her, so you're having her rotate beds the way ye want us to rotate crops? A different fella plows her field each month, is it?" the same old crofter laughed at him.

"It's worse than that, though, isn't it, Si?" Blair asked. "Elicit trysts in the glade? Trips to the village unaccompanied? *Reading lessons* in the dark? She made a cuckold of ye and left this very day."

"How dare you." He took another step towards Blair, eager to separate the bastard's head from his body, but Blair held up a handful of folded parchments, stopping him in his tracks.

"It's all right here. Letters to a secret lover. And now she's *missing*. Who was he?" Blair asked, grinning broadly. "One of us? Or someone she knew before?" He swung around to face the crowd. "Doesn't matter. He couldn't even keep a wife. He let your lands fall to ruin under his father's leadership, a father who can't even be arsed to come downstairs and name him tanist. If we went up to his chamber, would we even find the old man still breathing?"

Si barreled towards him once more, but Angus jumped in to drag him back with a ferocity he wouldn't have expected from the farmer.

"I *will* kill him."

"And I will sharpen your blade myself, but not today."

Si caught the man's eye and there was something earnest there. Like Angus believed in Si, and Si was letting him down—like he'd let *her* down. Like he'd been letting his father down for years.

Mrs. Kynoch, watching from the kitchen, had the very same fire burning in her eye, and his Auntie Alys, even the blacksmith.

"The laird is upstairs in bed," Norval said in a bored voice.

Start as you mean to go on, Si's father always told him. He took a deep breath. "No. He isn't. You want the truth, I'll give you all of it. Norval has been poisoning my father. Slowly. For weeks now."

The steward paled. He'd never expected an outright accusation.

"I wasn't certain until tonight, so I sent him away to keep him safe."

"Lies," Norval scoffed.

"It's the truth. I put him in a carriage with my wife this very day, and if your son has interfered with that carriage, he's not only endangered my wife but the life of his laird as well."

Norval searched the faces of the silent crowd. "He's as far gone in the head as his father," he protested weakly.

"Am I? You brought that castor plant into our garden. And then you used the seeds disguised as incense—"

"Is this because you think they'd vote for Blair? You've always hated him, but I never imagined you'd make up such heinous falsehoods—"

"He was like a brother to me. And you to my father. He trusted you to take care of his lands and his people in his absence. But that was his greatest mistake of all, wasn't it?"

Norval glowered, but Blair pushed into the crowd. "You've heard the phrase, 'Don't shoot the messenger,' surely, Silas?"

"Aye," Silas agreed. "But this messenger grew rich off the backs of his people, while their homes and this very castle crumbled around us all."

A collective gasp went through the room.

"Don't listen to him. He's an impotent fool who cannot even please his wife."

"I'll thank you to stop speaking of my wife, unless you'd like a newly blackened eye to match the other."

"Is she upstairs then, Si? Only, you did say you sent her away with your father," someone asked. He couldn't see who. It didn't matter.

"Aye," he admitted. "Blair's right on that score."

Si glanced at Angus, and his steward shook his head. In the kitchen doorway, Mrs. Kynoch crossed her arms, glaring daggers at him. But Si's father had reminded him that he could always read a crowd, and the only recourse with this one was to tell the truth. They'd heard far too many lies already.

"He's right. I couldn't please her. I haven't loved her so well as I should." He swallowed, the words sticking in his throat like month-old bread. "You've but to look at her to see that she's everything light and good and pure."

"And what are you, Si?" his Auntie Alys called from the stairs. She didn't look disappointed in him. Just sad.

"I'm... broken," he admitted. "I grew up broken, and I left here broken, and I came back more broken than when I left."

The crowd around him quieted, their murmurs replaced by uncomfortable shuffling.

"I haven't done anything so well as I should have, and I'll be the first to admit it." He didn't just mean with Len, and he hoped they would understand on some level. "Because I was scared—that I couldn't be what she needed, that she was so fragile I'd crush her just by looking, that she'd despise me for my brokenness."

He looked out at them all, pushing his shoulders back to stand straight and tall before them, and took a ragged breath.

"But she saw me," he whispered, emotions straining his voice and eyes. "She put me back together just like she did that wee chapel. First my sight, so I could see what you need clearly. Then my soul," he added, putting his hand to his heart, "so I could believe myself worthy of serving all of you."

Saying it out loud in that moment, he realized it was true.

"I'm not perfect. I will make mistakes, but I will own them and make them right. So yes." He turned to the cousin who had demanded to know what was more important than the ceremony. "This once, I'm afraid there is something I must put before the clan. I must be a husband first, because if I do not find her—if I *lose* her—then I will stand before you an empty husk, completely worthless to you all. If that means there's to be a ceremony without me, so be it, but there is no *me* without her."

The rumble started up again, with shouting from the kitchen, and Si grew desperate. He'd waited far too long already.

"Please, forgive me, but I must go search for my—"

Those blocking the kitchen door were jostled aside and a bedraggled figure stepped in, swathed in MacKenzie plaid closed with his mother's Luckenbooth brooch, long blonde hair matted with twigs, and mud smeared on her face.

"—wife," he finished. "Because she is the Lady Kintail you all deserve."

"Ye should've seen the wee girl," Fraser the groom gasped, carried in between Leask and the blacksmith, his legs looking worse for wear. "Strength of ten men, I tell ye." He beamed at Len, who stood quite still, staring at Si, until he pushed forward into the crowd, and then she was moving again, towards him, and nothing could keep them apart.

THE MOMENT THEY'D ENTERED LEOD, ELLEN HAD INSTRUCTED Ced the piper and his brother to settle the laird comfortably and then ride for a physician with all due haste. She believed his shoulder was separated and several fingers broken, but with proper care, he could recover.

Now she was shaking, and not just from being cold and wet and in pain. Hearing Si's voice addressing the clan even before she could see him made her stomach run circles around her heart.

She needed to get to him, urgently, but she had feared the whole way back to Leod that he wouldn't wish to see her, and for a moment, when their eyes met and before her ears caught up to his words, *I must go search for my wife*, a small but noisy part of her brain was still trying to convince her heart he might not want her.

But then he came to her, breathless, and the crowd parted to let them meet, and Si stared at her in wonder like he was watching the first dawn of creation.

"You're alive?" he whispered. "It's really you?" He reached towards her, but then hesitated, afraid to touch. She turned to kiss his palm and pressed it to her face with her good hand.

"I'm not a ghost."

His countenance softened, but then he frowned again. "My father?"

"Upstairs."

"I was coming to find you. I'm so sorry, I—"

"It's all right," she said, touching his cheek in a way that she knew would relax his creased brow. "I'm here now. May I speak?" she asked, because even though she'd interrupted his ceremony, she'd practiced her speech the whole way back.

"Aye. As much as you like. Or as little. You should never feel you have to, not with me, not ever, though I do love the sound of your voice," he babbled.

Ellen smiled. "I meant to them."

"Oh." The tips of his ears grew pink. The tips of his ears were one of her favorite parts of him. "Of course, if you wish."

She turned to face them, and he caught her hand.

"*Only* if you wish."

She smiled and drew a tremulous breath, but then Si tucked her under his arm, safe, and she was strong again.

The new man, Angus, whistled to get everyone's attention, and she nodded her thanks when the crowd fell quiet.

"Apologies for my tardiness. We had a wee misunderstanding."

The gathered MacKenzies nodded and chuckled appreciatively because she and Si were still newlyweds, and most of them remembered what that could be like.

"My cousin always did say that marriage means war, so I guess those are bound to happen from time to time."

The MacKenzies laughed again.

"Not entirely his fault," she hurried to explain. "I've never been one for talking things through. But I'm learning," she hastened to add.

As the clansmen murmured amongst themselves, Ellen glanced nervously around the Hall, taking in their faces. Morag nodded her approval, and Mrs. Leask offered a warm smile. Behind Sam MacPherson, Greer sent her a tiny wave. She could do this.

"I understand some of you might have reservations about making your pledge to my husband." Next to her, his posture stiffened, but he kept his arm around her, grounding her. "Let me tell you a few things you should know about Silas MacKenzie.

"He'll take care of you all, whether you give him your oath today or not. That's who he is. He takes care of things. Of people. Even at his own expense.

"He's honest and loyal and clever. You may find some of his notions unusual, but that likely means they're brilliant. And he'll be happy to teach you anything you want to know. That's how I found my way home tonight. Because he taught me how the stars are worth more than just being pretty."

Next to her, his breathing changed, like he hadn't been breathing at all before, and now he might be doing it a little too fast, and Ellen became very aware that she was sweaty under her damp clothes and heavy plaid shawl. She needed to finish this.

"I left the only family I ever knew to become a MacKenzie." She hadn't expected her voice to wobble quite so much when she said it, and she bit the inside of her cheek. "That's no small thing. And though I spent a lifetime being afraid, I'm not afraid now. Because I know that the Mackintoshes will be stronger for this alliance, just like I know that any clan with Si as laird will thrive. I haven't regretted it for even one minute.

"So if you're going to give him your oath, please do it quickly," she said, craning her neck to look up at Si instead of out at the men. "Because my laird is needed urgently in the bedchamber."

The last made the MacKenzies roar with laughter and slap Si heartily on the back, as she knew they would, but it needed saying, and she chewed her cheek again, fair certain she was only still upright because he was holding her.

His ears were scarlet now, and she couldn't see his eyes, but he held her even tighter and kissed the top of her head as they were jostled back through the Hall.

The quaich was brought and the men lined up before Si. Angus brought over a chair for Ellen, and she gratefully sank into it.

Bram was first in line. He looked up at his cousin with all the adoration in the world and took a dirk from his belt. "On the graves of my forefathers, the cross of my Lord Jesus Christ, and the blessed iron that I keep ever at my side, I pledge this day my fealty and my honor, to you and to the Clan MacKenzie—to defend, to thrive, to shine, not burn, until such a time as death may claim me."

Then Silas nodded and offered his cousin a drink from the quaich to seal the oath, and Angus stepped up for his turn. He repeated the pledge, cementing his position as the new steward, and after him came old Gawyn, and then Sam MacPherson.

One after another they came, and pledged, and drank, and it

was amazing to behold. Ellen watched the muscles in Silas's jaw, almost invisible behind his beard, twitching back his emotion at their loyalty.

Morag came and knelt before Ellen, cleaning the mud and dried blood from her face, and wrapping a poultice around her wrist to reduce the swelling.

After she'd managed to get Fraser and the Kintail on Buttercup's back, she'd asked Fraser which direction they'd been coming from, and then she'd found the North Star in the handle of the small ladle and guided them towards home.

But when the sky had clouded over again and Fraser could barely stay upright from the pain, she'd begun to despair, trusting only that Buttercup knew the way as she plodded painfully alongside the trusty steed. When the rumble of hoofbeats had preceded Mr. Leask emerging from the fog with the blacksmith close behind him, Ellen had nearly wept.

"I shouldn't interrupt his ceremony," she'd confessed to Mr. Leask who laughed, embracing her in his warm arms. "Dinna fash yerself about that, lass. I'm verra sure he'll be pleased for the interruption."

Even now, her stomach twisted with uncertainty. There was so much left to say.

A plate of warm food and a cup of wine appeared at her elbow, and Ellen looked up to see Angus nod at her. It seemed she had an additional protector now, and it warmed to her to realize she had real friends, not just one on paper.

As if reading her thoughts, Angus slipped her a letter from his sporran addressed in the mysterious writer's familiar hand. After everything, though, Ellen wasn't sure she ought to read it. At the very least, not before confessing it all to Si.

Chapter Twenty-Three

Norval MacKenzie gave Silas his oath near the end of the line, not breaking eye contact even as he drank from the quaich. It was the former steward's way of admitting defeat along with his intention to remain in Strathpeffer, though he knew well enough Si would never let him anywhere near his family again. Likely he'd liquidate his assets and leave the country soon after. Blair had already fled into the darkness, and good riddance.

When the last man had pledged and attention finally shifted away from Si, he reached down for Len's hand and led her away. He wanted to take her straight up to the bedchamber and maul her like a dog in heat, but there was too much unsettled between them, so he led her instead to neutral ground: the chapel.

She looked around it, a small smile tugging at her lips, allowing herself pride in the work she'd accomplished, delighted to see it again. He could watch her look that way for the rest of his days.

"This is incredible," he said, and her smile deepened.

He took both of her hands, being extra gentle with the one that was bandaged.

"Do you still wish to leave?" He tried to keep his voice steady and devoid of emotion.

The smile vanished from her lips, and she looked pained as she focused on the stained glass window. "I didn't want to leave *today*," she said, shaking her head. "But if you still think it's best—"

"Think it's best?" Si wrapped his arms around her. "Did you not hear anything I said before? You humble me, Len MacKenzie, and I will live out my days in service to you, if you'll allow me."

He sat down on a bench, pulled her onto his lap, and took a shaky breath. "Until tonight, I always believed—I knew—that my mother died trying to bring my worthless giant self into this world."

She looked up at him, tears swimming in the pelagic depths of her eyes.

"And I swore I would never cause the same."

She nodded her understanding.

"I cannot lose you."

"So the choice is to be together, happy and in love, until such a time as we're forced to part, or to start grieving each other now, before we have to?"

Si's mind juddered to a halt. "In love? Do you mean it? Because I love you, Ellen Mackintosh MacKenzie."

"Yes, you daft thing," she laughed. "Yes, I love you, and I don't think... I don't *accept* that we have any choice other than to spend every moment we have left loving each other as well as we possibly can."

Tremendous relief washed over Si, and then it drained like a receding tide as he remembered everything he'd not yet told her.

"What is it?" she asked, searching his eyes.

He set her beside him, pulling back, standing and pacing under the watchful eye of the crucifixion.

"I wrote you a letter," he said finally. "Angus was supposed to deliver it to you at the inn."

"You gave Angus a letter?"

He nodded.

She withdrew a folded parchment from her pocket. "This letter?"

Si nodded again, clasping and unclasping his hands behind his back. "I never meant to deceive you. It took on a life of its own, being someone else, being the person I wished I could be."

"Oh, Si," she whispered.

"Can you ever forgive me?"

She shook her head, staring at the floor and Silas's heart fell.

"I wanted it to be you," she said, shaking her head again in disbelief. "I always wished that it could somehow be you. I wanted it so badly, I was afraid to pray for it, my most selfish prayer." She peered up at him through damp lashes, and Silas knew then that hope smelled like damp lavender.

"Aye?" he asked, needing her to say it again.

"Aye," she whispered back with a giggle, and he fell to his knees before her and took her mouth with his, kissing her until he began to see sparks for lack of air.

"Should we go upstairs?" she asked when he pulled away, panting.

"There's just one last oath to be taken here tonight," he said, rubbing one thumb over her wedding ring, and from the sheath at her waist, drawing the matching sgian dubh.

"Milady Kintail, on the graves of my forefathers, the cross of my Lord Jesus Christ, and this blessed iron, which I gave you to keep ever at your side, I pledge to you this day, my fealty and my honor—to defend, to thrive, to shine, not burn, until such a time as death may claim me."

She smiled up at him and it was like the heavens parting to accommodate an endless blue.

"There's no quaich," she whispered.

"I can think of a better seal," he replied, catching up her lips once more to kiss her, deeply, to tell her anything he'd left unsaid.

And then he stood, sweeping her up in his arms as he did, delighting in the sound of her laughter. He kissed her as he carried her to the stairs, and he kissed her as he climbed them, and Ellen kissed him back, hungry and exploring, as though desperate to swallow every last piece of his soul.

In their room, he unwrapped her from the MacKenzie tartan she'd finally worn, then helped her out of each damp stitch of clothing until she stood naked before him, her rashy skin almost healed.

She reached for his belt, and he stripped the sark over his head before watching her lithe, nimble fingers unfasten the buckle. When his kilt fell to the floor, her eyes widened, taking him all in. He wanted to hide himself, but he reached for her hair instead, tucking a stray curl behind her ear.

Len lay back upon the bed and he stretched himself alongside her. She turned, and kissed him, playing her fingers along his chest hair and down to his navel.

Si pressed his forehead to hers. They could do it spooned together as they had before, but he wanted to see her face, so he rolled onto his back. She tilted her head at him curiously, and he almost wasted himself right then. But he guided her to straddle his belly, and when she bent down to kiss him, he whispered, "Like this, you're in control."

Tilting her head to the other side, she smiled and kissed him, and when she was ready, she eased onto him and gasped, but not with pain.

After a moment, she took him deeper and began to rock against him, undulating like the currents at the hot spring, tiny gasps and moans escaping from her lips, driving him to distraction, and he tried to hold perfectly still lest he explode.

Then she tipped her head back, moving faster, and Si synced himself to her rhythm, following her lead, as he would follow her for evermore. And when at last she reached her peak, her voice was the loudest Si had ever heard it, and he joined her, surrendering to the agony and ecstasy of whatever might come next.

Epilogue

Ellen stooped to lay a bouquet of purple hydrangeas on the old laird's grave. The recent rain had just about washed away the newness of the earth. Beside her, Si laid his own flowers at his mother's headstone.

The loss still weighed heavily on him after only a few months. Ellen wasn't sure she had the right words to comfort him. What did she know of being an orphan, except that she'd loved the Old Kintail dearly and had watched Jory experience the same loss as a girl?

"I know they're both so proud of you," she told him.

"D'you think so?" he asked, drawing her close to him under the shade of the large rowan tree. "D'you believe there's an *after* from where they're looking down on us, then? Watching every-thing we do?"

His voice was laced with concern, for if the dead could see acts that would make them proud, they could see cowardice and failure too.

"I think," she said slowly, trying to draw all her thoughts into focus and put them into words. "I think they're aware. And they remember better than we do what it's like to be human, so our successes are all the sweeter."

Si wrapped his arms around her and hunched to rest his chin upon her head.

"Besides, your father told me exactly how proud he was before he died."

"Did he? When?"

"Every day for three straight years. Every time I read to him. I never saw a more delighted father. Except for you."

A squeal and a cry sounded from the far side of the kirkyard, and she and Si both spun to see baby Marjorie fall to the ground, two-year-old Alex standing over her looking half-guilty.

"Oi," Si yelled. "Play gentle, mind. Both of you." He shook his head and rolled his eyes.

"I knew we'd be in for it as soon Marjie found her legs," Ellen moaned.

"They'll be fine," Si shushed. "They bounce at this age. And she'll keep the lad busy," he added with a bemused chuckle.

That made Ellen laugh, and she stood on her tiptoes to pull him down for a kiss.

"Well, if they're proud of me, 'tis your doing," he whispered in her ear. "All that I am is because of you."

Despite the aching loss of his father, beneath it and between it, Si was content. Two healthy bairns who had been their grandfather's absolute delight, the crofts were finally producing, and Len, well—she was a wee wonder. The whole of clan MacKenzie would be literate by the time she was through, and little by little she'd seen Leod restored.

Si remained convinced there was nothing she couldn't do.

"Glad you stayed?" he whispered, because he liked the way she wriggled when his breath tickled her neck.

It was a jest they shared, but he meant it in earnest every time he asked, and it soothed his soul like dock leaf when she whispered back, "Even Buttercup couldn't drag me away."

With his arm around her, tucking her close to his side, they walked over to their children, where the one-year-old was attempting to bury the two-year-old in fallen leaves.

"We should get Bram to watch them tonight."

"I suspect Bram's a bit busy these days."

"Busy?"

"Surely you've seen the way he moons after Greer."

"Does he? Should I speak to him?"

She laughed. "I ken someone should."

"Dorrie, then. She'll be keen for an excuse to leave the kitchen."

Len laughed again. "Why? Is there some bard coming to play, I've not been informed of?"

"Dinnae ken about all that," he said. "I hope not, because you and I are going to be very busy."

"Are we?" she asked in a low growl that made his cock jerk to attention.

"Aye. You've had a letter," he whispered, his lips very nearly touching her ear.

The ensuing flush spread across her cheeks like so much red ochre. "Oh?" she asked, biting her lip. "I wonder what it could say?"

"Perhaps that 'tis a new moon. Not a cloud in the sky," he gestured at the endless blue above them, as endless as the blue of her eyes. "And I had them move our mattress to the battlements for airing."

"Did you?" she asked in that same low purr, and Si had to smother several creatively indecent notions from his mind. It wouldn't do for the laird to be caught tupping his wife in the kirk while their children murdered each other outside.

"Aye," he murmured, taking her face in his hands and stroking a thumb down her cheek and along her bottom lip before kissing her again.

"Well," she gasped. "I'm sure Morag can spare Dorrie for one night."

"Only one?" He smirked and then bent down to scoop up the children.

"C'mon, you two heathens," he said, popping Alex onto his shoulders to leave one arm free to hold his wife as the four of them walked home together.

Author's Note

Silas and Ellen were delightful characters to write, and I love them so much, as well as their little corner of history and the Highlands, with its natural hot springs. The sulfur springs in Strathpeffer were said to have been discovered sometime in the 18th century, and by the 1800s it had become a popular spa town, though I like to think Ellen and Silas still had a secret little spot just for friends and family who visited Leod, which has been the seat of Clan MacKenzie since about 1513.

Despite the distance, Silas was sent away for his education and spent most of his life in Aberdeen, home of Scotland's third oldest university, which began as King's College before later becoming part of the University of Aberdeen. It was founded to train doctors, teachers, and lawyers, and after matriculating, Si stayed in the area, visiting the farms of classmates, and learning modern techniques such as crop rotation, which was first introduced in Scotland about two hundred years earlier, but in this fictional account, Si's stubborn clan was late to embrace the idea.

I've also taken some liberties with the history of clan MacKenzie. Bram's late father, Laird Alex Kintail's brother, is based on William MacKenzie, the Earl of Seaforth, who was laird for forty years and did not actually die during Simon Fraser of Lovat's siege of Inverness. It was actually William who was exiled in 1719, having a steward collect his rents while he was overseas, and who was eventually pardoned and allowed to return to Scotland.

The poison used against Alex is the 18th century version of what's known today as ricin. Highly poisonous, it occurs naturally in the raw beans of the otherwise benign castor plant, which have long been processed into oil for use in everything from laxatives to skin moisturizer to break fluids. Castor oil is safe and ricin free, however raw, the beans are quite toxic. Traces of ricin have been found on sticks dating back to the Paleolithic Cro-Magnon era, suggesting prehistoric peoples used it on arrow heads.

When inhaled as a mist, ricin can cause typical flu-like symptoms such as fever, nausea, and body aches, as well as severe respiratory symptoms including pulmonary edema, killing within days of exposure. In small doses, however, victims can recover. In Alex's case, he was exposed little by little over time, enough to sicken and weaken him, but still allowing him to somewhat recover.

According to some internet sources, the Mackintoshes were an ally of Clan MacKenzie. Though I suppose that ally-ship could have been owing to any number of mutual interests, I like to think it was because of the ill-conceived plotting of Ellen's father, which luckily just so happened to work out.

Acknowledgments

Writing is a funny thing. Sometimes you bang your head against a manuscript for months and it's just not ready to be written. And then one day you're in a cabin in the mountains surrounded by friends and you start over *almost* from scratch and the thing practically writes itself (in between episodes of *Ted Lasso*).

So thank you, first and foremost, to my beloved husband, DJ, who always understands my need to disappear into the cabin in the woods, even when the woods are on fire.

And thank you to my cousin-in-law, Josh Dickson, fire-fighter and all around good guy, who I recently learned helped preserve our writing cabin on more than one occasion. I owe you more than you could ever know, especially since you don't even know I wrote this book.

Mark Benson, who I can always count on for a late-night chat —or to stay up and keep an eye on said fires.

To my Word Warrior, DeAnn Hays, for tirelessly helping me sort out my vocabularic conundrums. I couldn't finish a single book without you.

My beta readers: Angie Griffee-Black, first reader of these words. I can't tell you how much I treasure all of our chats. You encourage me to be brave and take risks; Jessie Parker, your generosity knows no bounds; Jennie Ritz, an inspiration. You gave me exactly the words I needed to hear, right when I needed them most. And Krista Walsh, for everything, over and over and over again. You make me a better writer every day.

And to the rest of my Writerly crew: Christian Berkey, Sarah Henning, Jennifer Iacopelli, Trisha Leigh, Tabitha Martin, Megan

Paasch, and Sarah Blair, who let me name a baddie after her, I treasure you all.

To my big sister, Susan Semadeni. Hopefully I was never as much of a pain as Maggie. Know that even if I fight you on the em dashes, there are far fewer than there would have been if not for your influence. I wish that we lived closer together, but I content myself with knowing that we can look up and see the same stars. Or, you know, send a text.

To my mom and dad. Your love and support mean the world to me.

And to my brilliant cover designer, Poshie—you continue to bring my characters to life in a way that amazes me. Thank you for coming on this delightful journey!

When my aunt read my first book (she was forbidden from reading this series), she said, "I had no idea so many people were involved in writing a book," and it really is true. Like raising a child, good books take a village. Thank you for being my village.

Resources

- The 'Hurt Yourself Less' Workbook: http://www.arwtraining.com/wp-content/uploads/2015/02/01-The-Hurt-Yourself-Less-Workbook-Self-Harm-Self-Management.pdf

- NAMI collection of resources for people who self-harm: https://namimass.org/selfharm/

UNITED STATES

- Crisis Text Line: Text HOME to 741741 | WhatsApp 1-443-787-7678 | Chat https://www.crisistextline.org/

- 988 Suicide & Crisis Lifeline: Dial 988

- Trevor Project Lifeline: Text START to 678678 | Call 1-866-488-7386 | Chat https://www.thetrevorproject.org/get-help/#lifeline

UNITED KINGDOM

- Alumina: Under 19 self-harm support: https://selfharm.co.uk/

- Childline: Under 19, Call 0800 1111 (won't appear on phone bill)

- Samaritans: Call 116123 | Email jo@samaritans.org

- Shout Crisis Text Line: Text SHOUT to 85258 (under 19 Text YM)

About the Author

Rose Prendeville is a librarian living in Middle Tennessee with her husband and a garden full of bees, writing stories about found families and flawed people doing their best. The first place winner of the 30th annual Writer's Digest Awards for her debut *Last Blue Christmas* is passionate about books with happy endings and their ability to brighten a sometimes dismal world.

If you enjoyed this book, please consider leaving a review at your favorite marketplace.

To stay up-to-date on this series and other news, scan the QR code and sign up for Rose's newsletter or visit: 
    roseprendeville.com

Books by Rose Prendeville

Last Blue Christmas

The Unknown Birds

Brides of Chattan

Mistress Mackintosh and the Shaw Wretch

Lady Len and the Mysterious Mac

Maggie and the Pirate's Son

Tennessee Hebrides

Grace on the Rocks

A Faire Affair

www.ingramcontent.com/pod-product-compliance
Lightning Source LLC
Chambersburg PA
CBHW061535210726
48287CB00006B/1968